Also by Blossom Kan and Michelle Yu

China Dolls

Young,
Restless,
and Broke

Young, Restless, and Broke

Blossom Kan
and
Michelle Yu

Thomas Dunne Books
New York

For our grandmother—
the strongest woman we know

To our friends who inspire us by being the most memorable characters in our lives. Special thanks to Mark Teschner, truly the most dashing casting director in soapdom. Thanks to Arianne Zucker and Loudsuga, for their great support. Thanks also to Natasha Kern, our indefatigable agent, and our great editors, Karyn and Diana.

This is a work of fiction. All of the characters, organizations, and events portrayed in this novel are either products of the authors' imagination or are used fictitiously.

THOMAS DUNNE BOOKS.
An imprint of St. Martin's Press.

ISBN 978-0-312-37420-4

First Edition: May 2010

10 9 8 7 6 5 4 3 2 1

New York

1

Sarah knew in her bones that tonight was the night.

She'd been biding her time all these years. From the moment she'd first laid eyes on Rafe, she'd been determined to make him hers. With his chiseled, muscular build, square jaw, and thick, tousled chestnut hair, Rafe was like a modern-day descendant of the gods. When he turned his smoldering dark gaze upon her, Sarah felt as if she'd been impaled, struck immobile by those intense, passionate eyes. There was a connection between them, an electricity that couldn't be denied—and she knew he felt the same way about her.

Of course, there was that pesky business of him being married to her sister. But that was Amy for you—trust her to have everything. All her life, Sarah had had to deal with Amy's one-upmanship. Money, career, their mother's approbation: Whatever brass ring Sarah might desire, Amy would somehow find a way to snatch it up first. Of course she would have Rafe. But not after tonight.

Striding through the glittering, fabulously ornate Two of Hearts Ball, Sarah Cho smoothed back her sequined Versace sheath. As she pushed through gold lamé curtains, copper-tinted balloons, and a never-ending shower of tinsel confetti, she noticed Lin, the mistress of ceremonies, looking ever resplendent in fire red ruffled chiffon on the stage. The crowd parted before Sarah as she approached her target: Amy.

"Well, well, well," Sarah spat out, "if it isn't the queen bee herself. Lovely party."

Amy whirled around in her ice blue satin Dolce & Gabbana gown. She planted her immaculately French-manicured hands on her hips.

"Sarah! What are you doing here?" she demanded.

"When I heard you were throwing this gala, there was no way I could miss it." Sarah tossed back her lustrous ebony mane. "My invitation must have gotten lost in the mail."

Amy groaned in frustration. "Oh, come on, Sarah. After what you've done, you know you're not welcome here."

"Why?" Sarah demanded. "Because you're ashamed to have a stripper for a sister?"

"Your sordid past is the least of my concerns." Amy glared at her. "I'm more worried about what you're going to pull tonight. Let's think—you've already got kidnapping on your dossier, what are you going to add to your rap sheet now?"

"I didn't kidnap anyone," Sarah snapped. "I love that child more than anyone!"

"Except that she's not your child!" Amy shrieked. "Get it through your head—she's my daughter, not yours. They should have sent you away to Sing Sing, instead of letting you get off with a cushy stay at Shady Pines!"

"I'm fully recovered from my stay at the asylum," Sarah declared, "and I'm here to reclaim what's mine. I should have had Rafe's child, not you!"

"That will never happen," Amy said, sneering. "Once Rafe knows that you slept with his brother, you'll never have him."

Sarah's eyes narrowed. "Careful, or I might have to lock you in that secret room in the basement again."

Amy gasped. "You—you—bitch!"

She tossed her drink in Sarah's face. Blinking gin out of her eyes, Sarah gaped at her for a second. Then she snatched up a nearby vodka tonic and hurled the contents at her sister. Dripping wet, Amy looked down in horror at her ruined designer dress, while out of the corner of her eye, Sarah noticed Lin and Rafe staring at them from the other end of the room. . . .

Amy looked up with mascara-streaked eyes at Sarah—and lunged toward her with a feral scream. The next minute, the two girls were careening around the party, shattering china, knocking over tables, and sending flower arrangements flying as they screeched and yanked at each other's hair. . . .

"Sarah! Yoohoo!"

Sarah blinked, abruptly shaken out of her reverie. Glancing down, she saw that she was still clutching a vodka tonic in her fist—

"Earth to Sarah!"

Sarah whirled around and saw her friend Chad Lockhart waving frantically from the bar. As she stared at him, he gestured wildly at the irate crowd around the bar, all clamoring for their drinks . . . and her even more irate manager, Donnie, who was barreling toward the bar. Uh-oh.

Snapping into action, Sarah swung toward the bar and started throwing together martinis and Cosmos at warp speed.

"Okay, there—" She whisked three olives into one of the martinis. "Now, who likes theirs extra dirty?"

As she handed off the drinks, Donnie appeared at her elbow, a stormcloud hanging over his overgrown eyebrows.

"What's up, boss?" Sarah said gaily as she shoveled crushed ice into the shaker.

"Don't think you're fooling me, Cho," he snarled. "I've had my eye on you for a long time now, and you ain't foolin' me for a second. Just give me an excuse—and you're out of here."

With that, he stormed off. Sarah sighed and closed her eyes.

"Wow, that guy really has it in for you, doesn't he?"

Sarah looked up to see Chad leaning across the bar, the lone sympathetic face in a crowd of irate drunks.

"Tell me about it," she groaned. "That douchebag has been gunning for me since day one—probably because I told him I wasn't going to wear a push-up bra."

Chad laughed. "Maybe you should just tell him to spring for a boob job."

Sarah giggled. "I should totally tell him that. Right before I tell him where he can shove his fat ass!" She raised the pomegranate martini she'd just made and toasted a laughing Chad. Then, after glancing around to make sure Donnie wasn't lurking in the vicinity, she took a quick, restorative sip of her drink.

"So"—Chad popped an olive in his mouth—"what were you daydreaming about back there?"

"Oh, that." Sarah shrugged. "My drama teacher has us doing these immersion exercises where we imagine people we know in these soap scenes. She says it will help us 'bring the characters to life.'"

"Hm . . ." Chad rubbed his jaw. "Interesting. So what scene are we talking about here?"

Sarah shrugged. "Oh, your standard two-sisters-one-guy love triangle degenerating into a screaming, drink-throwing, hair-pulling catfight."

"Ooh, I like!" Chad exclaimed. "Let me guess, you channeled some of that long-simmering sibling rivalry you have with your sister Lin."

Sarah tossed her head. "Don't be ridiculous. I was obviously in a catfight with Amy, not Lin. There's no sibling rivalry between me and Lin—we've always gotten along fabulously. Me and Amy on the other hand . . . well, that's a whole other story."

"I don't know," Chad said. "I think the lady doth protest too much. I mean, Lin's beautiful, smart, supersuccessful. What's not to be jealous about?"

Sarah sighed. "Thanks, you're such a pal."

Chad chuckled and drained his martini. "You're welcome,

darling." He leaned back on his stool. "So who was the hunk in this burning triangle of love?"

At that moment, the busboy approached.

"Can I get you more glasses, Miss Sarah?" he asked.

Sarah turned and flashed him a smile. "That would be great. You're always so thoughtful, Rafe."

As she turned back to Chad, she saw that he was frowning at her in disapproval.

"What?" she demanded.

"Really, Sarah?" Chad said. "Now you're fantasizing about the help?"

Sarah laughed. "Welcome to my life."

The next afternoon, Sarah headed from her Hell's Kitchen hood to Lincoln Center for her audition, walking briskly in the light spring rain from the number 1 train stop. According to the Craigslist description she'd read on the Internet, the audition was for a musical called *United Nations*. Sarah was auditioning for the part of a FOB (fresh-off-the-boat) Asian who finds love in her new country. Dressed in silk black bloomers and a *qipao* top, Sarah yanked her slightly wet hair back in a sleek ponytail and took a quick look at herself in her compact as she strolled into the large glass building. Yep—she definitely looked the part.

As she rode up the mirrored escalator, her thoughts flashed back to her first audition. She'd been only seventeen then and had to play hooky from school to make it to the open audition for some new teen Disney musical. Even though she couldn't belt out pitch-perfect vocals like Mariah or shimmy like a pre-Federline Britney—and had zero possibility of getting the role—the experience had been exhilarating. Getting up onto the stage and having all eyes turn on her, that feeling where everything else receded and the only thing that mattered was the scene, that magical moment when she transformed into someone altogether different . . .

"Hi," Sarah said when she reached the casting table. "I'm Sarah Cho. I'm here for the *United Nations* audition."

"Great." The woman at the table didn't even look up as she jabbed a pen toward the right side of the stage. "Go towards your right, grab a script, and wait on that line."

Obediently, Sarah turned—and gaped at the dozen-plus other Asian females on the line, all waiting to audition. Some sat on the polished tiled floor, while others propped themselves up against the glass-and-beechwood-paneled walls, but they were all furiously scanning the same stapled script pages. Checking out the competition, she realized she was going up against some of the most stunning Asian women she had ever seen: They all seemed to have the same long, silky jet black manes, size two figures, and flawless skin. *Hold it together, Sarah,* she ordered herself, *you can hold your own with these girls—and you can actually act, unlike most of these no-talent bimbos.*

As she got on line, Sarah checked out the casting director. She hadn't seen him before at any other audition; he looked like he was in his mid-forties and was wearing Diesel jeans and a Ralph Lauren polo shirt. Although he had some funky rectangular glasses, he was nowhere near as dashing as Sarah had imagined (like the legendary *General Hospital* casting director Mark Teschner, for instance). Leaning against a table, he was reading with a drop-dead gorgeous Korean beauty.

"Excuse me . . ." A woman with a clipboard walked up to Sarah. "I'm Laura. You're up next with Abe Cohen, our casting director."

"Oh, great, thanks." Sarah smiled. "How much longer, do you think?"

"Just another few minutes," Laura said. "Here's how this works: You're going to read this one-page script with Abe, and once you're done, you'll step down and exit to your left. We'll contact you for callbacks, if necessary."

"Sounds good." Sarah nodded. "Thanks."

As Laura walked off, Sarah quickly glanced down at her crisp, white, brass-bound script. That was when she heard one of the girls next to her reciting her lines noisily.

"America is my dream!" the girl repeated in an overly loud voice.

Sarah couldn't resist anymore; she sneaked a glance at her neighbor. Dressed all in black—à la "Black Widow" pool shark Jeanette Lee—her Asian rival glared at her.

"You a lesbian?" she demanded.

Sarah jerked back, taken aback by the scowl being directed at her. "Uh . . . no." She hesitated, wondering if she had taken a detour to the land of the loonies.

"Good. Then mind your own business and stop looking at me," the woman snapped.

"Calm down." Sarah rolled her eyes. "No one was looking at you."

At that moment, a nearby woman shushed them. As Sarah swiveled around, the woman started taking a series of deep breaths, as if she were meditating in a yoga studio, while simultaneously reading her script. Sarah shook her head, wondering if she had just walked into the wannabe-actress version of *Girl, Interrupted*. She couldn't believe how fanatical some of these women were—after all, it was just an audition. Sarah considered herself to be pretty focused, but these women were verging on psychotic.

"Sarah Cho!" Laura called out.

Sarah hurried up onto the stage. She'd been so distracted by the crackpot women around her that she hadn't had a chance to properly study her lines. . . .

"Hi, I'm Abe Cohen." The casting director shook Sarah's hand. "Ready?"

"Yes." Sarah smiled, hoping she looked infinitely more prepared than she felt. She took a deep breath.

It was just as she was about to say her first lines that the Asian tigress screamed and dropped to the floor.

"This girl pretended to faint while I was reading my lines!" Sarah groused.

"Oh, how dramatic!" Chad burst into delighted laughter. "You Asian gals really bring out those claws, don't you? I love it!"

Sarah shook her head as she nestled her cell phone into the crook of her neck. It was several hours after her ill-fated audition, and she was seventeen minutes away from starting her shift at the Buddha Bar in the meatpacking district. At the moment, the place was lifeless and smelling faintly of dried alcohol and bleach, but come happy hour the bar would come spectacularly to life as a raucous, pulsating mass of bodies. It was Sarah's favorite time at the club—a little respite of quiet before the deafening, frenetic crush of the evening. . . .

"Chad, it's not funny. Those people were seriously deranged!" Sarah exclaimed. "She completely ruined my audition. I totally screwed up after her little scene." Sarah seethed just remembering the slick smile the woman shot her when no one was looking. The one that had "Here's to you, sucker!" written all over it.

"Now, now," Chad said, "no one likes a complainer. So stop being a whiny bitch and just go out there and get them next time. I mean, you didn't really want the part of a FOB that bad, did you?"

"I guess not," Sarah admitted. "But it's just so frustrating. It feels like I've been going on these auditions forever and I'm just not getting anywhere. . . ."

"Don't think like that!" Chad admonished her. "You just have to keep going to auditions, keep doing those immersion exercises— you can even use me in one of your scenarios. I'm thinking *General Hospital*, and I'm your long-lost lover—the one who was presumed dead in a tragic plane crash over the Bermuda Triangle."

"Ah, yes," Sarah said dreamily. "Or maybe it will be *All My Children*, and you're the half-brother my mother gave up years ago when she was knocked up as a teenager."

"Ah, the old incest story line," Chad said. "I always wondered what it would be like to be the blond, blue-eyed child of a Chinese woman."

Sarah laughed. Chad was one of her best friends, and there was nothing more that Sarah loved than their soap opera dissections. It didn't hurt that Chad was the spitting image of a soap opera Adonis—tall, sculpted, with immaculately moussed blond hair and a wardrobe to match. When she'd first met Chad in art history, Sarah had developed an insta-crush on him, drawn to his impeccable good looks and male-model outfits, which stood out in the crowd of jeans and sweatshirts that most of her male classmates sported. For a while, Sarah continued to harbor fantasies of being with Chad—until she discovered him in the rec room one day glued to an episode of *General Hospital*. Sarah had always considered herself to be the number one soap opera fan of any of her acquaintances, but Chad could recite whole lines of dialogue from *General Hospital* episodes from ten years ago. Not long after that, Sarah and Chad became fast soap buddies, and three o'clock on weekdays became appointment television for them. Too bad Sarah was pretty sure that Chad batted for the other team—even if he wasn't ready to come out of the closet because of his consultant day job.

"Well, hopefully, this will all result in you getting the role," Chad said. "You realize that's the only way you'll be able to legitimize your revenge fantasies against your sister."

Sarah smiled. It would be nice to be able to show her family that she was actually getting somewhere in her acting endeavors. If only getting this role were all that was needed to change their perceptions. . . .

"Sarah?" Chad said. "Did you hear me?"

Sarah blinked. She shook her head, trying to rid herself of thoughts of her family.

"I'm sorry, Chad." She took a deep breath. "I totally spaced there for a second. What were you saying?"

Chad sighed. "Uh, only that there's a huge *Soap Opera Digest* party this Friday that my friend Karen invited me to. Remember her? She's the one who works for their marketing department."

"Of course!" Sarah exclaimed. "The one I used to pepper for spoilers! I'm sure she was so sick of me asking her whether Blair and Todd were ever going to get back together again."

"Well, she never said anything to me about it, but I know I was pretty sick of that," Chad said archly. "Anyway, she invited me to this party—apparently, there's going to be cast members from all the soaps there. You wanna come and work your charm?"

"Do you need to ask?!" Sarah gasped. "I can't believe you held out on telling me this long! Omigosh," she mused, "there's probably going to be producers and casting agents and all the top execs there. I can't believe I have less than a week to buy an outfit!"

Chad gasped in mock horror. "Well, you better start hitting Barney's, or at least the Coop. By the way, before I go—have you poisoned Donnie's vodka martini yet?"

Sarah broke into laughter. "Don't tempt me."

After hanging up with Chad, she hugged herself, practically doing a jig of glee. Her very first *Soap Opera Digest* party! A soiree like that positively abounded with networking possibilities. Who knew what famous producer she might run into at the hors d'oeuvres table? She couldn't wait to leave those Asian tigresses and their histrionics in the dust. . . .

"So are you coming to dinner Sunday night?" Lin asked.

"Yes." Sarah sighed as she tossed down her apron on the counter at Balloon Burger in SoHo. "For the hundredth time, yes."

It was just before noon, usually the busiest time of day. But the kitschy, faux-fifties-inspired restaurant was experiencing one of those rare lulls before lunchtime, so Sarah had risked answering her sister's call—a strict no-no during work hours. Even though the burger joint was considered to be a step up from the McDonald's of the world, Sarah was feeling as beleaguered as any teenage fast-food employee at the moment.

"Sorry," Lin said, "I'm really not trying to be a pain, but Mom only left me four messages today about how I had to make sure you were coming."

"Doesn't she have anything better to do?" Sarah ran a greasy hand across her brow. "Like maybe plan Amy's wedding?"

"Well, I don't know about that," Lin said. "I mean, you know Amy had everything planned two years ago."

Despite herself, Sarah had to laugh in agreement. As both

she and Lin knew, their sister Amy had been chomping at the bit to get married long before Lin had even thought of uttering her vows. Amy and her fiancé, James, had been high school sweethearts, and they had planned on tying the knot after college—that is, until Lin had derailed those plans by engaging in a disastrous love affair during a break from her now husband, Stephen. Now that Lin had gotten back on track—and the Chinese tradition of the eldest being married first had been fulfilled—the path was finally clear for Amy's long-awaited nuptials.

"She made another comment yesterday about how her dress didn't cost half a year's salary," Lin remarked. "Think that was another jab at me?"

"Of course it was." Sarah leaned back against the counter. "She's been fixated on the Vera Wang dress you wore for your wedding since the moment she laid eyes on it."

Sitting next to Amy at the wedding, Sarah had witnessed firsthand her sister's jealousy—and had been the recipient of a few of Amy's jabs herself. Amy had a habit of taking out her pent-up resentment on Sarah, especially when she was angry with Lin. All her life, Amy had seethed over her inherent inferiority to Lin. Lin was smarter, more successful, and infinitely more beautiful. While Sarah had enjoyed her own spotlight as the baby of the family, Amy was the prototypical Jan Brady, consumed with Marcia envy—and it was only made worse by the fact that there was nothing she could do to combat Lin's supremacy. Which was probably why Sarah always seemed to end up the target of her spite.

"Oh, Amy . . ." Lin sighed. "At least she'll have the pleasure of being the daughter who finally gives Mom the Chinese wedding of her dreams, since I couldn't do that."

It was true. Lin's wedding had been exactly what one would expect for Sarah's sister—a lovely, refined affair at the St. Regis Hotel, complete with copious bouquets of orange tea roses and cream-colored linen place settings. Amy, on the other hand, was guaranteed to opt for the stereotypical: football stadium–sized restaurant in Chinatown with a grating FOB emcee, caterwauling karaoke singers, and steaming tureens of shark-fin soup making the rounds.

"So true." Sarah sighed. "Poor Amy. For the record, I thought your wedding was perfect."

Lin laughed. "Thanks, Sarah. I thought it was pretty perfect, too."

And that was Lin to a tee—perfect. Sarah could picture her vividly on the other end of the phone, no doubt sitting in her enormous glass-and-metal office in some elegant Prada sheath and her Jimmy Choo stilettos, hair expertly pulled back into a sleek chignon. Sarah, on the other hand . . . Looking at her reflection in the cracked glass above the potato fryer, she blew a stray strand of hair off her forehead and thought how it was a good thing that casting directors never seemed to grace the premises of the Balloon Burger. Not that she was down on herself; most of the time, Sarah thought she could pull herself together rather decently. She had her mother's delicately arched eyebrows, Amy's long, silky mane of jet black hair, and Lin's delicate, heart-shaped face. Someone once remarked that she was a composite of the women in her family—a description Sarah had never been particularly fond of. She liked to think of herself as an individual unto herself, not a bouillabaisse of bits and pieces from her mother and her sisters.

Ring! Ring! Ring! The phone on the wall was clanging insistently.

"Shit," Sarah groaned. "I have to go. It's the burger hotline."

"Okay," Lin said. "Burger duties today?"

"Yup, it's a party here." Sarah sneaked a peak to make sure her boss wasn't in the vicinity. "I've already flipped a hundred burgers today for all these orders that came in, and it's not even noon."

"Sounds . . . lovely," Lin said. "See you Sunday."

Pocketing her cell phone, Sarah quickly picked up the restaurant line. "Balloon Burger. How can I help you?" she answered.

"I'd like to place an order, please," a male voice intoned. "I'd like three hundred fifty cheeseburgers with bacon, avocado, and mushrooms on top."

Three hundred fifty burgers? Sarah wondered if she'd inhaled too much of the butane fumes during her manic patty-flipping phase.

"You want how many?" she asked.

"Do you need a hearing aid?" the caller demanded. "I want six hundred twenty-five cheeseburgers with anchovies, peppers, and tomato."

"Excuse me—is this a joke?" Sarah was fast losing her cool. "That's not what you said two seconds ago. And large orders like these need to be made twenty-four hours in advance."

"Advance?" the male voice echoed. "Ma'am, you're providing really lousy service. Are you that busy over there? Maybe I should come in sooner rather than later to help you out."

Sarah closed her eyes and breathed a sigh of relief. She heard her friend. "Owen, you jerk!" she yelped. "You almost gave me a coronary!"

Owen couldn't stop laughing at the other end of the line.

"Wow, I can't believe you fell for that. Have you been inhaling the butane again?" he snickered. "So what's shakin' over there?"

"Nothing much." Sarah yanked a potato stick out of her hair. "Basically holding down the fort here until you come in. There were so many orders this morning, but it's died down, thankfully. Plus, I bombed another audition yesterday."

"What happened? Letting those crackpot actors get to you again?" Owen said cheerfully. "It was one minor audition. Don't go blowing it all out of proportion."

Sarah knew he was trying to cheer her up. Owen Fletcher was Sarah's co-worker at the Balloon Burger, and they'd been working together for almost two years now. Laid-back and free-spirited, he was someone Sarah could always count on to bring her back to reality. While Chad shared her love for soaps and fashion, Owen was all about good times and beer. Put them together, and it was almost like having the perfect friend.

"You're always so positive." Sarah sighed. "I wish I could be, too, but I feel like I'm not getting any breaks. Plus, my family's been getting on my case. They're saying that I don't have a real job, and my dream is dumb, blah, blah, blah."

"Ouch," Owen said. "Not exactly the Brady Bunch, huh?"

She shrugged. "They're supportive in their own way, but when it comes to acting . . . well, let's just say they're not going to be supporting me like they would if I was in med school," she explained as she hauled out a bag of frozen fries from the fridge.

"Look, babe," Owen said, "you'll get there. Maybe you do need to move to L.A.—still thinking about that?"

Just hearing the word *move* was enough to make Sarah's pulse beat double time. Of course she knew that L.A. was the acting mecca of the world, but leaving New York had never crossed her mind as a real possibility. She'd always believed that if she made the right sacrifices, she'd be able to work her way to the top. And yet . . . Sarah was starting to question if that was ever going to happen here. What if she really had to move? Could she deal with being so far away from her friends and family? And would her family think that she was even more of a failure if she left town to chase a pipe dream—and didn't make it?

"I don't know." Sarah sighed. "The idea of moving to L.A. makes me think of—fries!"

"Fries?" Owen queried.

"As in burning spud alert!" Sarah gasped as she ran toward the source of the burned potato aroma. "Gotta go—talk to you later!"

Sarah slid her tray across the counter and leaned against the bar at Buddha to wait for her drink orders. It was almost midnight and she was only midway through her shift. Most of the time, she didn't mind the pushy customers or the deafening music or the spilled drinks. Tonight, though, she felt as if she had a sledgehammer pounding against her skull . . . and every single customer seemed intent on making her life miserable.

She wished that she could blame it all on Buddha, but the truth was she'd been out of sorts since her shift that morning at

Balloon Burger. For some reason, the conversation with Owen had lingered in her mind all day. She wasn't exactly sure why; maybe because even though it had always been a possibility, this was the first time she'd really thought about her future minus New York—and the thought was a scary one. . . .

"Here you go, Sarah." One of the bartenders slid a half-dozen assortment of Cosmos and mojitos toward her.

Smiling her thanks, Sarah hefted the tray of drinks and snaked her way through a maze of gyrating B&T couples to the waiting table under the beaded curtain in the corner. After depositing them, she turned to the newly arrived party at the next table.

"Hi, would you guys like to order some drinks?" Sarah whipped out her pad.

"Sarah? Is that you?"

Sarah looked up sharply to see the familiar face of Dana Teng—a fellow passenger on the Asian cruise that Sarah's parents had sent her on when she was a teenager. As she stood there looking at Dana, she quickly flashed back to the experience: the *Shanghai Sail*, designed for American-born Chinese youth to travel to China while also meeting "friends" and learning about their heritage. Sarah was fifteen when her mother decided to send her, and initially, the thought of spending an entire summer in a country full of strangers a world away had seemed worse than a year's worth of detention. In the end, though, Sarah had found herself surprisingly tearful. There was something about being around people who understood her in a way that only those from the same culture and background could that made the experience unforgettable. . . .

"Dana?" Sarah smiled. "Is that really you?"

"Oh, my gosh!" Dana jumped up and gave her a hug. "Sarah! I haven't seen you since we got back from the *Shanghai Sail*. How are you? You look great!"

"Thanks." Sarah beamed. "I'm good. Still here in New York." In surreptitiously giving the newcomer a once-over, she couldn't help noticing how matronly Dana looked in her pearl choker and beige cashmere turtleneck—a far cry from Sarah's silver lamé tunic dress.

"Really? Where are you living now?" Dana asked.

Sarah glanced over at Dana's friends, but they were too busy gabbing with each other to pay attention to them. "Well, I'm sort of a nomad these days," she explained. "I was living in the city with a roommate, but then I moved back home, and now I'm living at my sister Lin's old apartment until she sells it. She just got married, so she's living with her husband at his place right now."

"Ah, yes." Dana nodded slowly. "It's smart to be frugal in this economy."

Sarah pursed her lips. Dana's eyes were innocent and guileless, but Sarah felt somehow stung by the remark.

"No, not really." Sarah shrugged. "It's just that I'm deciding what I should do. Until then, I'm doing my own thing—which right now means being a nomad, like I said."

"But . . . what does that mean?" Dana looked confused.

"Well, I'm working at Balloon Burger during the day and bartending here at night," Sarah said. "I also try to squeeze in acting auditions the rest of the time. It's hard, but I'm doing what I gotta do."

"Huh." Dana raised her eyebrows. "Balloon Burger . . . Are you a cashier or something?"

Sarah frowned, not liking Dana's tone. "As a matter of fact, I am." She tossed her head. "Flipping burgers, the whole nine yards. It's actually kind of fun."

"I bet it is," Dana said noncommittally.

Sarah's back stiffened as all her nostalgia about the *Shanghai Sail* evaporated. "So, what do you do?" she asked.

Dana's eyes lit up. "Well, remember Chris Chung, our R.A. on the cruise?"

"Yeah." Sarah shrugged, faintly recalling a scrawny, bespectacled guy who always seemed to be reprimanding her for one infraction or another.

"He and I just got engaged." Dana broke into a gleeful smile.

"We're getting married next year at the Ritz in Maui. I'm a real estate broker, and we got this great deal on a time-share out there for the honeymoon!"

Sarah wasn't sure if she was more disgusted by Dana's ill-concealed gloating or the fact that she made her feel fifteen again. It was amazing how gloating and competitive Asian people could be, she thought. Whether it was family, friends, or frenemies, both family functions and chance encounters in a bar were opportunities to boast.

"Well, isn't that lovely?" Sarah forced a smile. "Anyhow, it was nice talking to you, but I better get back to work now."

"Oh, of course," Dana exclaimed. "But wait—let me give you my number. We should meet up sometime. Chris and I can treat you to some congee and dim sum."

Treat her? Sarah fumed. Did she sound like she was in such dire straits that she couldn't afford her own bowl of pork with thousand-year-egg congee?

Even though the last thing she wanted was Dana's number, Sarah politely took down her digits. Inwardly, though, she told herself there was no way in hell she'd be seeing Dana again.

2

While her encounter with Dana left a sour aftertaste, Sarah was quickly distracted from it by the promise of Friday night, the evening she had been waiting for ever since Chad's call. It was the annual *Soap Opera Digest* party, and she couldn't be more excited. Dressed in a silky black strapless Diane von Fürstenberg dress that she'd spent a whole month's paycheck on, Sarah accompanied Chad to the Waldorf-Astoria Hotel for the festivities.

"This is so amazing." Sarah was starry-eyed as they strolled up the plushly carpeted stairs. "I owe you a whole month of Pinkberry for this!"

She gazed around the ornate, sumptuous lobby, where gigantic gilt mirrors glittered above mahogany leather chairs nestled among discreetly placed palm fronds. Growing up, she'd always loved the Waldorf; it wasn't as crassly touristy as the Plaza or as aloof and intimidating as the Palace. There was something very old world about the Waldorf, something that always made Sarah imagine flappers and their escorts sauntering down the hallways toward some Gatsby-like soiree. . . .

"It was the least I could do." Chad tossed his head. "I know this is nirvana for you. And look"—he pointed toward one of the ballrooms—"I think that's Drake Hogestyn over there! He's with the divine Deidre Hall on the buffet line."

"Omigosh," Sarah gasped. "It really is John Black!" She sighed. "Who would ever believe I'd be eating out of the same serving bowl as him?"

"Well, you can believe it," Chad announced. "It's all a reality now."

Sarah flashed him a grateful smile. As they continued checking out the soap celebs, someone called Chad from behind. Turning, they saw a woman in a glittery amethyst evening gown heading toward them. It was Karen Winters—Chad's friend and contact to the soaps.

"Hey, Chad . . ." Karen kissed him on both cheeks. "Thanks for coming! So excited to have you here."

"Hello, dear," Chad responded in kind. "Pleasure being here."

While Karen and Chad exchanged pleasantries, Sarah noticed a tall, chiseled man hovering behind Karen. A moment later, Karen was all hugs and exclamations as she realized who was standing behind her.

"Where are my manners?" Karen joked. "I'd like you guys to meet Daniel Wong. Daniel is a producer for *Asylum*."

Sarah's jaw dropped. *The* Daniel Wong? To other people, Daniel might be an ordinary guy with a job in television, but to Sarah, he was a celebrity on a par with the president.

"Nice to meet you." Chad shook Daniel's hand. "I'd like you to meet my friend Sarah Cho—probably the biggest *Asylum* fan in this room."

Sarah blushed. Normally she wasn't shy about meeting someone new, but she couldn't help being in awe of Daniel. For several seconds, she just stood there admiring him. She remembered reading an article in *Backstage* magazine about him a few years ago. He was in his mid-thirties, majored in theater at Brown University, and was the first Asian male actor to appear on an American soap opera. Before he became a producer on *Asylum*, he played the sexy villain Desmond on *Another Time* and appeared in a few off-Broadway plays. Since then, though, his career had taken off. After winning several *Soap Opera Digest* Awards, he'd become a top producer on *Asylum*. Looking like a cross between Korean actor Rick Yune and *Survivor: Cook Islands* winner Yul Kwon—tall, handsome, with that healthy California glow—Daniel was drop-dead gorgeous, and Sarah was instantly smitten. It was unbelievable that he was here, standing mere inches away from her.

"Hi." Sarah smiled shyly. "It's a pleasure to meet you. And yes, I really admire your work and the show."

Chad gave Sarah a strange look, no doubt marveling at her uncharacteristic formality, but Sarah ignored him.

"The pleasure is all mine." Daniel smiled. "Are you enjoying the party?"

"Yes, the party is wonderful," Sarah said, beaming. "It's my first time at the *Soap Opera Digest* Awards."

"Really? Well, as these award shows go, this isn't a bad one to start with," Daniel said. "The *Soap D* Awards are pretty laid-back. So, are you part of the industry? What type of work do you do?"

"I'm working on being an actress." Sarah licked her lips. "Done a few Off-Off-Broadway plays, but it's not exactly Broadway."

"Well, Broadway's not what it's all cracked up to be," Daniel said. "I did some plays back in my day, too, so I've been through the drill."

Karen cleared her throat. "I'm sorry to interrupt," she said, "but I have to go tend to some other guests—and get a drink. See you later, Daniel. It was nice meeting you, Sarah."

"You too." Sarah smiled.

"I'm following Karen," Chad chimed in. "I'm dying for a dirty martini."

Sarah suppressed a grin. One of the best things about having Chad as a friend was that he was a brilliant wingman. She winked her thanks to him.

"Nice meeting you," Daniel said.

"Likewise," Chad replied. "I'll be back in a bit."

As Sarah watched Chad walk away, she felt uncharacteristically nervous. She wasn't usually shy with guys and never had a problem making conversation with them, but she felt a bit out of her element—especially standing in the middle of the Waldorf with such a big-time soap opera producer. After all, he was famous, talented, and extraordinarily successful. And here she was—struggling with her life, flipping burgers and bartending.

"So, I'm guessing you're from New York?" Daniel asked.

"I grew up on Long Island." Sarah hesitated. "I do have a confession to make . . ." She bit her lip. "I'm probably the biggest soap opera geek in this place."

"You're kidding!" Daniel chuckled. "Not about the geek thing, but—I'm from Long Island. What part?"

"My parents are from Syosset," Sarah replied.

"Get out of here." Daniel shook his head. "My family is from Muttontown. I used to go to Roosevelt Field all the time as a kid."

"Probably not as much as me!" Sarah laughed as she flashed back to her formative teen mall years. Suddenly, she felt much more at ease. It was comforting to hear that Daniel was a Long Islander—or, as they would say, "Strong Islander." Two minutes ago, she'd felt they had nothing in common, but now she felt they almost had some sort of bond.

"And since you were so honest with me, I'll let you in on a secret," Daniel said. "I grew up a huge soap fan, too. Why do you think I became a soap opera producer? I grew up watching *All My Children* with my mom and kept following the story lines even when I was in college."

"Impressive." Sarah raised an eyebrow. "I never thought any guy other than Chad watched *All My Children*—or would admit to it without being tortured."

Daniel winked at her. "This will be our little secret."

He was smiling at her in a way that gave Sarah a little shiver of delight. What a novel thing, she marveled, to meet a guy so secure in his manhood that he had no trouble confessing to watching soap operas with his mother. . . .

"So I assume you live in Los Angeles since the *Asylum* studio is there?" Sarah asked.

"I do. I'm one of those New York transplants to Hollywood," Daniel replied. "Been in L.A. for five years now, and I really like it. It's laid-back, and the weather's nice all the time." He gazed at the heavily curtained windows across from them. "There's nothing better than waking up in the morning, taking a run on the beach, then having my morning coffee while I'm looking out to the ocean."

"Sounds like paradise." Sarah sighed. "I'd love to move out to L.A. one day, but right now I don't think I'm ready."

"How come?" Daniel asked.

"Well, all of my family and friends are here, so it's a little difficult, I guess." Sarah tried to imagine herself three thousand miles away from everyone she knew . . . but couldn't.

"I get it," Daniel said. "But sometimes you have to take the plunge." His eyes were understanding but serious as they met Sarah's. "There's a lot more opportunity in L.A. for actresses. There are acting classes, showcases, auditions every day. Being out there really might be better for your career—at least for now, anyway."

As Sarah listened to Daniel, she felt herself being carried away by both his words and his gaze. He was so knowledgeable and persuasive—and he seemed to really care about her career and her future. . . .

That was when she felt her cell phone vibrating in her clutch. She dug through her bag, pulled out her phone, and saw a text from Owen that read: "Call me ASAP, babe. Where are you?"

What could he possibly want at this inopportune moment? This better be an emergency, Sarah thought, trying not to feel too worried.

"Oh, crap, I have to make a phone call." Sarah sighed. "I'm so sorry."

Daniel shook his head. "No worries at all. Do what you have to do."

"Are you leaving soon?" Sarah asked.

"As a matter of fact, I think I am," Daniel he said, nodding. "I have a few meetings in the morning."

"Oh." Sarah tried not to look too disappointed. "When are you going back to L.A.?"

"I won't be going back until the end of the week, actually," Daniel said. "This is my little yearly East Coast break, so I want to stay out here as long as I can."

"Well, I'm sure you're really busy, but if you have any free time at all, I'd love to get any tips or advice you might be able to give me," Sarah blurted out.

As soon as the words left her mouth, though, she wished she could take them back. She didn't know what had possessed her. Daniel was an important producer who no doubt had a packed schedule and numerous obligations. If he had a moment of free time, why would he want to spend it with some nobody he barely knew?

Fortunately, Daniel didn't seem to have the same thoughts. "Sure, I'd love to grab a coffee with you or something." He paused. "I know better than anyone how hard it is to get into the biz— especially when you're not blond-haired, blue-eyed, and a product of Southern California." His eyes were sincere and empathetic as he held her gaze. "So if there's anything I can do to help, it would be my pleasure."

Sarah's heart suddenly started beating like competing drums in a high school band. "Let me get your number, and I'll give you mine" she said as she reached for her phone.

After a hurried explanation to Chad, Sarah walked outside the Waldorf to ring Owen, shivering a little in the night breeze. The balmy spring weather had been a welcome relief after winter, but the evenings still had a bite.

"Daaarling!" Owen yelled.

"Where are you?" Sarah demanded. "Are you okay? I got your text."

"I'm at Brass Monkey," Owen said, slurring his words. "Come now."

He hung up. Sarah knew Owen was drunk, but was he in trouble? Deciding that thinking about it wasn't going to help, she waved for a cab to take her down to the meatpacking district.

During the cab ride, she kept thinking about her conversation with Daniel. She couldn't believe that he was willing to meet up with her. After all, he was wildly successful, an established man with a powerful job. He wasn't some drunk goober like Owen partying his life away.

Just thinking about Daniel made Sarah smile. There was something exciting about an older man. Sarah had always dated men her age or even younger, but thinking about them now, she realized how immature they all were. Not sophisticated like Daniel. . . . Sarah shook her head. What was she thinking? She should just enjoy the evening and her time with Daniel at the party. It wasn't as though anything would come out of it. He lived in Los Angeles, anyway.

As she was pondering this, the cab pulled up in front of the Brass Monkey. After paying the driver, she walked carefully into the bar, trying not to ruin her dress. Taking a look at the crowd, she noticed they were all in jeans and tanks while she was still in her designer dress.

Owen better have a good reason for me to come down here, Sarah thought as she jostled her way through the crowd. Finally, she spotted him in the back with a bunch of guys in T-shirts.

"Owen!" Sarah hurried over. "Are you okay?"

"I'm perfect." Owen took a swig of his Yuengling. "So glad you're here, Sarah!"

"So, where's the fire?" Sarah asked.

As the words left her lips, she glanced at the group of guys milling around them. They were slapping one another and chortling over nothing discernible as they struggled to stand upright without the aid of a wall. For a moment, she thought she was in a scene from a poor man's *Animal House*. At the same time, she realized there was no emergency or apparent reason for her to come to the bar—other than to play audience to another of Owen's drunken adventures.

"Well, I puked a few times already in the bathroom," Owen said. "But I'm fine now. Have a beer and meet the guys." He handed her a Yuengling. "I was just telling them about how you and I served someone a booger burger last week."

Sarah had to smile at the thought of the incident. "That *was* hilarious," she conceded. "We'll have to serve another one when our fat boss comes in next week for inspection."

"So why don't you sit down and have a beer with us?" said one of Owen's friends, grinning.

Sarah started to sit on a stool, then paused as she noticed a suspicious-looking substance on the cracked black plastic. Suddenly, she remembered she was supposed to be deep in conversation with Daniel at the Waldorf—and would have been, but for Owen and his non-emergency. Instead, she was here in some beer-soaked dive, surrounded by these drunken fools. . . .

"No thanks. I'm going to leave," she said icily. "Owen, I'm actually really pissed off that you texted me with no emergency. I was at a nice party at the Waldorf talking to this mind-bogglingly handsome man before you interrupted us!"

"Handsome man?" Owen laughed. "Since when do you call men 'handsome'?"

"I'm being serious." Sarah scowled at him. "Please don't call me to tell me you want to puke. I'm out of here."

Sundays were always reserved for the Cho family dinners. Sarah and Lin would take the 10:38 train from Penn Station back to Syosset, while Amy would drive a whole five blocks to have dinner with their parents. Ever since Sarah began dorming in college and Lin moved to Manhattan, their mother Kim had named Sunday as the day the entire family would "reunite." For dinner, each of the girls would be responsible for cooking and bringing a different dish. Sarah's staple was steamed fish made with her own special garlic, ginger, and black bean sauce concoction. Lin's was double-cooked pork with onions, red and green peppers, and sesame chili sauce. And Amy always opted for her old standby: tofu-and-mushroom casserole.

"How was your week, girls?" Kim asked at the dinner table as she scooped some rice for the girls' father, Harry.

"The stock market was great." Lin took a bite of the pork. "Our unit made a killing this week."

"The pharmacy was really busy." Amy sighed. "I'm beat."

Sarah silently took a bite out of her own fish dish.

"Good—means business good!" Harry chimed in as he scooped up some rice with his chopsticks.

"What about you, Sarah?" Kim asked. "What happen to audition?"

"I won't hear until next week—but I did go to the best *Soap Opera Digest* party!" Sarah said excitedly. "It was so much fun. We saw John and Marlena from *Days of Our Lives!*"

"No audition?" Kim frowned. "How come?"

Sarah took a sip of her tea. "Just a slow week, I guess."

Her mother pursed her lips. "No such thing as slow week—just slow work."

Repressing the urge to roll her eyes, Sarah forced a patient smile. "I work very hard, Mom. Trust me, if there's an open call anywhere in the city, I find it."

"Then why nothing?" Kim demanded. "Even when I had small interest to be actress in Hong Kong, I got audition every week."

"Ma, this is different," Sarah protested. "New York is a really competitive market. There are so few roles out here and so many people vying for them. Some weeks there might not be anything casting. This week just happened to be one of them."

Kim waved Sarah's words away. "You need to work harder, look harder," she said, repeating the immigrant mantra Sarah had heard all the time as a kid. "Every day, you go and look for audition. No time to be lazy."

Sarah resisted the urge to throw up her hands in frustration. "This isn't about being lazy, Mom. And considering I'm working two jobs right now, I don't think anyone could say I'm lacking in effort."

"Then you not meant to be actress," her mother countered. "When things don't work out, you try something else—like me."

"Mom, I'm in a totally different situation from you—you can't even compare the two," Sarah exclaimed, feeling as if she were under a very unwelcome spotlight. She could tell her father and sisters were listening carefully even as they pretended to be chowing down.

"No different." Kim shook her head. "Sarah, I know what it's like to want to be actress. I was young, too. I try it. I fail. I don't want you to be like me." She waved her chopsticks at Sarah. "I come here to give you better life—we want you to have everything."

"Mom, you're worrying about nothing. Even though things are a little slow, there are still a lot of opportunities here." Sarah's voice rose. "Maybe if I didn't have to worry about being in New York all the time, I would move out to Los Angeles and finally get my break. But I know you would worry, so I don't go. Instead, I stay here—"

"Hey," Lin interrupted, "isn't my dish especially delicious today?"

Unfortunately, the rest of the family ignored her.

"How dare you?" Kim pointed her chopsticks at Sarah. "You should want to take care of your family and be with them. Look at Amy—she live at home during college and now she lives around the block."

"That's not fair," Sarah retorted. "I know you don't want me living in the city, but Lin didn't live at home either before she got married."

Kim shook her head. "Lin different. Lin banker and make money so she can afford apartment in Manhattan. You actress and don't have real job!"

And there it was again—her mother's ill-disguised contempt for her chosen profession. In her mother's eyes, she would never measure up to Lin in all her investment banker glory. Even worse, though, was the fact that Sarah was pretty sure she was second best even to Amy—as if anyone really wanted to be a pharmacist anyway.

"Acting is a real job!" Sarah sputtered. "And even Lin wasn't an overnight success. She moved to London for a year before she got her big promotion. Why didn't you yell at her for not taking care of her family and being with them?"

"Actually, she did yell," Lin tried to interject.

But Kim had had enough. Nostrils flaring, she made a sweeping dismissive gesture toward Sarah. "You know what? You want to fail at being actress so bad, then you go ahead. Move! Let me see how you survive. You crawl back to us in no time."

Sarah inhaled sharply. At that moment, all her usual patience with dealing with her mother's attitude abandoned her, and she suddenly knew how Lin felt back in the days of her daily battles with their mother.

Meanwhile, Lin, Amy, and Harry were silent, as if they didn't know quite what to do. Without saying a word, Sarah got up and left the dinner table. Lin called after her, but Sarah kept going.

When Lin turned back to the table, Kim was eating as if nothing were wrong. Harry and the girls looked at her.

"I'm not sorry," Kim said as she calmly took a bite of duck. "She is becoming actress-crazy. I bring her back to reality."

Shivering in the dark, Sarah all but ran to the railroad station near her parents' home.

Luckily, a train came quickly and she hopped on, taking the first seat she could find on the train heading back to Penn Station. She gazed out the window somberly . . . and that was when the tears came. Not even caring if people were looking at her, she started crying uncontrollably. Why couldn't her mother be supportive of her, especially when she too had once wanted to be an actress? If anyone should have understood, it should be her.

The rest of the train ride back to Manhattan took an eternity. Was she ever going to get anywhere if she stayed in New York?

What if she really did need to go to L.A. in order to fulfill her dreams? And if she stayed in New York, could she accept the possibility that she might never make it as an actress? Trying to imagine herself with a desk job, Sarah realized that she just couldn't give up her dream. Wearily, she trudged off the train and onto the crowded platform.

As she walked out of Penn, her phone rang.

"Hi, Sarah." It was Daniel!

"Oh, hi," Sarah said as casually as she could. "How are you?"

"I'm good. Yourself?"

"Not so good. I was just visiting my parents and got into a huge fight with my mom," Sarah began, then stopped. Why was she boring Daniel with such childish problems?

"I'm sorry to hear that." Daniel's voice was sympathetic. "What happened?"

"Long story," Sarah said. "Let's not talk about me. How were your meetings?"

"They were good," he replied. "But the reason I'm calling is that I can't meet up. Unfortunately, we're a little backed up with shooting, so I have to take a red-eye back to L.A. tonight."

"That's too bad." Sarah's heart sank. "Sorry to hear that."

"Well, listen, I'm sorry I couldn't have that coffee with you," Daniel said, "but I owe you a rain check when you make it out to L.A. It really was a pleasure meeting you the other night."

Daniel's words brought a little bloom of warmth within Sarah. Suddenly, the night didn't seem quite so cold as she massaged his words in her head. *It really was a pleasure . . .*

"Thanks." Sarah smiled. "It was so great of you to call. And who knows? Maybe I'll be coming out to L.A. sooner than you think." She paused. "Would it be all right if I called you sometime for some advice about the business?"

"You better," Daniel said warmly. "Take care."

3

Even though it was a Monday, the crowds were out in force at Buddha Bar. Which translated to more work for Sarah that evening at the swanky, chic lounge. The past weekend had been particularly tough, with at least five bridge-and-tunnel birthday parties. Sarah counted at least five hundred dirty martinis served and umpteen hundred people yelling at her.

Stifling a sigh, Sarah pushed back a stray hair. Normally, she enjoyed bartending; she liked meeting new people, and there were worse gigs than serving drinks. Except for the skimpy spandex minidresses, it was actually a pretty amusing job and a relatively easy way to make cash fast. The past week, though, had taken a toll on her. Sarah didn't know if this had anything to do with the fact that she and her mother had yet to speak since their fight more than a week ago, but she did know that she'd been steadfastly avoiding her family—even Lin.

"Hey, girlie," a Wall Street type bellowed from the bar. "I need my drink refilled, and this time on the rocks, please."

Sarah nodded. "I'll be right there," she said as she fixed a Cosmo for another customer.

"Lady!" a drunk blond girl yelled out. "I've been waiting for five minutes now! Where's my vodka tonic?"

"I'm making it next," Sarah said as calmly as she could.

She shook her head as she streamed Grey Goose through a strainer. Why was everything getting so stressful? Maybe it was a sign—a sign that she had to make some changes in her life.

"What the fuck?" the Wall Street type said, scowling. "You said you were making mine first!"

Sarah glared at him, then bit her lip. She had to force herself to remember her boss's number one motto: "The customer is always right."

"Coming right up, sir," she said cheerfully.

As she started to make his drink, a group of guys ambled up to the bar. It was Owen and his buddies.

"Sarah, babe!" Owen smiled broadly. "A round of Yuenglings, please, for the five of us. How's my favorite Asian bartender?"

"Hi, sweetie." Sarah gave him a wan smile. "This is a nice surprise."

"Get in line, asshole," the Wall Street type interrupted. "The China doll is fixing me my drink."

Owen gave him a look of utter disgust. "Excuse me—who are you?"

"Stop it, Owen," Sarah ordered. "I'll take care of this."

She started to hand the drink to the Wall Street type, but as she was leaning forward, a busboy jostled her accidentally—and the drink went flying into the Wall Street type's face. Seeing his dumbfounded, dripping wet countenance, Sarah began to laugh.

"I'm so sorry!" she cried, trying desperately to look appropriately appalled.

"You fucking bitch!" yelled the Wall Street type. "You're going to pay for this!" Furious—and drunk—he slapped Sarah's arm hard.

Stunned, Sarah jerked back. "I said I was sorry! It was an accident!"

"Did I just see you slap her?" Owen suddenly appeared at Sarah's elbow, his expression outraged.

Before the Wall Street guy could even respond, Owen took a big swing at him—and punched him straight in the nose. That was when the whole bar started screaming: "Fight! Fight! Fight!"

"Owen," Sarah yelled amid the chaos, "you shouldn't have done that!"

"Why not?" Owen demanded. "He shouldn't be hitting anyone, especially not a woman and especially not you!"

That was when the manager came out of the back room.

"What's going on here?" Donnie pushed his way through the crowd.

The Wall Street type staggered up, clutching his bloody nose. "That fucking asshole punched me," he bellowed. "And he's friends with your crappy bartender!"

"You asked for it, you jerk," Owen yelled.

"Shut it!" Donnie pointed at Owen. "There will be no fighting at my club. Get out now, and don't come back here again."

"But, Donnie," Sarah protested, "that guy hit me first. My friend was just trying to protect me."

Donnie turned around, the vein on his forehead throbbing. "What did I always tell you?" He jabbed a finger at her.

Sarah looked down at the floor. "The customer is always right, " she muttered.

"That's right," Donnie snapped. "And you want to know something else? You're fired!"

Sarah's jaw dropped. No, she thought, she must have misheard him. There was no way—no way that he had just said what she thought he'd said. . . .

"Donnie—," she began.

"Don't Donnie me!" he snarled. "I don't need this bullshit! My club isn't some crappy dive bar, and I don't need your little frat-boy friends to come in here and disrupt business. You're fired! Now get out!"

Head buzzing, brain barely processing what was happening, Sarah grabbed her purse from beneath the counter and fled toward the exit. Pushing her way through the crowd and out the doors, she felt her eyes well with tears.

This couldn't be happening to her. Sarah Cho wasn't someone who got fired. Well, okay, so maybe she had been fired one other time in her life—but the Gap gave her the ax only after she didn't show up to work for three weeks straight while flagrantly abusing her employee discount card. At any rate, that wasn't really comparable. It was only the Gap, after all. This . . . this was different. This was the primary gig supporting her financially while she pursued her acting dreams, not some insignificant after-school job that she'd taken for pocket money and 20 percent off her favorite jeans.

Her cell phone trilled. Blinking back her tears, Sarah answered it.

"Hello?" she said, sniffling as she stumbled across the cobblestone street.

"Sarah!" Owen's voice blared. "Where are you?"

Sarah glanced around through wet eyes. "In front of the Gansevoort."

"Stay put," he ordered. "I'll be there in a sec."

Sarah snapped her phone shut. She cast a forlorn look at the throng of B&T clinging to the velvet rope outside the hotel. They seemed so carefree, so happy, their only concern whether they would make it past the scowling, black-suited bouncers on patrol. . . .

"Sarah!" Owen yelled from across the street.

Looking up, she saw her friend's familiar figure. As she rubbed her eyes, he quickly beat the traffic light and jaywalked across to her. The minute he reached her, he wrapped his arms around her.

"I'm so sorry, babe." Owen's expression was contrite. "I know you probably hate my drunk loser self right now, but I just couldn't let that asshole treat you like that."

Sarah sighed. "I know, I know—the guy was a total jerk. I know all of that . . . but I just got *fired*, Owen. What am I going to do? What am I going to tell my parents?"

"Don't tell them anything yet," he advised. "You still have enough rent money left for another month. In the meantime, just keep working at Balloon Burger with me, and we'll find you another bartending job."

Looking up at him, Sarah couldn't help but smile. Sometimes it seemed she'd known Owen forever. In reality, though, it was only about two years ago that she'd reluctantly dragged herself into the Balloon Burger, forced to suffer the indignity of flipping burgers so that she could make ends meet. As she'd tried not to cry into the chocolate milkshake she was pouring, someone threw a French fry at her. Glancing up, she saw Owen giving her an impish grin as he made faces behind their dorky boss's back. Despite herself, Sarah began to giggle. After all, who couldn't use some harmless entertainment, especially when it came from such an endlessly amusing source? Working at the Balloon Burger wasn't exactly a thrill a minute, but Owen's wisecracks made the job infinitely more tolerable.

Still, for a long time Owen was just this drunken buffoon who was good for a few laughs. It was only after listening to his morning-after stories for a few months that Sarah had finally agreed to venture out with him and his crew one night. They had been exactly as she'd envisioned them: loud, rowdy, ridiculous in their drunken antics. What Sarah hadn't counted on was how much she enjoyed being with them—whether it was cheap wine at a streetside café in the afternoon or PBR at the dingiest college dive.

Even so, that didn't mean she and Owen agreed on everything. In their friendship, at least—although not necessarily in any other phase of her life—Sarah was the responsible one. Owen, on the other hand, lived every day by the seat of his pants.

"It's just not that simple." Sarah shook her head. "My parents already think I'm a failure. If I can't even keep a bartending gig, I don't want to think about the hell I'm going to be in for. . . ."

"Like I said," Owen told her soothingly, "we won't tell them about it. Just keep this on the DL—especially from Amy—and everything will be cool."

"Ugh," Sarah groaned. "She's the worst! I bet she'd hightail it to my mom's as soon as she found out."

Owen put an arm around her. "Let's get a beer and forget about this—at least for tonight, okay?"

Sarah hung her head, but after a long moment, she nodded. "Okay."

The morning came too soon for Sarah.

Sunlight flooded her bedroom as she squinted at her alarm clock. It was barely eight—crack-of-dawn time for her. Making things worse, she was extremely hung over—no surprise, given how she'd thrown herself into drinking her sorrows away the night before. Levering herself up gingerly, she squinted toward the ear-splintering noise that had woken her up again. It was her phone—ringing at the hearing-impaired volume level. *Stupid, crazy Owen must have been playing with her phone again!*

Fuming, she flipped open the phone. "Hello—," she began.

"The best show is on SOAPnet right now," Chad exclaimed. "It's from season one of *I Wanna Be a Soap Star*, and one of the judges is the *General Hospital* casting director Mark Teschner. He's great—and sooo nice. He just let this woman down gently even though she basically sucked ass! Not to mention the fact that she lied about her boob job—season one was such a good season."

Sarah shook her head, her morning-addled brain refusing to process Chad's babble. "Chad, why are you up at the crack of dawn watching this? And more importantly, why are you calling to tell me this?"

"Uh-oh," Chad said. "Did our little Sarah wake up on the wrong side of the bed today?"

Sarah rubbed her eyes. "I got fired last night," she mumbled.

"What?" Chad gasped. "How did this tragedy happen?"

She sighed. "It's a long story. This jerk was at the bar, and I accidentally spilled a drink on him. Anyway, he kind of slapped my arm, and then Owen came and punched him—"

"Wow!" Chad gasped. "That sounds exactly like this one

scene from *All My Children*—except that Susan Lucci wouldn't be caught dead bartending. How excit—"

"No, it's not exciting at all," Sarah interrupted. "I got fired! How can I tell my parents? Not only am I the only Cho daughter making menial wage, but now I can't even keep a job mixing drinks! As if I can go any lower on the family loser scale."

"Yikes." Chad sighed. "You better not let Amy find out."

"Owen already said that," Sarah groaned. "She'll rip me to shreds if she finds out."

Just thinking about Amy was enough to make any prospect of further sleep disappear. Finally managing to get out of bed, she grabbed a Kleenex on her desk to dab at her suddenly watery eyes. Phone in hand, she sniffled and plopped herself down on her desk chair to check her e-mail.

"Well, you do have some money saved up, don't you?" Chad asked. "You can probably pay the rent for a couple more months. Hopefully by then something good will have happened or you'll have found another bartending gig."

Sarah chewed her lip. "I guess . . . but I've never lied like this to my parents before. I mean, there was the time I flunked chemistry, and I didn't tell them about all those times I broke curfew, but I— Holy shit!" Her gaze froze as the words on the computer screen caught her eye.

"What? Don't keep me in suspense!" Chad demanded.

"I was just checking my e-mail," Sarah said excitedly, "and guess what? Daniel Wong just wrote me an e-mail!"

"Well, don't stop there—what does it say?"

Sarah took a deep breath and began to read:

Hi Sarah—

    Hope you're well. Just wanted to drop you a line and see how things were going in New York. L.A.'s good—busy as usual. Anyhow, I'm writing to you because I wanted to let you know that *Asylum* is actually having a huge 25th anniversary party this coming weekend, and I wanted to see if you were interested in coming out here. There will be tons of industry people, including casting directors and other producers. It would be a great opportunity for you. I know it's a bit late notice, but it might be something to think about.

—Daniel

"You should totally go," Chad exclaimed. "Can I come, too? If you see that hot Australian actor from *General Hospital* there, I will die and hate you forever—"

"Chad," Sarah interrupted, "control yourself! It's too early in the morning to be gushing over Jax. I really do want to go this party, though . . . too bad I'll never pull it off."

"Sure you can," Chad egged her on. "Tell your parents that you have an audition in L.A. Don't tell them you're networking—they wouldn't know what that means. Just tell them you're auditioning and that you have to go out there ASAP!"

Sarah shook her head. "It's not that simple. They're going to ask me where I'm getting the money to go out there. Then they're going to ask me where I'm staying, how long I'm staying, what kind of an audition it is, will there be a love scene—"

Chad burst out laughing. "Come on now. What is this, the Addams Family or something? Who cares?"

"Oh, my crazy family does," Sarah groaned. "Even when I'm an hour late for dinner, it's where were you, who were you with, why didn't you call—"

"You're twenty-four years old," Chad interrupted, "not twelve. You should be free to do whatever you want—it's your life, after all."

Sarah snorted. "I don't know, Chad. I already got fired. I would feel really guilty if I went away to a party in L.A."

"Sarah, you'll never be where you want if you listen to everything your family tells you to do," Chad admonished. "The only way to break out of your rut is to show everyone that you'll do whatever it takes to make it." His tone turned serious. "Remember Lady Macbeth? You stayed up four nights straight trying to perfect your monologue."

"I know." Sarah sighed. "But that was different. This whole situation is different. I just don't know . . . I feel like my life is such a shit show right now." She took a deep breath, thoughts of her unceremonious firing replaying in her head. "I promise I'll think about it. Thanks for listening, though. Time for a fun lunch with the family now—I'll talk to you later."

After hanging up the phone, Sarah sat back and propped her legs up on her desk. Looking at the azure sky outside her window, she thought longingly of the prospect of being three thousand miles away from her disaster of a life. How amazing would it be to party with Daniel and the cast of *Asylum*? And how fantastic would it be if that actually led to an opportunity to star on a soap?

"*Har gow, shui-mai!* Shrimp, pork dumplings!"

A beleaguered-looking woman carting trays of dim sum strolled past the Cho family table at the Min Min Garden restaurant. Hailing her, Sarah's new brother-in-law, Stephen, ordered a tin of the shrimp dumplings.

"I know you love these," Stephen said to Lin as the woman shoveled the steaming metal tin onto the table.

"Thanks, hon." Lin bestowed a smile on her newly minted husband.

Kim beamed at the picture of domestic bliss presented by her eldest daughter and new son-in-law. They couldn't have been closer to perfection if they tried—a young, attractive, professional couple who conscientiously followed all the old Chinese traditions. As opposed to Sarah, who was picking silently at her beef noodles.

"Sarah, look at your sister," Kim instructed. "She happy and find good man. Amy marry soon, too. What about you?"

Sarah looked up, rendered temporarily speechless. What about her? She was only twenty-four and had the whole world ahead of her, as Chad would say. Why would she want to saddle herself with a husband right now?

"I'm not even twenty-five yet," Sarah protested. "I'll find someone someday. Right now I need to concentrate on other things in my life."

"Yeah, like finding a real job," Amy chimed in. "Not like that pretend bartending thing. Or being a starving actress!"

Sarah resisted the impulse to throttle her sister. "Whatever." She glared at Amy, her hangover swiftly making a return appearance. "Not everyone finds pharmaceuticals as thrilling as you do, Amy."

"At least I know where my next paycheck is coming from." Amy lifted her chin. "You claim to want to be an actress, but I don't even see you go on auditions. All you do is hang out with your drunk white friends." She wrinkled her nose in distaste. "The Cho sisters are not like that—look at Lin and me."

"Hey, hey, hey," Lin jumped in. "Amy, no need to go down that road. We're all grown up, and we make our own decisions here. Let Sarah be—let her make her own mistakes and learn."

Mistakes? Furiously, Sarah blinked as she put down her chopsticks. She couldn't believe it. Lin was supposed to be her big defender—the only one in her whole ridiculous family who was ever in her corner. How could she turn on Sarah now? And what kinds of mistakes did she think Sarah was making?

"So you agree with them, Lin?" Sarah's voice rose. "You think I'm making a mess of my life, too? Kind of like when you dated Drew Black and made the mistake of bringing him home to meet the family?"

The table fell silent. Lin's whole relationship with the infamous Drew Black was one of those things never discussed among the family—and Sarah knew it.

"Uh . . ." Stephen cleared his throat. "Maybe we should talk about something else. Why don't we just all try to enjoy our dim sum and relax?"

But there was no way that Sarah was going to relax after this. It was bad enough that she had just gotten fired—a miserable mess that hung over her like an ever-present stormcloud. But while she felt terrible keeping it secret from her family, this whole episode showed exactly why she had no choice. Even though they had no idea about the firing, they were already attacking her with unrelenting ruthlessness. And that was when she did the unthinkable.

"You guys are all wrong," Sarah said, the words tumbling out of her mouth as if of their own volition. "I have news. . . . I—I . . . actually have an audition."

Amy stared at her, surprise creeping its way across her face. Meanwhile, the rest of the table stopped midmastication as all eyes turned toward Sarah.

"Wow . . ." Stephen was the first to recover. "With who? That's so great. Congratulations!"

Sarah smiled at him. "Thanks, Stephen. It's with *Asylum*— the soap opera—and . . . it's in L.A."

Kim's eyebrows rose at the mention of L.A.

"Los Angeles? You go fly for an audition in Los Angeles? That is too much. Where you get the money? Where you stay? When you going? Love scene?" Kim asked.

Sarah smiled grimly; as she'd told Chad, she was a fortune-teller with her family.

"I'm going next week," she said quickly. "The producers are paying for me to go out there."

"Paying for you?" Kim frowned. "How come? What they want from you?"

Inwardly, Sarah cringed. As usual, Kim's radar was spot-on. But even though she felt guilty lying to her family, this was the only thing that was keeping them from attacking her. If they knew the truth . . . Sarah swallowed. It seemed like every time she opened her mouth she was telling another fib, but Sarah knew she couldn't stop.

"Yes." Sarah forced her voice to remain steady. "*Asylum* is a big-budget soap opera, which is why they're flying me out there. I'll be staying at . . . a friend's place."

Good thing her family didn't know anything about the acting world!

"I don't believe you," Amy burst out. "Ma is right—they have to want something from you."

"Don't believe me"—Sarah tossed her head—"but I'm going—this weekend. There's even a big *Asylum* anniversary party, so I'll be going to that, too."

Finally, she'd told the truth about something. Sarah knew she was probably more guilty than most of telling a little fib here and there; in fact, she often liked to think of herself as a great scam artist who could talk her way out of everything. This whole *Asylum* lie, though . . . even Sarah felt that this particular "story" was going too far.

"I'm sorry if it sounded like I doubted you," Lin spoke up. "I guess I'm just surprised you didn't tell us earlier. I think it's great that you have an audition with them. Just be careful. People in the industry can be kind of fake sometimes."

Sarah stared at her. Even though this whole thing was a lie, she was taken aback by how Lin seemed only semisupportive.

"You better call me every day when you there." Kim shook her finger at Sarah. "I'm not happy, but you do what you want to do. I don't want to argue with you anymore. Bad for my health."

And just like that, Sarah had solved her problem. For now, anyway.

4

The first thing Sarah did when she got home was turn on her computer and book a flight to L.A. The second thing she did was write an e-mail:

Hi Daniel,
    Great to hear from you. Thanks so much for the e-mail and thanks so much for the invite! This is so exciting that I actually think I am going to take you up on the offer. I'm booking a flight as we speak. So, I assume the party is Saturday night, right? More importantly, what am I supposed to wear?! ☺ Any cheap places you can suggest for me to stay near the party?
                                        Look forward to seeing you,
                                        Sarah

As Sarah clicked "Send" on her computer, she broke into a smile. Yes, she had just told her family the biggest lie of her life. And yet . . . she couldn't help but feel a rush. So this was what it felt like to be Owen—to be spontaneous, devil-may-care, living only for the moment. As Owen would say, what was life without a little insanity?

All her life, Sarah had listened to her mother's lectures about how to be a proper Chinese daughter. Before Lin married Stephen and became the apple of Kim's eye, she was the cautionary tale that Kim liked to trot out at every family gathering. Lin was throwing her life away with that evil white man and on and on and on. While Amy had gleefully played the peanut gallery from the sidelines, Sarah had watched her sister's debacle with a certain wistfulness. Sure, she knew as well as anyone else that Drew had disaster written all over him. But he was handsome and charming, and Lin seemed to be having the adventure of her life with him—so why shouldn't she? Wasn't everyone entitled to a little adventure? That was all Sarah had ever wanted, too. Sometimes it seemed everyone had their crazy stories but her. Now, though, L.A. might just give her that story—after all, she was going not only for the *Asylum* party, but also to spend time with Daniel Wong.

Thinking about Daniel, Sarah felt a smile creeping involuntarily across her lips. She had never been one of those girls with an obsession for older men, but there was something about Daniel that drew her to him—something other than the obvious facts that he was hot and successful and sophisticated. For some reason, he actually seemed . . . genuine.

"Would you like your Balloon Burger superburst size?" Sarah smiled brightly at her customer Thursday morning.

"Yes, please." The middle-aged pencil pusher type barely glanced up from his Sudoku puzzle.

Sarah tapped in the order. As she did, Owen walked up from behind her and gave her a little nudge.

"Hey, killer," he greeted her. "What's the latest?"

"I'm going to L.A. this weekend," Sarah blurted out. "I've decided to go to the *Asylum* party and do some networking!"

"Fuck yea!" Owen gave her a high five. "Is this an invite from that Asian dude you keep talking about?"

Sarah felt herself blush as she handed the burger meal to the customer. "Yes." She smiled. "It should be fun."

"You are so going to get laid," Owen hooted. "I love it! That's my girl! Now remember, while you're there, find me a hot young emaciated actress."

"You are such an idiot!" Sarah burst out laughing. "But I'll see what I can do."

"I'm really happy for you, babe." Owen squeezed her shoulder. "You deserve to go and live a little after everything that happened last week."

"I know." Sarah took a deep breath. "I just wish I didn't have to lie to my family to do this. I mean, I told them I was going there for an audition, and I still haven't even told them that I got fired!"

"Really?" Owen's eyes widened. "I have to admit—I'm shocked . . . but good for you. All you got to do is carpe diem, and you'll be fine."

"I hope so. I'm running pretty low on cash." Sarah ran a hand through her desperately-in-need-of-a-salon-visit bangs. "Not only is this trip going to cost me a fortune, but I only have a couple of months' rent left in savings. If something doesn't pan out soon, I don't know what I'm going to do."

She frowned glumly down at the counter. That was when Owen tucked something into her hand. Looking down, Sarah blinked at the wad of bills suddenly nestled in her fist.

Owen lowered his voice. "Sar, here's three hundred bucks. I just went to the bank—use it for L.A."

Sarah opened her mouth, but for once words escaped her. Of all the things she would have expected—this was definitely not one of them. Knowing how tight Owen was with money himself, Sarah was genuinely touched.

"What are you doing?" she protested. "I didn't tell you all of this so you would give me money. Believe me, I'll be fine."

"No, you won't—you'll be behind on rent if you don't find a bartending gig ASAP, and then you won't be able to go to L.A. to become rich and famous." Owen busied himself with refilling the ketchup bin. "And since I'm partly responsible for you losing your job, I really can't let that happen. Besides, it's no big deal.

I made some overtime last week, so I'll be okay for a while. Right now, you need this a lot more than me."

Overwhelmed, Sarah suddenly felt teary, not sure how to respond. Here she was, always saying that Owen didn't have a care in the world—and here he was, showing that he really did care.

"I don't know what to say," she mumbled finally.

"I do." Owen's voice was firm. "Take the money, go have a great time, and in return, I ask only that you tell me a story about getting laid."

Sarah swatted him playfully. "Hmm . . . no promises, but thanks so much, Owen. I'm really touched." She threw her arms around him.

Owen hugged her back. "No prob. You know I love ya, babe." He chuckled. "When you become a big star, you can pay me back triple the amount and take me as your date to everything."

"You and Chad will have to fight for that right," Sarah teased.

"Ha!" Owen snorted. "I can take Chad anytime." He tapped her on the head. "Okay, catch you later—gotta run an errand for the boss man now."

Smiling after him, Sarah took off her apron and whipped out her cell phone. That was when she saw the text message from Daniel.

HEY THERE . . . JUST GOT YOUR E-MAIL. SOUNDS GREAT—GIVE ME A CALL LATER. PARTY IS ON FRIDAY NIGHT. LOOK FORWARD TO SEEING YOU.

Sarah held back a squeal. While it was always nice to get a text from someone she had a crush on, this was different—this was a text from one of the top producers on the very soap she dreamed of starring on. This was one of those opportunities that every aspiring actress dreamed about, and Sarah vowed to make the most of it as she reread the message. And if anything romantic was to happen with Daniel, well, that would just be the icing on top of an already scrumptious cake. . . .

Sarah shook her head. *Get hold of yourself. Daniel Wong is a big-time Hollywood producer. He probably has six girlfriends and sixty other women on speed dial. He's just trying to be nice,* Sarah tried to reason with herself, *and he probably hasn't given you a second thought.*

And yet, she mused, as she closed her phone, she couldn't help but hope.

Fortunately, Sarah didn't have too much time to obsess over Daniel's text because she had to leave work and meet Chad for their pre–L.A. trip dinner. For the occasion, she had made reservations at the Dos Caminos Soho, their favorite Mexican restaurant in the city.

"Your story is so going to be a great *E! True Hollywood* story," Chad said dreamily. "Girl lies to parents, goes to Hollywood, falls in love with Tinseltown producer mogul, makes it big, and tells parents to fuck off!"

Sarah felt a twinge of guilt at the reminder of her not-so-little lie.

"That's not true." She took a hasty sip of sangria. "I would never tell my parents to fuck off. They're just a little uptight, that's all. I just wish I didn't have to lie to them to prove I can make it."

Chad waved her concerns away. "Enough about the Chos—talk to me about the man." He leaned forward. "So where do you think Daniel will take you to dinner . . . some high-powered hot spot like Spago? Or some romantic hideaway trattoria in Redondo Beach? And where will you share your first kiss? Will it be at some West Hollywood lounge or up in some Hollywood Hills mansion out of *Cribs*?"

"Whatever, Chad!" Sarah pushed him, laughing. "I haven't thought about Daniel at all, much less about if and where we're kissing!"

Chad held up his hand, catching her gaze. "Sarah, how long have I known you?"

For a moment, they just looked at each other in silence. Then they broke into simultaneous laughter.

"Okay, okay." Sarah giggled. "Definitely the Hills. Maybe in his Mercedes—while we're looking out on the city from the mountaintop at night." She chewed her lip. "What kind of a kisser do you think he'll be? I mean, he's probably kissed a ton of beautiful women. Plus, he's ten years older than me, which means he must be so much more experienced—"

"Oh, my God." Chad pretended to faint. "I'm getting all weak-kneed just thinking about it! Forget about getting thrills from looking at profiles on MySpace—I'm living vicariously through you!"

Sarah laughed and happily sipped her second glass of sangria. Feeling suddenly ebullient, she raised her glass to make a toast.

"To L.A.," she announced. "Let's hope it lives up to the billing!"

Chad clinked glasses with her. "To L.A.! May you come back with a story that would make Luke and Laura jealous."

Sarah took a hearty swig from her glass, feeling her worries start to evaporate. "I know I've been kind of dishonest, but we all have to get our hands dirty sometimes to get what we want . . . right?" She looked at her friend hopefully.

"Absolutely," Chad agreed. "Look, you're not doing anything bad. You're just protecting yourself from the inevitable hissy-fit your family would throw. And once you become rich and famous, it'll all be worth it."

Sarah felt a rush of relief. "Okay, good." She exhaled. "I wish you could come out with me. It would be so much fun."

"I know. . . ." Chad sighed. "You know I'd be there in a sec if I could. I mean, who would give up the chance to check out Deidre Presley on *Asylum?*"

Sarah cast a fond smile at her friend. While she often envied Lin's ever-present support network of girlfriends, Sarah decided that there were worse things than having Chad and Owen as her own support system. Even though they were guys, she had always been able to share anything with them. In some ways, they were easier to deal with—never caring if she was wearing last year's style and also having that all-important male perspective on things. Chad was an even better listener than any of the girls Sarah knew. If he could be a bridesmaid at her wedding, she would let him in a heartbeat—he would probably even be able to pull off the purple taffeta.

"Well, my plane leaves tomorrow." Sarah took a deep breath. "You can be sure I'll be texting you all weekend. I just hope this whole thing doesn't turn out to be a total disaster."

Chad looked her squarely in the eye. "Sarah," he said sternly, "this is not the end of the world. You're just living a little. You're all grown up now—and that means that you have to learn to function without your parents' say-so."

Sarah exhaled. "I know, I know. It's just that I keep thinking about all the things that could go wrong. Like—what if my plane crashes or something and then Amy finds out I lied about everything? Instead of mourning for me, my family'd probably be talking about how it was all my own fault that I got killed."

Chad rolled his eyes. "Either you need therapy, my dear, or you need to just snap out of it. You're going to have a great time, network, and possibly get some really good leads. Then you'll fly back and that will be the end of that."

"I hope so." Sarah pasted on a determined smile. "How am I going to get by without you?"

"You should be able to get by for forty-eight hours, and if not, I'm only a text message away." Chad grinned. "Now let's get the check and get outta here so you can go home and raid your closet. I want to see you showing those L.A. girls how it's done at the *Asylum* bash!"

The moment Sarah walked in her apartment, her cell phone rang.

"Hey there, it's Daniel . . ." Daniel's increasingly familiar baritone came through the phone.

"Hi!" Sarah burst into a gleeful smile. "I was just going to call you. How's life in the fast lane?"

He laughed. "It's treating me pretty well. Everything's been really hectic getting ready for the anniversary event. There's going to be a ton of media—it'll be a madhouse, but it should be great."

"Sounds amazing. I can't believe I'm coming tomorrow." Sarah hugged herself at the thought. "I do have a question, though—I still need to book a room for my stay. Any ideas?"

"Well, that's actually why I'm calling," Daniel said. "I was thinking about your situation, and well, I'm going to go out on a limb here. My sister's out of town, but I have her keys. I know she won't mind if you crash for a couple of nights—just as long as you don't have a keg party."

"Well . . ." Sarah heaved a mock sigh. "I throw a keg party every night, so I'm afraid that won't work."

Daniel chuckled. "Well, there's always the Super Eight motel a few blocks down from the party."

Sarah giggled, but there was a nervous taste in her throat. She felt suddenly at a loss, not sure what to do. After all, she barely knew Daniel. How could she stay at the home of someone she didn't know *and* accept an offer from someone she barely knew? If Amy—or her mother—found out about this, they would have a nervous breakdown . . . after they locked her in her room for the next five years. But then there was the part of Sarah that was thrilled at the thought of Daniel taking such a personal interest in her. After all, he *was* Daniel Wong—and he was opening up his sister's home to her. How could she possibly refuse such a generous offer, especially one from a top Hollywood producer?

"Your offer sounds great, Daniel," she said, then hesitated. "But I feel a little weird about this. I mean, I wouldn't want to impose on you—or your sister. I don't even know her. Would she really want a complete stranger in her home? It might be a little strange if I crashed at her place, if you know what I mean. . . ."

"Believe me, you wouldn't be imposing," Daniel assured her. "I've rented the place out to some of our visiting actors because my sister spends so much time in London. I remember what it was like starting out, and since I'm the one that invited you, I don't want you having to spend a fortune on this party." He paused. "I know we've only met once, but for some reason, I have a good feeling about you. But . . . if you feel uncomfortable about this, I completely understand."

Hearing the words uttered by Daniel, Sarah felt a sudden flutter. Was it her imagination or did he sound a little disappointed? The last thing she wanted to do was upset him or make him regret his generous invitation. Feeling torn, she chewed her lip in dismay. She desperately wanted to spend every minute she could with Daniel, and this would be a perfect way to do it. And it certainly would help her financial situation to not have to pay for a hotel; in her excitement at talking to Daniel, she'd forgotten about the money issue. That was when she had a sudden flashback to her firing from Buddha and the subsequent dim sum outing where her family had chewed her out so mercilessly. Given all that, how could she let some puritanical streak keep her from achieving her dreams?

"No, I think it sounds wonderful." Sarah cleared her throat. "Actually, Daniel, if your offer still stands, I would love to accept the invitation. You're being very kind and generous, and I would definitely save some money."

"Are you sure?" Daniel asked. "The last thing I would want to do is make you feel uncomfortable."

"Not at all," Sarah said firmly. "I just didn't want to impose on you or your sister. Thanks so much! You've been so kind—I hope you'll at least let me buy you dinner."

Daniel chuckled. "Absolutely. I could always use an In-N-Out burger."

"In-N-Out?" Sarah's eyes lit up. "That's my favorite. I can't wait to order a cheeseburger, Animal Style."

"I'm impressed," Daniel teased. "You already sound like a true Angeleno."

Sarah blushed. "Well, I do love my In-N-Out. And of course we can go there, but I'd like to take you out to more than just a fast-food joint to pay you back."

"We can talk about that later. I'm just glad you're coming," Daniel said. "Hopefully, this will be worth it for you."

"Are you kidding me?" Sarah exclaimed. "This isn't just the highlight of my year—it's the highlight of my decade! You'll be sorry you invited me after I chew your ear off about how much I love every actor at the party."

"I'm willing to take my chances," Daniel said. "Being the self-centered producer that I am, I can hear people sing praises about my show forever."

All of a sudden, Sarah felt immeasurably lighter. It was almost as if she were already in Los Angeles and far, far away from all of her problems. It was amazing how talking to Daniel could made her feel so free and invincible, as if there weren't an obstacle in the world that could keep her from becoming the star she was meant to be.

"Careful—you might get your wish," Sarah said, beaming. "So where should I meet you after I land?"

"I'll text you the address of my sister's place, and I'll meet you there," Daniel replied. "If you need a ride, just let me know and I can pick you up at the airport."

"Sounds fabulous." Sarah was almost bursting with glee. "Thanks so much again! I really appreciate this."

"You bet," Daniel said warmly. "Safe travels."

Sitting at JFK and waiting to board her flight the next day, Sarah felt strangely different. Every other time she'd been to the airport, she'd been about to head off on some family vacation or some weekend lark with her friends. But this time, she thought as she watched the sweatered crowds shuffle by, this time she was escaping from New York in a wholly different way, taking charge and embarking on a new episode of her life. This could be the beginning of something huge—something that could change her life forever.

It better, Sarah thought grimly. Because if it didn't and she came back home jobless and broke, having bankrolled all of her worldly possessions on this trip . . . well, she didn't even want to think about the repercussions. Taking a deep breath, she leaned back in the hard plastic chair, trying to cleanse herself of the negativity.

As she paged through a copy of *Life & Style* magazine, scanning the latest gossip on Hollywood's newest weight loss fad, Sarah thought back to Owen's parting advice to her when he'd called her the night before to wish her a good trip.

"Remember your roots, killer," he'd warned. "Try not to get sucked in by the L.A. scene. And I expect you to come back with lots of new contacts and plenty of juicy stories for me."

"You are too much sometimes." Sarah sighed. "Here I am trying to be serious for once, and you have to turn it around and make this into a circus. Do you know how much I have riding on this trip? I'll be totally screwed if something doesn't come out of it."

"What a freaking tight-ass you are," Owen groaned. "Why can't you just have a good time and let things run their course? This isn't life or death, babe—you're going away to a blowout casting party, and you'll be hanging out with a great guy. Live!"

Sarah had made a face at the phone, but she didn't really have a retort. Sitting in the airport now, she thought of how much she hated it when Owen was right. Why did everything in her life have to be so complicated? Especially when none of it was actually complicated at all in the grand scheme of things. Maybe it was because her family always made it seem like every step she took had massive repercussions for the rest of her life. Or maybe she was scared that her actions weren't amounting to much at all.

At that moment, the boarding announcements began.

Taking a deep breath, Sarah gathered her bags and stowed away her magazine. Owen was right, she thought as she got up and headed toward the gate, it's time to stop obsessing and start living.

5

Growing up in New York, Sarah had always had a secret fascination with Los Angeles. While she loved her native town and all it had to offer, she couldn't help but be entranced by the allure of Tinseltown—the sun-swept surf, the celebrity spottings, the perfectly engineered hard bodies of Hollywood. As a teenager sitting in her room on yet another snowy February day, she would comfort herself with *Beverly Hills, 90210* episodes, which only reinforced her conviction that life in L.A. was one nonstop, glamorous Kelly Taylor and Brandon Walsh saga.

Unfortunately, by the time she'd disembarked from her excruciatingly long, six-hour cross-country flight and had fought her way through the crowds to get her luggage at the LAX baggage claim, Sarah was feeling anything but glamorous. Her neck ached, her hair was a tangle of hairpins and unruly cowlicks, and she was just thankful that she had turned down Daniel's offer to pick her up at the airport. As her cabdriver sped down the scenic Pacific Coast Highway to Daniel's sister's apartment, she gazed out the window at the pristine white beaches and tried to soak in the sun-drenched moment. She was finally here.

That was when her phone rang. It was Kim.

"Sarah, where are you?" Kim's piercing voice reverberated through the phone. "Why you not call me? We worry you didn't land yet and something happen!"

"I'm fine, Mom." Sarah yawned. "I just got off the plane. I was going to call you."

"You must call when you land," Kim admonished her. "You know that—you make me worry. Remember, get lot of sleep, and bundle up. It's cold in L.A. this time of the year."

Sarah sighed. "It's never cold in L.A., Mom. And stop trying to find me every five minutes. I'm a big girl, I can handle stuff—really. I'll talk to you later."

She hung up before her mother could get another word in. Every time she talked to her mother, she felt a twinge of guilt about the fabrications she'd fed her family. Which was why she had to stop thinking about them immediately—and concentrate on the present.

As she stuffed her phone back in her bag, Sarah tried to immerse herself in the passing L.A. landscape. She was so absorbed in her study of a particular sun-bronzed Greek god jogging by that she was startled to realize the cab was heading into Malibu. So Daniel's sister lived in Malibu? This was incredible—the only people Sarah knew who lived in Malibu were Jennifer Aniston and Angelina Jolie. This was already turning out to be a great experience, and she hadn't even gotten out of the cab!

As they drove along the Pacific Coast Highway, Sarah could barely contain her excitement. Everything was so picturesque and perfect—the white sands, the golden sun worshippers, the cerulean blue of the surf. Watching the palm trees waver back and forth above the gently lapping waves was remarkably soothing and therapeutic. That was when the cab pulled into an enormous white-walled apartment complex atop the Malibu Hills. Getting out of the cab, Sarah felt as if she were visiting Mt. Olympus itself. Was she really staying in this paradise? Dragging her luggage up the stairs behind her, she knocked on suite 8D, which bore the nameplate "K. Wong."

The door swung open. Looking as polished as Sarah felt disheveled, Daniel greeted her from the threshold.

"Sarah!" He smiled and gave her a kiss on the cheek. "You made it! Let me help you with this luggage."

Just looking at Daniel was enough to make Sarah blush. He was impossibly handsome in his Ermenegildo Zegna blazer and Rock & Republic jeans. Just like when she'd first met him, his hair was perfectly coiffed while his tanned olive skin glowed. Then there was the way he towered over her. Sarah was reasonably tall, but she felt positively Lilliputian next to Daniel. Incredibly, he seemed even more attractive now than he had at the *Soap Opera Digest* party. If she wasn't careful, she could seriously embarrass herself with this teenybopper adoration.

"Hi!" Sarah shoved a tangled strand of hair behind her ear. "This place is amazing! I can't believe I'm really here. It's so great to see you."

"Thanks." Daniel grinned. "Let me give you a quick tour. As you will soon see, the bathroom's to the right and the bedroom is all the way down to the left. As for the kitchen . . . well, it's here."

Looking at the kitchen, Sarah couldn't resist a wry smile. Not only was it immaculate and massive compared with the typical cramped New York City kitchen, but Sarah's entire studio apartment could probably fit in it. There was a minibar counter and a pristine marble island in the middle of the room that was graced by a bowl of kiwi and pomegranates. For a moment, Sarah fantasized about living in this beautiful apartment with Daniel, whipping up culinary masterpieces in the kitchen with Daniel, sharing adorable little kisses with Daniel . . .

"So what do you think?" Daniel asked.

Sarah snapped out of her daydream. "It looks like it should have its own photo spread," she said, beaming. "So . . . your sister doesn't mind you coming and going in her apartment? She doesn't think it's a little too literally Big Brother?"

"Well, I actually own this place, but I rented it out to my

sister so she would have a place to stay when she's in town. So technically, I guess you could say I'm her landlord."

Sarah laughed. "Ahhh . . . so you're playing super right now?"

"Something like that." Daniel smiled, dimpling as he did. "I live down the block, so it's no big deal for me to come over and check on things." He wiped an imaginary speck of dust off the kitchen counter. "Anyway, how was your flight? Are you hungry?"

"I'm actually starving," Sarah admitted. "They served peanuts on the plane, but that's not gonna cut it for me."

Daniel's eyes crinkled. "She wants to eat—a girl after my own heart. What do you say we get out of here and grab a late lunch?" He leaned toward her, his bedroom eyes making a perfectly innocent suggestion seem somehow illicit.

Sarah wondered how much glee she could exhibit without being completely uncool. "Sounds great," she said with as much nonchalance as she could muster.

"So, here's the plan," Daniel announced as they sped down the Pacific Coast Highway in his gleaming, silver blue Porsche. "We grab some food now. Then I'll take you back to the apartment so you can settle in for a bit." He put the top down, giving Sarah an unobstructed view of the windswept beach adjacent to the highway. "I'll have to go to a couple of meetings after that, but you'll be able to do your own thing regardless. Cool?"

"Sounds perfect." Sarah beamed. "I really appreciate you looking out for me and letting me basically invade your world for the weekend. Especially since you really don't have to do this. I mean, you barely know me."

Daniel turned to glance at Sarah. "I'm happy to be invaded." He flashed her a crooked smile. "Like I said, I'm glad you're here—and I look forward to getting to know you."

Sarah started to respond but stopped as Daniel held her gaze. It was then that she knew beyond a shadow of a doubt that Daniel Wong really was flirting with her.

* * *

"If I could only eat one dish for the rest of my life, it would be this," Sarah enthused. "Pesto's my absolute favorite sauce in the world."

"Doesn't hold a candle to what you can get in Florence, though." Daniel took a bite of his penne. "Have you ever been? I haven't gone in a while, but every time I do go, I can't help wondering what kept me away so long." His gaze turned distant. "Damn, I could really use a trip there right now."

They were dining in what Chad would have called "a *très* fancy" hot spot right by the ocean. Wearing her Prada sunglasses—the ones that she had blown two whole Balloon Burger paychecks on—and her dark Abercrombie & Fitch jeans that made her look almost statuesque, Sarah was feeling quite Hollywood as the wind blew her hair back against the majestic Malibu backdrop.

"I know what you mean. Italy is the most beautiful place I've ever been to," Sarah agreed. "I went there with my mom a few years ago when I was in college."

"That's sweet," Daniel said, his eyes crinkling with amusement.

Sara maintained her smile, but inwardly she groaned. Sweet? That was the last thing she wanted Daniel to say. Whoever Daniel went to Italy with, she was pretty sure it wasn't his mother.

"Well, that was a long time ago," she mumbled.

But then Daniel smiled at her with not even a hint of scorn in his eyes. "It's great that you went with your mom," he said. "My parents wish that my sister and I would go to more places with them, but, well . . . I'm thirty-four now, and people might think I'm a little too old to be following my mom everywhere."

Sarah laughed, feeling immeasurably better. "So who did you go to Italy with?"

Daniel paused, toying with his pasta for several seconds before answering. "I went with my ex-girlfriend," he said finally.

Okay, so she hadn't expected that Daniel Wong would be in

Florence with anyone other than a woman—and no doubt a beautiful one at that. But the awkward silence that followed the word *ex-girlfriend?* Judging by his facial expression, the mere memory evoked strong emotions in him. She just couldn't tell if it was lingering resentment from a bitter breakup, sadness that he wasn't with her anymore, or absentminded reverie about being in Italy with her. Or there was always the obvious explanation— which was that she was once again overreacting and reading way too much into nothing.

"Ahhh," Sarah said, trying to look as casual and unbothered as she possibly could. "That must have been romantic and all."

Immediately, she winced. *What a brilliant choice of words*, she chided herself. Now, he was probably thinking about having mad, passionate sex with his ex-girlfriend in some sunflower field under the blazing Tuscan sun. Why did she have to go there?

"It was nice," Daniel said finally. "Like you said, that was a long time ago."

Deciding that the best course of action was to change the subject, Sarah started chattering about how she couldn't wait to go to the *Asylum* set. But although Daniel responded to all her comments, his tone remained remote and detached. Finally, after he absently said the same thing twice, Sarah decided to give in. After all, she was dying to find out more about this mystery woman. So what better time than now? Besides, technically they were friends, and didn't friends talk about their exes?

"So what happened with you and your ex-girlfriend?" Sarah asked, trying to sound casual. "I mean, if you don't mind my asking."

"We broke up almost six years ago." Daniel poured some more wine into his glass. "We were together for a while— almost four years—before we moved in together. But once that happened, well . . . it didn't quite work out the way I thought it would."

Sarah tried to look noncommittal, but the truth was that she was blown away. Four years? Living together? The only commitment that she had ever made lasting four years was to finish high school—and, later, college. Relationshipwise, the longest one she'd ever had was her three months with Darren Lee, freshman year of college. After meeting during orientation, the two of them had been inseparable for the entire fall semester. They lived down the hall from each other, and between eating all their meals together and taking the same classes, they were practically joined at the hip.

Which was probably why they broke up the minute they came back from winter break. In retrospect, Sarah knew she had latched on to Darren out of loneliness and insecurity. He reminded her of home, and as long as she was with him, she didn't have to remember that she was away from her family for the first time in her life—and that she had no idea how she was going to get through the next four years without them.

"Wow, that sounds pretty intense," Sarah remarked. "How could things not work out after you guys spent four years together?"

He sighed. "It's a long story. There were lots of communication issues once we moved in together. We'd talked about getting engaged, but, well, living together sort of ruined everything for us."

"I hear you." Sarah took another bite of her pasta. "I could never live with someone until after I'm married to them."

And there she was, running her mouth again. *Bold statement there, Sarah*, she thought. Since when did she become "Dear Abby"? And who was she to be making judgments about whether Daniel should have been living with his ex-girlfriend or not? She really needed to stop talking.

Fortunately, Daniel didn't seem offended. "That's probably a wise choice," he said, taking a sip of his Pinot Noir. "Anyway, it was all for the best, I think."

"Do you still talk to her?" Sarah asked.

"We e-mail once in a while." Daniel drummed his fingers on the table. "She was a big part of my life, so I can't help but want to know that she's doing okay."

Sarah nodded. "That's completely understandable."

"Well, enough about me." Daniel cleared his throat. "What about you?"

What about her? Sarah thought. Anything that might have been going on in her life—her spats with her family, her outings with Chad and Owen, her inane Balloon Burger exploits—seemed terribly juvenile and silly compared with what Daniel had been up to the past couple years.

"What do you mean?" Sarah tried to look innocent.

"Are you seeing anyone?" he asked as he took a bite of penne. "I'm sure a beautiful girl like you must have guys lined up around the block for you."

This time, the smile extended to his eyes. Sarah smiled back. Finally, it felt like he was back in the real world with her instead of in the past with his ex.

"Oh, I'm not dating anyone special, if that's what you mean," she replied. "Men in New York are either single, attractive jerks—or they're single, unattractive jerks."

Daniel laughed. "Uh-oh, that sounds like some male bashing to me!"

Sarah blushed. "Okay, well, maybe not all of them are bad, but I'm not dating anyone serious. I'm more into the whole finding myself thing right now. I can tell you that my latest drama has nothing to do with my love life."

"What's that?" Daniel asked curiously as he refilled Sarah's wineglass.

"I was fired from this club I was bartending at." Sarah sighed. "It was really bad. Truth is, it was so bad that I really shouldn't be out here because my budget is so tight. This asshole at the bar slapped my arm when I accidentally spilled a drink on him, and my friend Owen punched him in the face. Of course, my boss came out at that exact moment, and I got fired immediately."

"Wow." Daniel knitted his brows. "I can't believe it. Why didn't you tell me that over the phone? I'm so sorry."

"It's not as bad as it seems." Sarah shrugged. "Besides, we were having such a good time talking that I didn't think it was a great time for me to jump in with a 'Hey, I got fired!' comment."

Daniel nodded slowly. "I guess you're right. Well, I hope this at least takes your mind off of things. This weekend is all about you meeting new people and advancing your career."

Sarah raised her glass. "I couldn't agree more. To the present and forgetting the past," she said, touching her glass to his.

As they took sips of their wine, Daniel reached over and squeezed Sarah's hand comfortingly. She felt a little anticipatory tingle. Everything was going to work out, she told herself—she knew it was.

After lunch, Daniel dropped Sarah off at the apartment and sped off to his meetings. Left to her own devices, Sarah quickly unpacked, did a survey of the apartment, and jotted down a quick list of necessities that she would have to purchase ASAP. While Daniel's sister had a beautiful apartment that was immaculately outfitted in almost all the creature comforts, there were some things that could be taken care of only with a trip to Walgreen's.

Slipping on her shades, Sarah strolled out of the house—and came to an abrupt halt. What was she thinking? More important, where did she think she was going? There was nothing but white sands and palm trees and empty roads for as far as the eye could see. There certainly was no Walgreen's in sight. And with no car and no apparent means of transportation, how the heck was she going to be able to get her "necessities"?

Chill, Sarah, she instructed herself. *You can certainly figure out something as simple as this.* Glancing around the complex, she noticed a little old lady with a halo of puffy gray curls puttering around a plot of roses. Perfect.

Hurrying over, Sarah flashed the woman her most winning smile.

"Hi there, I'm Sarah. I'm going to be staying upstairs for a few days," she introduced herself.

The elderly woman blinked up at her. "Oh, that's nice."

"Yes, I'm so excited to be here." Sarah paused. "Although I

could really use a pharmacy right now. Could you happen to tell me where the closest one is?"

The woman pursed her lips. "There's one about ten minutes down the road."

"Great," Sarah exclaimed. "Thanks so much! I'll head over there now."

"They have a really small parking lot, though," the woman said. "You might have to park down the street."

"Oh, that's okay." Sarah shrugged. "I'm going to walk there anyway."

The woman blinked. "You're going to walk there?"

"Oh, yeah." Sarah nodded. "It's okay. I'm from New York, so I walk all the time."

The woman just stared at her. Waving a cheerful good-bye, Sarah sailed out of the complex, shades in place.

These L.A. people, she thought scornfully, they're so dependent on their cars. For a town that's so body-conscious, the inhabitants seem to have no clue how good walking is for them.

One hour later, Sarah was no longer feeling quite so superior. Perilously faint, she stumbled into Daniel's sister's blessedly air-conditioned apartment like a parched wanderer stepping into an oasis. Her hair was a damp beehive, and she was dripping with sweat as she collapsed onto the expensive white leather couch. As it turned out, ten minutes in L.A. was an eternity, especially when there were no actual sidewalks. As she clung to the narrow path on the side of the road, passing cars honked at her. While some drivers chose to make derogatory comments about her intelligence and/or sanity, others were apparently convinced she was some highway prostitute, begging to be propositioned. By the time she got to the pharmacy, Sarah was feeling exhausted, dizzy, and pretty sure she had a serious case of heatstroke.

Lying on the couch, Sarah thought how wonderful it would be if she could simply lie there for the foreseeable future . . . except that she hadn't flown three thousand miles to veg on a couch, lovely as it was. She had the *Asylum* party in a mere few hours to worry about, along with all the primping and pampering that was needed to turn her into a Cinderella all of the soap opera execs would be clamoring after.

It will be fine, she tried to reassure herself. All she had to do was make sure that she didn't show up looking like an oil slick—and that was when it hit her. How the heck was she going to get to the party? She didn't have a car; no budget for that. And Daniel had done so much for her already. She really couldn't impose on him any further and ask him for a ride. And wouldn't she seem incredibly lame if she did that? Which meant . . . she would have to walk from Malibu to West Hollywood?

Get a grip, Sarah. Remember you're a street-smart New Yorker. If you were in New York right now, what would you do? Well, that was easy. If she were in New York, she would just hail a cab. So . . . why couldn't she do the same here? Or at least the L.A. equivalent?

Sarah dragged herself up from the couch and started digging through closets and under tables until she unearthed the phone book. Voilà! Maybe this wasn't going to be as hard as she'd thought. After flipping through the book until she got to "Taxis," she dialed the first number she saw.

"Hi," she said brightly, "I'd like to order a cab from Malibu to West Hollywood."

"Sure," the dispatcher rumbled, "what time's pickup?"

"Six-thirty." Sarah paused. "Um, about how much would that be?"

"Well, everything depends on traffic," the dispatcher said, "but I would say about a hundred."

Sarah's jaw dropped. "A hundred *dollars?*"

"That's right."

Swallowing, Sarah mumbled, "Um, I'll call you back."

Hanging up, she sat back, stunned. A hundred-dollar cab ride? Going from one end of Manhattan to the other cost only about twenty dollars.

Checking her wallet, Sarah studied her meager reserve of cash. She had about two hundred dollars for this entire trip, and that was supposed to cover food, drink, and any other expenses she might have. Could she really justify spending half her money on a cab ride to West Hollywood? And that wasn't even counting the ride back!

This can't be happening, Sarah thought. How was her Hollywood career supposed to take off when she couldn't even afford the trip to the *Asylum* party?

Feeling her temples close in on her, she threw herself down on the couch again. What was she going to do? Hitchhike to West Hollywood? Take the bus? Was there even a bus from Malibu to West Hollywood? Maybe she would just have to suck it up and pay for the cab, then hope that some Good Samaritan would give her a ride home. . . .

That was when her cell phone rang.

"Hello?" Sarah said bleakly.

"Hey, Sarah . . ." Daniel's voice echoed through the receiver. "Just calling to see if you need a ride to the *Asylum* party."

Thank God.

"Yes," Sarah said calmly, "that would be lovely."

It was six forty-five, and Sarah was frantically trying to find her chandelier earrings in her suitcase. Daniel was supposed to pick her up at seven thirty and she hadn't even done her makeup yet. As she rummaged through her bag, her Sidekick phone beeped.

"So, tell me everything. What are you wearing, and what time is he going to pick you up?" Chad immediately peppered her with questions.

"I can't talk right now," Sarah exclaimed. "I can't find my chandelier earrings!"

"The emerald ones?" Chad asked. "I love those!"

"This is terrible." Sarah rifled through her jewelry case. "I can't find these damn earrings anywhere!"

"Okay, take a deep breath and talk to me for just two minutes," Chad instructed. "How is everything going, my dear? Are you and that producer on the verge of making cute Asian babies yet?"

"Chad!" Sarah shook her head. "You're starting to sound like Owen, but in a slightly more classy way." She rummaged through her suitcase again. "No, we aren't making Asian babies yet."

"Awww," Chad sighed.

"But we did have a nice lunch by the ocean this afternoon, and he's giving me a ride to the party," Sarah said dreamily.

"That sounds *so Santa Barbara*," Chad exclaimed. "I loved that show. And that's so romantic of Mr. Producer."

"Do you have to make everything a soap opera?" Sarah said half-mockingly. "But yes, it was nice. He's picking me up in a few, so I have to go now. My makeup isn't done, and I haven't even put on my dress yet."

"Okay, okay," Chad said, "Be beautiful and take *lots* of pictures, and if you see Luis from *Passions*, tell him I would clean his house for him if he wanted me to."

Sarah laughed. "Bye, darling."

As she hung up the phone, she received a text message from Owen:

TONIGHT'S THE BIG NIGHT. BRING CONDOMS! HOPE YOU'RE HAVING FUN. LOVE YA, BABE.

Shaking her head, Sarah laughed. Oh, Owen.

Glancing at her watch, she winced. It was already six fifty, and she really needed to get herself together. She had everything done except her makeup and the earrings—aha! Sarah snatched up the earrings triumphantly from her makeup bag and headed to the bathroom for her final preparations. That was when her phone rang again. Sarah flipped the phone open without looking at it.

"What's up, sis?" Lin asked.

Lin? Well, this was quite a surprise. Between Amy and Lin, Lin was definitely the more supportive one. Even so, Sarah knew that Lin didn't completely understand her obsession with becoming a soap opera actress. Which was why Sarah wasn't sure why Lin was calling her now.

"Hi, Lin." She frowned. "How are you? Is everything okay?"

"Everything's fine," Lin assured her. "Stephen and I just wanted to know how you were doing. We're sitting at home right now flipping through the channels, and we came across SOAPnet and thought of you."

"Thanks . . ." Sarah hesitated, still a little puzzled. "I'm doing great. I'm about to head to that *Asylum* party now, so I'm actually in a little bit of a rush."

"Gotcha," Lin said. "Well, I hope you have fun, and good luck on your audition this weekend!"

Audition? Sarah had forgotten all about it. But of course, it was her "audition" that she was supposed to be here for. And here was her sister calling her ever so nicely to wish her well on it, and she didn't even have one. Feeling suddenly awash with guilt, Sarah swallowed. *Come on, Sarah,* she told herself, *there's no time for guilt right now.* Daniel was coming to pick her up in about a half hour, and she still had a face to put on.

"Thanks, Lin." Sarah smiled. "Tell everyone I say hi."

As she got off the phone, she ran to the bathroom to start putting on her eyeliner. She was going for a sleek, Veronica Lake look tonight and had spent the past hour straightening her hair with the help of her handy CHI hair-straightening machine. All she had to do now was make sure her complexion was flawless. She already had her Diane von Fürstenberg dress—the one she'd bought at Woodbury Commons for Christmas—sitting on the bed. Once she put that on, she would be ready to go.

The next fifteen minutes were a marvel of makeup and getting dressed. Walking to the living room to don her heels, she saw Daniel's headlights flash through the windows. He was here already! Glowing, she swung open the door.

"You look stunning." Daniel's gaze lingered on her as he gave her a peck. "That's a lovely dress."

"Thanks." Sarah giggled. "You mean this old thing? I love your suit, by the way."

Daniel certainly did look amazing. Sporting an überfashionable, slim-cut black suit with satin lapels, Daniel looked as though he'd been born on a soap opera set. Gazing at him, Sarah couldn't help wondering—again—why it was she never met men like Daniel in New York. Giving new meaning to debonair and dashing, Daniel was a far, far cry from the clueless galoots at the Brass Monkey.

"Thank you," Daniel answered. "By the way, while the dress is lovely, it is missing one thing."

Sarah stifled a gasp. Was there a rip in her dress? Was a button missing? What else could possibly be missing from the dress? Yes, it was an outlet dress but could it really be a defective Diane von Fürstenberg gown? Sarah felt beyond mortified.

But before Sarah could utter any of these thoughts, Daniel reached over to the drawer underneath his coffee table and took out a small box. Sarah blinked, at a loss for what to expect. But as Daniel opened the box to reveal a necklace, she suddenly felt like Julia Roberts in "Pretty Woman."

"Wow, that's beautiful," Sarah broke into a delighted smile.

"I thought this necklace would look nice on you," Daniel smiled. "It was made by my friend Arianne. She has her own jewelry line and this is one of her newest pieces. She gave it to me last week to give to our wardrobe department, but it slipped my mind."

As Daniel slipped the necklace on her, Sarah gazed at her reflection in the hallway mirror. The necklace was gorgeous—a sterling silver rolo chain with black onyx beads and red Svaroski crystals. It looked picture perfect with her dress.

"I'm glad you like it, and that it's being put to good use," Daniel remarked.

Put to good use? Sarah wasn't sure what he meant by that but she just laughed. "Thank you so much for the necklace, Daniel. It's beautiful."

"You're welcome," Daniel said. "So, anyway, the casting director is definitely going to be at the party tonight. I saw him this afternoon and told him about you. Do you have any business cards?" Daniel asked as he opened a bottle of wine and poured out two glasses.

"Absolutely," Sarah said quickly. "I got some made at Kinko's the night before I left. You got to love Kinko's and their twenty-four-hour service."

"Great!" Daniel chuckled. "It should be a fun evening. The casts of *Days of Our Lives* and *General Hospital* are going to be at the party, too."

Sarah gasped. "My friend Chad would die if he were with me now."

"Chad?" Daniel asked. "Is that the guy I met at the party?"

"Yes." Sarah nodded. "He's a huge soap opera fan. We would go days without leaving our dorm room in college just watching soaps. It didn't matter which soap—we would channel surf to whatever was on at the time and watch until the next soap came on."

"That's hysterical." Daniel smiled and raised his glass. "Well, here's to a great evening of soaps tonight—and the beginning of great things for Sarah Cho."

He looked deeply into her eyes as he saluted her. Sarah wasn't sure if it was the intensity of his gaze or the wine, but she suddenly felt as if the evening were rife with endless possibilities.

Sarah brought her glass up to meet his. "From your lips," she said fervently.

6

The walk into the excessively opulent Beverly Hilton—yes, the one in the Brenda and Brandon 90210 zip code—was a blur to Sarah.

She didn't know what to focus on first: the buffed and polished, jutting-hip-boned actresses and models catwalking down the red carpet or the cameras flashing in the Chanel-perfumed and paparazzi-filled air. Chandeliers dangled from the ceilings like icicles, reflecting all of the Versaces and Armanis being modeled below. Sarah goggled at it all, dazzled into silence. Sure, she'd always imagined Hollywood to be all about glitz and glamour, but somehow seeing everything firsthand—instead of in the pages of *Us Weekly*—made everything aeons beyond her expectations. Walking into this on the arm of Daniel Wong, Sarah felt starry-eyed and light-headed, as if she'd been transported into her very own soap opera wonderland.

"Daniel . . ." A man with a luxurious walrus mustache and a shiny bald pate strode over. "Great to see you. Congratulations on reaching the quarter-century mark!"

"Thank you, Clyde—same to you." Daniel exchanged a hearty handshake with the newcomer. "Who ever thought that we'd make it this far? I always figured we'd land in an actual asylum before we ever saw season twenty."

"Trust me—there were days when I was ready to admit myself into one." Clyde laughed as he slapped Daniel on the shoulder.

"Tell me about it," Daniel said, chuckling.

They har-harred with each other. Sarah smiled politely through all the Hollywood-speak, waiting for her introduction.

"So, Daniel," Clyde said finally, "have you forgotten your manners? Who is this stunner with you?"

"My bad," Daniel said. "Clyde, this is Sarah Cho. Sarah— meet Clyde Turner."

Sarah flashed her best megawatt smile. "Nice to meet you," she said, her voice a half octave higher than usual. "Congratulations! You must be so proud of such an amazing accomplishment."

Clyde was certainly not too shy to give Sarah a once-over. He looked her up and down, eyeing her lace-strapped heels, her slinky black beaded dress, and her perfectly straight, sleek jet hair.

"You're a beauty." He gave Sarah a kiss on the hand. "Which show are you on?"

Sarah blushed. "I'm not on any show, but . . . maybe one day. I'm just visiting from New York."

"Clyde, Sarah's an aspiring actress. Sarah, Clyde is actually our casting director," Daniel explained.

Sarah's ears perked up. Casting director? How could Daniel not have given her some notice? This was her chance to charm the man who decided who would grace the set of *Asylum*!

"I love New York," Clyde said. "I lived there for five years while working on *Another World* years ago. I had this great place on Central Park West. It was really something to be able to wake up every morning and look out onto the park."

"Oh, but here in L.A., you can wake up every morning and look out onto the ocean," Sarah countered. "New York is really overrated—it's noisy and crowded and sometimes just plain ugly. It's also not as exciting as everyone makes it out to be. I grew up in New York, and even though it's such a big city, it seems like I'm always running into the same people." She had a sudden flashback of seeing Dana at Buddha Bar.

"She's feisty, isn't she?" Clyde arched an eyebrow. "I like her!"

Daniel nodded. "Yes, she's something. Sarah's looking for her first break, and I was telling her to just hang in there. I remember how hard it was for me to break into the biz. But if I can do it, anything's possible."

"I'll tell you what, Sarah," Clyde announced. "I don't do this very often—actually, not at all—but you have a fantastic look, and I think you might have something." He gestured toward Daniel. "Get my information from this guy, and I'll have you come in and read with me. We're always looking to cast new roles, so you never know. Now, I have to run. The matriarch of the show is expecting my presence by the martini bar. Sarah, it was a pleasure."

"The pleasure is all mine," Sarah said, shaking Clyde's hand. "Thank you so much! I really look forward to speaking to you soon."

The minute Clyde was out of earshot, Daniel turned toward Sarah and raised his eyebrows at her.

"Look at you!" He grinned. "The first person you meet, and you've already swept him off his feet. And believe me, Clyde is the kind of guy that you want to sweep off his feet. He's a little bit of a lech, but that's to be expected since you're a chick."

"Chick?" Sarah raised an eyebrow.

"I mean . . . beautiful lady." Daniel flashed her a crooked smile.

Sarah batted him lightly on the arm and smiled back. "Is that how you refer to women when you're with your cronies?" she asked.

"Oh, definitely. We like to sit at old-man alcoholic bars and break beer cans with our heads while chanting about our conquests. Followed by a big ol' belch, of course," Daniel said with a smirk.

"You wiseass." Sarah couldn't help but laugh. "I knew that

underneath that smooth Hollywood exterior beat the heart of a frat boy."

Daniel grinned. "What can I say? You got me."

Sarah smiled back at Daniel, trying to absorb everything that was going on. Here she was, all the way on the other side of the country, and she was having the time of her life with an older man who was actually—gasp!—mature. Why did they have to live three thousand miles away from each other? Why couldn't she meet a guy like this in New York? To her, it seemed that all of the men she met were either too stodgy-corporate or Peter Pan Lotharios with no inclination whatsoever to commit to a single woman.

At that moment, Daniel leaned down close to her. "Are you having a good time?" he asked softly.

"Are you serious?" Sarah gave him a radiant smile. "Of course. This is all so amazing—I still can't believe I'm really here. . . ."

As she babbled on, a petite blonde approached Daniel.

"Darling!" She kissed Daniel on both cheeks. "You look fabulous! Are you wearing the Ben Sherman suit we had Jasper Dixon don last episode? It's very retro."

Sarah gave her a long look. She wanted to find something wrong with her, something that made her not quite as gorgeous as she obviously believed herself to be—but she couldn't. The blonde was a certified bombshell. She had a perfect sun-kissed tan, an absolutely breathtaking Marc Jacobs dress that emphasized her tight, toned arms, and a gigantic sapphire-and-diamond-studded necklace. She was gorgeous enough to make Pamela Anderson look . . . ordinary.

"Actually, I am wearing the Ben Sherman," Daniel acknowledged. "After we shot Jasper's scenes, Liz in wardrobe had it pressed and sent over to me—apparently, she thought it would look good." He paused, then turned around. "Oh, this is Sarah, by the way."

"Hello," Sarah said brightly. "Nice to meet you!"

"Hi there," the blonde said without much enthusiasm. "I'm Cherisse."

She shook Sarah's hand limply before quickly turning her attention back to Daniel. "So, Daniel, I must have some spoilers for the show," she wheedled. "I'm dying to know if Arlene gets impregnated by that evil Julian, and if he'll sell his baby to the Ferris family in exchange for the love of his life, Kerry."

Sarah had to suppress a snicker. Hearing Cherisse ask Daniel that question reminded her of the weekly soap opera dissections she and Chad had over brunch.

"You'll find out in time." Daniel smiled. "Let's just say Arlene may be the cause of a major shake-up for everyone in town."

"You are such a tease, Danny." Cherisse gave him a pretty little pout. "I'm going to get a glass of wine. Meet you at the bar?"

"Sure thing." Daniel nodded as Cherisse headed toward the hall. "We'll see you in there."

"Aren't you Mr. Popularity," Sarah remarked. "People are just flocking to you."

"Not really." Daniel shook his head modestly. "I'm just an old dinosaur who's been around for too long. I'm glad that you're here with me. You're a breath of fresh air in this tired scene," he said as he slipped his arm around Sarah and led them out of the ballroom.

Letting herself be guided through the sumptuous, bullion-colored carpeted corridor and into the gold and black balloon-festooned main hall, Sarah knew she was becoming completely smitten. Aside from being handsome, charming, and a powerful soap producer, Daniel had a way of making her feel special, even though she was a nobody wannabe actress. Sarah knew the entertainment industry was teeming with disingenuous, insincere phonies, but Daniel seemed to belie the stereotype. Rather than being absorbed with glamour and celebrity, he seemed to be a genuine human being who didn't care about her nonexistent star wattage. Gazing at him, she wanted desperately to text Owen and Chad at that moment with some dramatic declaration—like "Hold me back—I'm in love!"

"So what's your drink of choice?" Daniel asked as they approached the bar.

"I would love a vodka tonic," Sarah replied, falling back on her staple nonmessy drink.

"Coming right up," Daniel said. "Why don't you go grab seats at our table? It'll have a place setting with my name on it."

"You got it." Sarah felt a warm glow spread through her at the unaccustomed—but more than welcome—attention.

As she entered the dining hall, Sarah was suddenly confronted with soap opera celebrities everywhere. The editor of *Soap Opera Digest* was being interviewed in one corner, while cameras flashed away at the *Asylum* cast members in another. For a few seconds, she allowed herself to drift away and imagined having her picture taken for *Soap Opera Digest*—

The vibrating of her phone jolted her out of her reverie. She whipped it out and saw two new text messages from Chad and Owen. One read: "So tell me everything. Set the scene for me!" The other read: "Have you gotten laid yet?!" It was no mystery to Sarah which one was from whom.

Shaking her head, she laughed—and almost crashed into a statuesque blonde in a gorgeous turquoise taffeta gown.

"I'm sorry, I didn't see y—," Sarah's jaw dropped as the blonde turned around and she recognized Arianne Zucker—aka Nicole from *Days of Our Lives*!

"Omigosh!" Sarah practically squealed. "Nicole—I mean Arianne! I'm a huge fan of yours!"

Arianne flashed her a gleaming smile. Wow, Sarah marveled, she's even more gorgeous in person than on TV!

"Thanks," Arianne said. She paused as she noticed Sarah's neckline.

"Hey—is that one of my necklaces?"

It took Sarah a moment, but suddenly she realized that Daniel's friend "Arianne" was actually Arianne Zucker! She couldn't believe it—she was wearing Arianne Zucker's jewelry!

Sarah beamed and touched her one of the Svarowski crystals. "Yes, my friend Daniel gave this to me, and I'm a huge fan of the Lowdsuga line. I have to stop myself from spending my entire paycheck on your jewelry every week! Oh, and you definitely need to get more of those crystal rings in stock!"

Arianne laughed. "Thanks! I'm glad you like my jewelry. And we're coming out with new bags the next few weeks, so look out for them!"

"Definitely!" Sarah exclaimed.

Still not believing that she'd just had a real, honest-to-goodness conversation with Nicole from *Days*, Sarah hurried over to the table with Daniel's place card on it and whipped out her phone. She couldn't wait to text her friends about this encounter!

"Hi there." Sarah looked up to see a debonair man with thick chestnut hair and olive green eyes smiling at her. "Are the rest of these seats taken?"

"Just the one next to me," Sarah responded, placing her clutch on Daniel's chair.

"Great! I'm Lucas Meyer." He extended a hand.

Sarah shook it. "I'm Sarah Cho—it's nice to meet you. Are you part of the show?"

"No, no, I'm just a guest of one of the cast members," Lucas replied. "I'm actually an agent."

Sarah shoved her phone back into her bag. "Very cool." She tried not to look overly excited. An agent—talk about catnip to an unrepresented aspiring actor. . . .

"And you?" Lucas asked. "Are you one of the actresses on the show?"

This was the second time that evening someone had asked her that question. Sarah would be lying if she didn't admit that it was a nice thought. Fortunately, she had enough sense to come back down to earth before uttering some delusional response.

"I'm actually a guest, too," she replied. "I'm visiting from New York."

"Wonderful," Lucas said. "What do you do in New York?"

"I'm actually trying to get into acting." Sarah cleared her throat. "I've been an extra in a few commercials, but nothing major yet."

"Ahhh." Lucas nodded. "Do you have an agent?"

"Not yet," Sarah admitted, repressing the tiny surge of anxiety she felt every time she thought of her unagented, unemployed status.

"Well, please give me a call." Lucas pulled out a business card and handed it to Sarah. "I don't often do these things at parties, but when you're ready for an agent, I'll be glad to talk."

"What's going on here?" Daniel appeared with two drinks in hand.

"So, you're the one sitting next to this pretty lady." Lucas grinned at Daniel. "Daniel, how are you, man?"

"Great. Long time no see, Lucas!" Daniel gave him a slap on the back.

"And how, may I ask, do you know our lovely Sarah here?" Lucas inquired.

"We met at a party in New York, actually. She wants to get into acting," Daniel explained.

"I knew that already." Lucas waved his hand dismissively. "We go way back, me and Sarah. Well, back to five minutes ago, anyway. I told her to give me a call when she's ready for an agent."

"Excellent," Daniel exclaimed. "Sarah, this guy is someone to know. He's responsible for getting Josh Duhamel his first photo shoot."

Sarah's jaw dropped. "The *All My Children* turned *Las Vegas* star?"

"You bet." Daniel nodded.

"So, Sarah, any desire to move out to L.A.?" Lucas asked. "You could go on so many more soap opera auditions out here."

Desire to move out to L.A.? She would love to! But of course there were so many things holding her back. Like . . . well, there was her family, of course. And . . . well, maybe her family was the only reason holding her back. She had never known any life outside of New York. In fact, she'd never even spent more than a week away from the Big Apple. How could she be away from it for good?

"I'd really like to. . . ." Sarah hesitated. "It's just that I've been in New York my entire life. Living here in L.A. would probably be like a vacation. I used to think that living in California meant going to the beach every day and meeting my very own *Baywatch* boy toy."

"You're hilarious," Lucas said, chortling. "This girl is all about the pop culture. Do you have your head shots yet?"

"I do. . . ." Sarah paused. "But I don't know how great they are."

Lucas held up his hand. "Look, when you get back to New York, send me your head shots. I'll send some out to these pilot shows that are always looking for young females. I know that there are a few things coming up—like *The Young and the Restless* is always looking for some extras, as is *General Hospital*."

"That would be so wonderful." Sarah clasped her hands. "Thank you so much—you have no idea what a dream that would be for me."

The rest of the evening was a blur of flashing light bulbs and designer dresses for Sarah.

As she stared with rapt attention at the parade of soap stars ascending to the stage, all she could think was how surreal it all was. Just a day ago, she'd been flipping patties at the Balloon Burger, and now here she was—sitting at the table next to Deidre Hall, sipping champagne with Drake Hogestyn, rubbing elbows with Joseph Mascolo, aka Stefano DiMera. It was all she could do not to gape at her childhood idols in an utterly uncool, drooling groupie way.

Fortunately, Daniel's presence kept her from lapsing into her crazy soap opera fan tendencies. Watching him meet and greet with such practiced ease, Sarah couldn't help but gaze at him in admiration. He was so smooth, so practiced, so self-possessed . . . it was as if he'd been doing this all his life. Was this what came with age and maturity? If that was the case, Sarah hoped she'd one day have a fraction of Daniel's sophistication.

As she watched Daniel mingle with the producers of *All My*

Children and *One Life to Live*, several young starlets sauntered over to blatantly flirt and banter without even the slightest bit of pretense. One of them said something that made Daniel laugh and duck his head as the girl ruffled his hair. Looking at them, Sarah felt a stab of something—jealousy? But what right did she have to be jealous? Why wouldn't he want to be with one of these pre–Kevin Federline Britneys?

Not wanting to watch anymore, Sarah turned and snagged a glass of champagne from a passing waiter bearing a tray of drinks. *Stop acting like some lovesick schoolgirl,* she admonished herself. *You came to L.A. this weekend to make your soap opera dreams come true, not to moon over some guy.*

Taking a deep breath, she turned to study the other guests, many of whom were leaving their tables for the dance floor as the band started playing a waltz. Noticing Tony Geary and Genie Francis chatting over by the chocolate fondue table, she tried to think of some nonstalking way to approach them and introduce herself. . . .

An arm slipped around her waist.

"So," Daniel murmured in her ear, "would it be completely inappropriate for me to ask you to dance?"

Sarah's heart did a little jitterbug of joy. She pirouetted around, her delight palpable.

"It would be completely inappropriate if you didn't," she breathed.

He smiled at her and led her out to the dance floor.

Midnight.

After seemingly endless hours of schmoozing and boozing, Daniel drove Sarah back to his sister's apartment. As the two strolled up to the doorstep, he took her hand and kissed her palm gently.

"I had fun tonight," he said. "I'm so glad you came out, Sarah. I hope you had a good time."

Sarah responded by pulling Daniel into a long, tender, passionate kiss. Maybe it was all the vodka tonics or maybe it was all the champagne she'd downed, but the kiss was something right out of the movies. Was it her imagination or did the waves crash behind them in a perfect operatic crescendo? It was as blissfully romantic as John and Marlena's first kiss on *Days of Our Lives.*

"I guess you had a good time, too," Daniel said playfully when they finally pulled apart.

Sarah laughed and wrapped her arms around his neck. "I did." She sighed happily. "All of this has been so perfect. This is the most insane thing I've ever done in my whole life—and I'm so glad I did it. Flying here and coming to this party has really inspired me."

Daniel smiled as he opened the door and pulled her in for another kiss. "I'm glad."

After what seemed like an eternity against the doorway, Sarah pulled away.

"So are you going to walk me inside?" she said softly.

"Do you want me to?" Daniel asked.

"Definitely," Sarah whispered. "I don't want this night to end yet."

Sarah opened her eyes to find the sun streaming through the blinds and bathing her in brightness. Yet the walls were all wrong— daffodil yellow and not Lin's yuppie eggshell white. Plus, instead of the persistent blare of sirens outside, all she heard was the sound of crashing surf. Blinking, she had a sudden urge to pinch herself. Was she still in L.A., living her romantic Hollywood fantasy?

She got her answer when she turned over and saw Daniel beside her.

"Hi." Daniel was propped up on one elbow and smiling down at her. His hair was tousled and his eyes were still hooded with that sleepy afterglow, but somehow he managed to look even more handsome than he had the night before.

"Hello," Sarah whispered, hesitant to break the spell. "How are you feeling this morning?"

"Pretty good. You?"

Sarah smiled. "Couldn't be better."

Daniel leaned over and kissed her tenderly. Sarah closed her eyes blissfully. It felt so wonderful to be here in Daniel's big, strong arms. Still, she couldn't help but think how everything would be over in a number of hours. Soon, she'd be back to flipping burgers with Owen and struggling to make her rent and listening to her family judge her.

"It sucks that I'll be leaving tonight," she groaned.

"It really does," Daniel said. "Last night was fun. It's really too bad that you're not staying longer."

"I know," Sarah said. "It'd be great if I lived here. I think I would be so much happier."

"You should think about it." Daniel leaned over to give her another kiss. "You and I would have so much fun."

"We would, wouldn't we?" Sarah smiled as she contemplated the prospect . . . and became aware of another, more immediate desire. "By the way, are you hungry? I'm starving right now."

"Ravenous," Daniel said. "How about I take you to this great place in West Hollywood?"

With her flight looming in just a couple of hours, Sarah took all her bags and stowed them in Daniel's Porsche. Once that was taken care of, Daniel drove them over to the Griddle Cafe in West Hollywood. Sarah was beside herself with excitement at the thought of sharing syrup with the likes of Ian Ziering and Rachel Leigh Cook, whom Daniel said he saw there all the time. Once there, Sarah was reminded of some of her own favorite brunch haunts in New York. Just like back home, the lines were long as people milled about on the sidewalk, awaiting their chance to chow down on the lighter-than-air, fluffily golden pancake confections inside.

Even though Sarah was afraid they would end up having to

wait for hours, the restaurant sat them automatically upon seeing Daniel. According to Daniel, he was often mistaken for Yul Kwon, the winner of *Survivor*; apparently, Los Angeles was such a celebrity-driven town that any resemblance to a celebrity could be used to one's advantage.

"I recommend the pancakes," Daniel announced as they sat down. "They're gargantuan, especially the one loaded with chocolate chips and powdered sugar. It's a food coma waiting to happen, I promise."

"That sounds heavenly." Sarah perused the menu, fascinated. "I actually think I saw this place featured on Rachael Ray's show."

"Yeah, it's a popular joint." Daniel nodded. "It's so funny how Hollywood works. I've been coming here for years, and they still haven't caught on that I'm not Yul Kwon." He rifled through the packets of Splenda in the sugar bowl. "I'm not sure if I should be offended because they thinks all Asians look alike or flattered that I look like a reality show winner."

"Look at it this way." Sarah put down her menu. "You don't have to wait on lines at restaurants. I would love to have a perk like that!"

"I guess so." Daniel didn't look entirely convinced. "But that's one of the things I don't love about this city. Everything is pretty plastic here. But since I'm in the business, I just have to go with it." He smoothed back a stray cowlick. "One of the things I miss most about New York is how people there don't obsess about celebrities. They're always on the go, and they actually care more about their own lives than what some actor is doing."

Sarah remained silent, not quite sure how to respond. New York always seemed so drab and boring compared with the glitz and glamour of L.A., yet here was Daniel waxing nostalgic about it. Maybe he was right, but it was hard to remember New York's virtues while she was in this sultry, sun-soaked oasis.

"Well, if I had more time in L.A., I would suggest we go have dim sum," Sarah said after they'd ordered, deciding the safest course was to change subjects to something she did know about.

"The dim sum here in California is so much better than what we have in New York."

Daniel raised his eyebrows. "Really? I had no idea."

"Without a doubt." Sarah nodded. "My grandmother says that the dim sum here is authentic because the chefs come from Hong Kong. There are so many more varieties of dim sum here—it's not just your standard old beef noodles."

"Sounds like you're quite the connoisseur," Daniel observed over the rim of his mimosa.

"Well, every time we come out here, we go to NBC Seafood." Sarah smiled at the memory. "No matter how hungry you are or how prepared you are to eat, you can never try everything. Plus, every time I've gone they've got some new and exotic dish freshly imported from the other side of the Pacific. Last time I went, they had something called Snow White buns. Sounds weird, but these little cakes were so amazing that they literally melted in your mouth."

"Wow . . ." Daniel rubbed his chin. "I've heard great things about the place. Of course, first time I heard of it, I thought we were talking about the Peacock's latest franchise."

"The name's pretty funny," Sarah admitted, "but it really is one of the best Chinese restaurants—and I'm not just saying that because my uncle is one of the owners."

"Really? Talk about being well connected!" Daniel looked distinctly impressed.

Blushing, Sarah couldn't help relish being able to contribute to the conversation. "I'll have to bring you there for dim sum. I'll make sure my uncle has some special delicacies whipped up for us!"

Daniel smiled. "My mouth's watering just thinking about it."

He gazed at her as if in deep contemplation. At first, Sarah blushed at the attention, but after a moment, she started to feel unnerved and self-conscious. Perhaps he wasn't so impressed with her dim sum know-how after all. What if he was just being polite and feigning interest as she blathered on?

"I hope I don't have anything stuck between my teeth," she said finally.

"Oh no," Daniel said, "sorry. I was just thinking how you reminded me of my family." He cleared his throat and took a sip of water.

Sarah furrowed her brow. "Oh."

"My parents are still back in Long Island," Daniel explained. "I try to see them every chance I get, but it's not the same. My sister's out here, but she travels a lot so I don't get to see her that often." He paused. "Here I hang out mostly with the soap opera set—don't really spend much time with anyone Asian, let alone eat dim sum."

Sarah colored. "Well, just because I like dim sum doesn't mean I spend all my time in Chinatown or anything. . . ."

"No, I think it's a great thing," Daniel said quickly. "It's nice to be with you and hear you talk about things like this because I don't get much chance otherwise. You remind me of what I've been missing."

He smiled at her, and Sarah felt herself smiling back. Maybe it really wasn't a bad thing that she apparently reminded him of all things Asian; after all, if she could provide something in his life that he didn't already have, he might just want to continue having her around.

At that moment, the waiter brought over their food. As Sarah poured syrup over her double chocolate-chip pancakes, she suddenly noticed that Daniel was drinking his coffee by sipping the liquid from his cup through a straw. She was staring at him when he looked up.

"Something wrong?" he asked.

"Oh, no." Sarah tried to laugh it off. "It's just that I've never seen anyone drink coffee with a straw before."

"It's so I don't stain my teeth," Daniel explained. "I love caffeine, but there's nothing harder to get rid of than coffee stains on the teeth. That's why I use the straw. It's a little Hollywood insider trick."

"Wow," Sarah said, "I'll have to remember that."

Inwardly, she thought that it was somewhat strange to be drinking coffee through a straw, teeth stains or not. Which just went to show how much she had to learn about Hollywood. "So . . ." Sarah cleared her throat. "What made you decide to leave your family and move out to Los Angeles?"

"A few reasons." Daniel hesitated. "I got offered this job right after I broke up with my girlfriend—you know, the one I moved in with. When things didn't work out between us, I decided that I needed a change, and that's how I came out here."

Once again, Sarah wasn't sure what to say. She never knew what to say about Daniel being with another woman, which was stupid because obviously, in his thirty-four years, he had dated numerous women. In some strange way, she saw him in some fairy-tale bubble where he was *the* Daniel Wong of *Asylum*. But hearing him talk about his ex, it all sounded incredibly serious and grown up to Sarah. After all, none of her friends were engaged or even on the verge of popping the question. And even though she'd spent less than twenty-four hours with him, a small part of her couldn't help feeling jealous of this ex-girlfriend/almost fiancée.

"Gotcha." Sarah did her best to sound nonchalant. "I'm not trying to pry, but you never did tell me what happened between you two."

"I'm not sure myself." Daniel took a deep breath. "I guess, in the end, it wasn't such a good idea for us to live together . . . the passion between us just sort of died."

Sarah chewed her pancakes slowly, thinking. Daniel's statement made no sense to her at all. How could passion suddenly die between two people who were so much in love? So maybe the honeymoon was over, she thought, but people didn't just fall out of love with each other—or did they? In Sarah's world, a marriage—or a near marriage—was a huge thing, and if two people could be together for such a long time, it seemed that it would take something more monumental than dwindling chemistry to break them apart.

"Well, like I mentioned before, I can't say I have much experience in the cohabitation arena," Sarah replied. "I always planned on waiting until I got married because it would be something to look forward to. I mean, isn't that part of what makes marriage so exciting—what you discover about each other when you live under the same roof?"

"You may be right." Daniel picked up a packet of Splenda and shook it.

Despite his apparently relaxed demeanor, Sarah could tell that Daniel was uncomfortable discussing the issue. She could already feel him withdrawing after that little bonding moment they'd had over the dim sum discussion. Maybe she was pushing a little too much . . . after all, it wasn't exactly as if the two of them had known each other forever.

Time to change the subject.

"Okay"—Sarah took a swig of orange juice—"enough from me. I mean, I'm hardly the poster child for perfect relationships."

Daniel peered up at her from his coffee. "Actually, you haven't talked much about your personal life at all. What was your longest relationship?"

Sarah swallowed, suddenly feeling out of her element. Whatever she said would end up making her sound like a teenager talking to an adult. After all, Daniel had just told her that he was almost engaged, and she hadn't had a relationship that lasted more than a few months!

"Um, just a few months," she finally admitted. "I've never really dated anyone serious. I was seeing someone in college for a semester, but he was a drug addict, so I'm not sure if he even thought we were together."

The minute the words left her lips, Sarah cringed inwardly. Here was a mature, adult man discussing serious life issues with her, and what was she doing? Telling him about a pot addict she used to hook up with in the dorm. *Try to sound a little grown up here, Sarah*, she chided herself.

"Drug addict?" Daniel looked amused as he leaned forward and grazed her wrist with his finger. "So you're into druggies, huh? Maybe we should have scrapped the breakfast and checked out the Viper Room instead?"

Sarah blushed. But she was glad that Daniel found the situation humorous and not as an indication of her immaturity.

"Very funny." She elbowed him. "I'm sure you were a pothead in college, too."

"Well, maybe occasionally," Daniel acknowledged. "I did go to Brown . . . and maybe I did smoke up with my golf team buddies sometimes before matches." His gaze turned nostalgic. "We would take turns hiding behind a tree, smoking up a storm."

Sarah raised an eyebrow. "I've learned so much about you in the past half an hour, Daniel Wong. I feel like we're on an episode of *Get to Know Your Date*."

"Same here." Daniel smiled. "Pothead lover."

Sarah swatted him playfully on the arm.

Post-breakfast, Daniel took Sarah on a tour of Hollywood, complete with visits to Grauman's Chinese Theatre and the Walk of Fame. Sarah tried to look blasé in Daniel's presence, but she couldn't help gazing around like a starstruck tourist. Yes, it was cheesy and perhaps the scene smacked a bit too much of Times Square, but there was no denying the old Hollywood allure. This was, after all, where movieland dreams were made. . . .

Afterward, Sarah reciprocated by taking Daniel to the promised land of dim sum for lunch.

Even though Sarah's uncle wasn't at the restaurant, the family connection was enough to help them bypass the hour-long wait for a table.

"Looks like I'm not the only one with 'special' connections," Daniel teased as Sarah poured them some chrysanthemum tea.

"Just because I don't look like Yul Kwon doesn't mean I can't score us a table," Sarah said smugly.

"Point taken." Daniel laughed. "This place is packed—it must really be good."

"Just wait until you actually try the food." Sarah held up a finger as she turned to order some fried breadsticks wrapped in shrimp noodle sheet and drizzled with hoisin sauce.

"This is amazing," Daniel remarked as they feasted on *char sui bao*, barbecued pork buns; shrimp and chive dumplings; and egg rolls filled with meat, mushrooms, and bamboo shoots. "I can't believe I've lived fifteen minutes from this place for the past ten years."

"Where do you and your family go for Chinese food?" Sarah asked curiously.

"Nowhere, really." Daniel shrugged. "Flushing sometimes when I go back home, but when they come out here to visit, I usually just take them to some American place." He speared a piece of steamed tripe and popped it into his mouth. "It's not that I don't want to take them out for Chinese, I just don't know where to go. My sister isn't around a lot, and most of my friends are in the industry. Their idea of real Chinese food is chicken and broccoli."

Sarah started to laugh, then stopped when she saw that he was serious. Growing up, she'd been indoctrinated early on about what "real" Chinese food was; her mother would turn up her nose at the mere sight of beef and broccoli, sweet-and-sour pork, General Tso's chicken. This was for the *gua loas*, she declared—food for the white devils—and no self-respecting Chinese person would ever touch such inferior fare.

Clearly, Sarah thought as she gazed at Daniel's innocent face, there were Chinese people out there who had different ideas.

"Well, now you know where to go," she declared. "You can take your family and friends here, and I promise you they'll be impressed with your Chinese food know-how."

Daniel smiled at her. "Thanks to you, Sarah."

Sarah felt her pulse flutter as she gazed back into his eyes. "You're welcome," she said. "It's the least I can do."

Several hours later, Sarah was clutching her stomach.

"I'm about to get on the plane and pass out from all this food," she groaned. "I think the pancakes have taken up permanent residence in my stomach."

"I told you." Daniel chuckled. "But that dim sum! I was stuffed, but I couldn't stop eating those turnip cakes. Now I'll have to go on that carrot juice diet to get back into shape."

Sarah laughed. It was early evening, and her Cali sojourn had finally come to an end as Daniel drove her to LAX for her flight back to New York.

"Dan . . ." Sarah took a deep breath as they pulled up to the Delta terminal. "Thanks so much for everything. I had a complete blast—and I really had fun with you."

She smiled brightly at him, doing her best Mary Sunshine impression even though all she could think about was how she might never see him again.

"Me too." Daniel parked his car by the curb. "I'm so glad you decided to come out. If things lighten up at work, maybe I can even fly out and come see you in New York."

He gazed intently into her eyes as his lips curved into a smile. Sarah's heart leapt.

"Please come visit me anytime," she urged. "I'll call you the minute I land."

"You better." Daniel smiled. "And don't forget what I said— you need to seize the moment when it comes to your career."

Sarah smiled back at him, not wanting this very *Casablanca* moment to end. She may have been young, but she wasn't a complete idiot; she knew that this thing between Daniel and her was not terribly realistic given that they lived on opposite ends of the country. Still, she couldn't help feeling they'd had something more than just a weekend fling—even if she had been with him for less than forty-eight hours. Looking at him now, Sarah couldn't imagine not even knowing him just a week ago. . . .

"Take care," she whispered as she leaned in to kiss him. "Until we meet again."

Sarah didn't notice anything as she walked to her gate.

Not even sure how she got to Gate 15—or how she managed

to pass both the food court and the restrooms without noticing them—she plopped down into an empty seat and gazed out a nearby window where a plane was taking off. What an amazing weekend. Leaning back against the mesh-iron airport chair, she replayed the scenes in her mind: Daniel greeting her at the apartment, the star-studded soap party, meeting Clyde and Lucas, she and Daniel falling into each other's arms . . .

Sarah closed her eyes, feeling simultaneously ecstatic and sad. It was strange how the same memories could elicit such conflicting emotions. The bottom line, though, was that she had to forget all of it. That was the only way she would be able to survive going back to her old drab, dreary existence.

Her cell phone vibrated. Shaking the thoughts from her head, Sarah picked up.

"You sneaky thing . . ." Chad's tone was accusatory. "You go to the party of the century, but don't immediately call to go over it detail by detail. Our friendship could be terminated!"

"Oh, stop it." Sarah laughed. "I've been busy! There was so much going on, I had the best time out here. Chad, I felt like I was in a soap opera."

"Enough with the scanty little tidbits," Chad ordered. "How was the weekend? I want details now!"

Sarah eased herself lower into her chair. "It was wonderful," she said dreamily. "The party was so amazing. I was sipping champagne with all these *Asylum* actors! It was like I was one of them," she said, recalling her encounters with Susan Lucci and Robin Strasser over the canapés on the buffet line. "And I met all these *Asylum* producers, and they were so nice. The casting director was beyond cool. He told me to send him a tape!"

"That's fabulous!" Chad exclaimed. "Sounds like the break you've been waiting for."

"I hope so." Sarah crossed her fingers. "It's just going to be hard coming back. I mean, being here, I really feel like I can do this—like I can be an *Asylum* actress." She paused. "It's just—I can't help feeling like it's all a dream, and soon I'll be back in New York, flipping burgers at Balloon Burger forever—"

"Don't say that," Chad interrupted. "You're on your way, Sarah. You just have to keep the faith."

Sarah sighed. "I'll try . . . I just wish I wasn't so far away from Daniel."

"Okay, now we're getting to the juicy stuff. You had sex, didn't you?" Chad said quickly. "Did I not call the story line? 'Aspiring actress sleeps her way to the top of Hollywood by doing a soap opera producer.' Am I a genius or what?"

"Chad!" Sarah yelped. "It's not like that. I really like him. He's an amazing guy." She thought about how he'd taken her—a complete nobody and a stranger to boot—and offered her a gateway to this dreamworld where producers and agents were actually offering her *their* numbers. And that wasn't even counting the way he made her feel—desired, cherished, as if she belonged in that glittery fantasyland. "Too bad we can't be together," she said sadly.

"Alas, that's the way it is," Chad declared. "You live in different worlds—him Malibu and you Hell's Kitchen. Not to mention the fact that when you were six, he was sixteen!"

"You always know how to put things into perspective, don't you." Sarah rolled her eyes. "Anyhow," she said, hearing her flight number called, "I miss you and I'm coming home. I have to board now. I'll tell you more when I get back. See you soon!"

7

Okay, I want a double bacon cheeseburger with no lettuce, no mustard, but one slice of tomato and a teaspoon of mayo. Oh, and instead of bacon, can I have mushrooms instead? Oh, and no pickles. And on the cheese, can I get Monterey jack?"

Sarah sighed and punched in the order. Maybe it was jet lag or just overall fatigue from her whirlwind L.A. trip. Or maybe it was the shock of being home after her glamorous Hollywood weekend. Either way, Monday morning at Balloon Burger was beyond excruciating.

As her customer finally bustled off, Sarah collapsed against the counter. Okay, so working at Balloon Burger was never exactly fun, but somehow things seemed so much harder this morning. Partly it was because she couldn't stop thinking about the *Asylum* party and how tantalizingly close she'd felt to being the star she'd always dreamed of becoming. But there was also the memory of Daniel and his soft brown eyes. . . .

Stop it, Sarah, she told herself. *You're not in Hollywood anymore—you have a job to do. Even if it's working in some disgusting greasy spoon.* And yet . . . it was so incredibly hard.

That was when her cell phone emitted its familiar purr. After checking to make sure her boss wasn't in viewing distance, Sarah pulled out her phone, hoping that it would be Daniel asking how her trip home had been. Instead, it was a text from Dana Teng, asking if she was up for dim sum with her and her fiancé. Thinking how that was quite possibly the last thing in the world she wanted to do, Sarah shoved the phone back into her pocket with disgust. To go from Deidre Hall to Dana Teng . . .

"Wahhhhhhhhhh!"

Snapping to attention, Sarah realized that a melee had broken out between two competing groups of toddlers in adjacent booths. Drinks had been spilled, fries were being flung across the aisle, children were wailing, and three harried mothers were trying unsuccessfully to quiet their charges.

Sarah hurried over and somehow managed to separate the two factions. After calling over one of the janitors, she set him to mop duty, all the while soothing the sniffling three-year-olds with promises of free ice cream.

Order temporarily restored, Sarah returned to behind the counter, where she stared forlornly at the potato fryer. Somewhere close by, she could hear her acne-ridden, barely-out-of-college boss calling for her. Sighing, she dropped her head and tried to focus on her memories of white sands and flutes of Veuve Clicquot.

After her shift ended, Sarah took an evening stroll through SoHo, trying to cleanse her mind with some soothing window-shopping. Even though it wasn't L.A. mild, it was still an unseasonably warm May night. Hopefully, though, they were still weeks away from the usual oppressive New York summer heat.

She was busy studying a Topshop dress in one window when her Sidekick beeped. Glancing down at it, she saw the following message:

"Hey, sis, you coming to dinner on Saturday, right? Remember we switched this week from Sunday? Lin."

Sarah looked up toward the heavens. She'd been waiting for

this—waiting for the inevitable. Ever since she got home from L.A., she'd done her best to avoid seeing or speaking to her family. After all, she knew exactly what to expect: They would demand to know how L.A. had been. They would ask her about her audition. And of course, they would ask her how long it would be before she was offered a job. Because there was no room for failure—at least not in the Cho family.

She snapped her Sidekick shut and shoved it back into her bag. She knew she would end up going to dinner on Saturday, but for now she wanted just to savor this blessed moment before she told her family that she hadn't gotten a job, that she wasn't going to be on *Asylum*—and that she had never had an audition to start with.

The Topshop no longer quite so alluring, Sarah trudged away. So maybe she was in denial, but what else could she do? Before she went to L.A., the idea had seemed so great, so bursting with promise, but now . . . Sarah shook her head. During the weekend, Daniel had occupied all her waking thoughts to the exclusion of anything else, and on the way home, the memories of being with him had been enough to sustain her through the trip. But now that she was back on East Coast soil, Daniel seemed far, far away and she had nothing left but the reality that she was no closer to achieving her dreams. Which meant that she was out six hundred dollars—and for what?

She wished that she could talk to Owen. He always seemed to know what she should do. And even if he didn't, he still made her feel better. Unfortunately, Owen was away in Philly visiting his folks and wouldn't be back until Sunday. Pulling out her phone, Sarah decided to call her only other real friend in the world.

"Sarah," Chad exclaimed. "How's my budding little *Asylum* starlet?"

"Not so good." Sarah took a deep breath. "I've been ducking my family since I got back. Lin's hounding me now about dinner on Saturday, though, and I'm not sure how much longer I can really avoid them. What do you think?" she said hopefully.

"Well, if they were my parents, I would avoid them forever," Chad cracked.

Sarah groaned. "Yeah, well, that could never happen because my mother would just camp out on my doorstep until I ran out of food and had to cry uncle. That's why I should just give up right now. I'm never going to outlast her!"

"Not unless you move to L.A.," Chad said. "It would be a lot easier to avoid your family if you were three thousand miles away."

Sarah shook her head. "Don't tempt me, Chad." Pausing at an intersection, she thought about L.A. and what she would be doing if she were there. "I'm going to have to face my family and admit to them what a complete failure I am."

Her phone beeped. Sarah glanced down at her call waiting: Lin.

"I gotta go," she groaned. "It's Lin, and if I don't answer, the family's liable to send out an APB. Talk to you later."

She clicked over to the other line. "Hey, Lin," she mumbled.

"Sarah!" Lin greeted her. "I can't believe I finally got hold of you."

"Um, yeah." Sarah rubbed her eyes. "It's been really busy. You know how it is getting back up to speed on everything."

"I completely understand," Lin said, "and I'm sorry to bug you. I just promised Mom that I would make sure you were coming to dinner on Saturday."

Sarah paused to stare into a nearby store window, her mind flipping through—and discarding—the catalog of excuses she could use to evade the dreaded dinner.

"Sarah?" Lin's voice echoed in the silence.

"Yes," Sarah said finally, "I'll be there."

"Great," Lin exclaimed. "Can't wait to see you. You'll have to tell us all about L.A.!"

"Yeah," Sarah said, "uh, I gotta go. I'll see you on Saturday."

She quickly hung up. Okay, she thought, there's no getting out of it now. But, as she'd told Chad, why delay the inevitable? Yet all she could think about was how Saturday was going to be a complete and utter disaster.

Her phone rang again. What was this, Grand Central Station? Without looking at the phone, she flipped it open impatiently.

"Hello?" she said curtly.

"Sarah? It's Daniel."

That stopped her right in her tracks.

"Oh, Daniel," she gasped, "I wasn't expecting you."

"Is this a bad time?" he asked.

"Oh, no." Sarah cleared her throat. "Actually, this is a great time. I was just thinking about L.A."

"Yeah?" Daniel said. "Good thoughts, I hope."

Sarah chuckled. "The best. Since I've gotten back, all I can think about is how great a time I had out there."

"I had a great time, too," he said. "Actually, I was thinking of you because someone was asking about good Chinese restaurants, and I told them all about NBC Seafood."

"Really?" Sarah said. "I hope they like it if they go—wouldn't want anyone to be disappointed."

"Actually, they loved it," Daniel said. "Which is why I had to call and tell you about it. After all, it's thanks to you that I finally got in touch with my Chinese roots."

Sarah laughed. "Oh, I don't know about that."

"Well, I do," Daniel declared. "I feel like a real Chinese person now after all that dim sum. Now I just have to find a date for the Daytime Emmys tomorrow night, since the person I was going with canceled. It's too bad you're not here in L.A., because I would love to go with you."

It was all Sarah could do not to drop the phone and yell out, "Daniel Wong wants to take me to the Daytime Emmys!" Fortunately, he couldn't see her twirling with joy on Broome Street. She didn't even care that she was his second choice— although she couldn't help wondering who the other "person" had been.

"That makes two of us." She smiled. "Don't make me feel any worse than I already do! You know I would love nothing more than to be out there going to the Emmys with you."

Daniel laughed. "You're right, I'll stop. By the way, I— Oh, damn it."

Sarah frowned. "What is it?"

"Just got a frantic e-mail from one of the writers," Daniel said. "Look, I better go—talk to you later."

Before Sarah could respond, he'd hung up. Sarah shut her phone sadly. Not only was their conversation tantalizingly short, but Daniel was off dealing with real-life, real-world soap opera problems. And then there was the fact that if she were in L.A., she would be going to the Daytime Emmys. Instead here she was, standing alone in the middle of the street, about to confess to her family that they were right about her being the black sheep of the family once again. Was there anything else that could go wrong in her life?

That was when she heard the crack of thunder. Of course.

"So how was L.A.?" Lin asked.

Sarah took a hasty sip of tea. It was the dreaded Saturday night dinner, and her family was at Congee Palace in China-town. Sarah had come armed and prepared for the onslaught of questions that would inevitably be hurled at her, but now that the moment was at hand, she could feel the butterflies return in force.

"It was amazing," she said brightly. "The party was total red carpet, and everyone looked so glamorous. Plus, it was an incredible opportunity for networking. I met so many people in the business, and they were all really happy to help any way they could."

"Sounds great," Stephen remarked as he poured her some more tea.

"And?" Amy prompted.

Sarah frowned at her. "And what?"

"And what came of all this?" Amy leaned forward. "It's all well and good that you met all these people, but didn't you say you had an audition out there?"

"Yes." Sarah's mother looked over attentively. "What happened audition?"

Sarah licked her lips. "The audition . . . was good."

There was a long pause. Sarah's father was focused on the menu, but the rest of the family was staring at Sarah—her mother frowning, Lin and Stephen perplexed, and Amy triumphant. Seeing the growing disappointment in their expressions, Sarah felt an uncomfortable tightness in her chest.

"What do you mean by 'good'?" Lin asked. "Did they think you were right for the part?"

"Um, yes," Sarah said, stalling, "they thought I—was perfect for the role."

"So they hire you?" Kim, as always, cut to the chase. "Where's contract?"

"Well . . ." Sarah cast about desperately for some diversionary tactic. "Contracts take a while. The legal department has to put all these papers together—"

"But you have job, right?" Kim persisted. "You are going to be on TV?"

Sarah froze, at a loss for a response. Her mind went blank as a wave of panic washed over her. What could she possibly say that wasn't a lie?

"I knew it," Amy said scornfully. "You didn't get the job, did you. That's why you haven't said anything. I told you this whole trip was a waste of time and money." She turned to their mother. "See, Ma? I told you that you shouldn't have let her go off, thinking she can become an actress."

And that was when it happened. Sitting there in Congee Palace, looking at the knowing sneer on her sister's face, Sarah felt something snap. She thought she could take her family's disappointment, but seeing such open derision and contempt . . . all she wanted to do was wipe that smirk off Amy's face.

"Actually, you're wrong, Amy," she snapped, rising. "I *did* get the job. The only reason I didn't say so earlier was because I was trying to figure out how to tell all of you!"

For a moment, there was nothing but stunned silence. Sarah

swallowed and sat back in her seat, her heart racing. Did she just say what she thought she'd said?

"Omigosh," Lin exclaimed. "That's fabulous. Congratulations, Sarah!"

"Yeah, congrats," Stephen chimed in. "Does this mean that you're going to move to L.A.?"

Sarah stared at him. L.A.? But yes, of course. That was where *Asylum* was filmed.

"Uh, yeah," she mumbled. "I will be moving to L.A . . . to start my new job."

Her family erupted in excited chatter at that. Sarah slid down her seat. What had just happened? What were these words coming out of her mouth? It was as though she'd been possessed by the *Exorcist* demon and was being forced by an evil spirit to say these things. Yes, she'd always been guilty of a fib here and there, and yes, the lie about the audition had been a big one. But that paled in comparison with this one—this crazy, life-altering lie that couldn't be faked by some fancy talking. Sarah suddenly felt as if she were on some dangerously slippery slope that she couldn't stop herself from falling down no matter what.

"L.A." Her mother clutched her jade necklace. "You mean California? How I take care of you then?"

Sarah opened her mouth, but no words came out.

Sarah ran into her apartment and slammed the door behind her. Her heart was pounding, her pulse was racing, and she felt she was going to lose the entire contents of her stomach at any moment. She couldn't believe what she had just done. She hadn't just told her whole family that she'd gotten cast on *Asylum*, had she? Because that would be the biggest lie she had ever told in her entire life—bigger than when she'd told Kelly Martin that Sarah Smith was after her boyfriend, bigger than when she'd told her teacher that she hadn't done her paper because her house had been destroyed in a fire, bigger even than when she'd told her mother that she was taking summer school to get ahead for the next semester.

No, this one blew all those out of the water. It was one thing to tell her family that she was going to L.A. for an audition, but to tell them that she had actually gotten the part? That she was going to leave New York and move to L.A. and start working on the biggest soap opera on television? How on earth was she going to get herself out of this one?

Suddenly feeling she couldn't breathe, Sarah pulled out her phone. Damn Owen for being away. She needed to talk to someone stat.

"Chad?" she said shakily.

Chad picked up on her tone right away. "Sarah, what's wrong?"

The story came tumbling out. By the time she was done, Sarah was tear-streaked and barely coherent.

"I don't know what to do," she wailed. "This isn't some little lie I can fake. How am I supposed to carry off moving to L.A. and being cast on *Asylum*? I'm such an idiot!"

"Don't say that, sweetie," Chad said. "You were feeling cornered—you felt like you had to tell them something. What you did was completely understandable."

"But what am I going to do?" Sarah cried. "If I tell my family the truth, they'll never forgive me! And even if they did, I wouldn't be able to look them in the eye ever again."

She dissolved into a fresh wave of tears.

"I guess you have to tell them the truth, then," Chad said.

Sarah sniffled. "What do you mean?"

"Well, haven't you always talked about making the move to L.A. so that you could pursue acting for real?"

"Well, sure," Sarah said, "but that was just talk. I mean, to really do it . . ."

She trailed off. Yes, to really do it—that was a whole different thing. Sure, she'd talked about moving out to L.A. where all the real acting jobs were rather than staying in New York and reading for the three roles that ever got cast here. But to do that would mean leaving the place she'd called home her entire life, leaving the life she'd made for herself here, and leaving the safety of her friends and family—who, for all their flaws, had been an ever-present safety net.

"Sarah?" Chad said. "You still there?"

"Yeah." Sarah sighed. "You're right, Chad. I've always talked about moving to L.A. It's just . . ."

"Just what?" Chad asked.

"Just . . ." Sarah suddenly realized that she had no response for Chad. What could she say? Did she or didn't she want to be an actress? If the answer was that she did . . . well, it was time to fish or cut bait. She wasn't getting any younger, and the roles weren't going to get any more plentiful. And now that she had met Daniel and actually had someone who wanted to help her get her career off the ground, what was really keeping her in New York?

"Just nothing." Sarah straightened up. "I'm done with excuses, Chad. Maybe this happened for a reason. All the lies, the mess I've gotten myself in . . . maybe it was all a sign that I need to get off my butt and start going after my dreams. I mean, what am I really waiting for?"

"So what are you going to do?" Chad said.

Sarah squared her shoulders. "I'm going to get on with my life."

After she hung up with Chad, Sarah spent the next hour looking at L.A. apartment listings on the Internet. So maybe L.A. apartments weren't exactly cheap, but having spent most of her monthly paycheck on a 450-square-foot studio, Sarah could deal with it. Now all she had to do was get someone to sublet Lin's apartment, give notice, pack, and buy a plane ticket. But before that, she had to do one more thing.

"Daniel?" she said, her hands shaking a little as she clutched her cell phone.

"Hey!" Daniel exclaimed. "How are you?"

"Oh, I've been good." Sarah paced around her apartment. "Busy, but good."

"I'm sure," he said. "Going on auditions?"

"Well, not quite yet." She took a deep breath. "Actually, that's kind of what I was calling to tell you. I, uh, have kind of made a big decision."

"Oh?" Daniel said. "What kind of decision?"

"Well"—Sarah swallowed—"I've decided it's time to really get serious about my career . . . and so, I'm going to move out to L.A."

Silence.

Sarah bit her lip. What if she had made a terrible mistake? What if Daniel was just being nice to her because he figured he was never going to have to see her again? What if he didn't want her to come—

"That's fabulous!" Daniel sounded genuinely happy. "Sarah, I can't tell you how excited I am for you. You know I think that the opportunities are all out here—and now you can finally take advantage of them."

Sarah felt a huge wave of relief wash over her. She suddenly realized that she'd been holding her breath, terrified of what Daniel's response might be.

"You're absolutely right." She felt herself relax. "This is the only way I'll ever be able to make it. I've been holding out because I was scared to leave home . . . but now that I've decided to do this, I don't know what I was waiting for all these years!"

"So how did your family take it?" Daniel asked.

Sarah shrugged. "As well as you can expect. It'll take them a while. In the meantime, I've got a ton to do. First and foremost, I need to find myself an apartment in L.A."

"Well, you don't have to do that tomorrow," Daniel said. "My sister is still out of town for the next couple weeks. You could stay at her place while you search."

"Oh, I couldn't do that," Sarah protested. "You've already done so much—"

"I think we've had this discussion before," Daniel said. "Do I have to give you my spiel all over again?"

Sarah laughed. "You're right. If I can't find an apartment in time, I will definitely take you up on your offer. Thanks so much.

You've been so great to me already. I don't know how I'm going to make it up to you."

"That's a dangerous thing to say, because I can think of all sorts of possibilities," he teased.

Sarah smiled. "Try me. I'm ready for anything."

The next week was a blur of activity for Sarah. After leaving messages for a couple of L.A. real estate brokers (none of whom apparently worked on Sunday—Cali slackers!), she started taking inventory of the apartment. Not that there was that much to take inventory of. After all, how many personal belongings could really be crammed into a 450-square-foot studio? For once, though, Sarah was grateful for Lin's minuscule pad.

She had just finished assembling a dozen cardboard boxes when the phone rang.

"Hello?" she said as she tried to carve a path through the boxes strewn around her bedroom.

"How's it shaking, babe?" Owen's familiar voice echoed through the phone.

"Owen!" Sarah dropped down onto her bed, breaking into a huge smile. "Oh, my God, I've been dying to talk to you."

"I know, I know," Owen said. "Just a few days without me, and you're a wreck. You know I'm always there for you, babe, but even Owen needs some alone time."

Sarah rolled her eyes. "Whatever, O!"

"So what happened?" he said. "How was L.A.? Did you get laid? How was the Asian Sensation?"

Sarah shook her head. "L.A. was great—and Daniel was great. But there's something I have to tell you."

"What? Did you get knocked up? I didn't give you that box of super-duper sheepskin condoms for nothing, you know."

"Owen, will you stop?" Sarah demanded. "I'm being serious here."

"Okay, okay, chill out," Owen said. "What's got your panties in such a twist?"

She took a deep breath. "I'm finally going to do it, Owen. I'm going to become an actress for real. I'm moving to L.A."

Silence. It was funny how a few little words like "moving to L.A." seemed to inspire the same reaction in everyone—first Daniel, now Owen.

"Owen?" Sarah said. "Did you hear me?"

"Wow," Owen said slowly. "I got to hand it to you—you got me good this time."

"Isn't it great?" The words came tumbling out of her. "I mean, I have to admit I was really scared at first, but now that I've had some time . . . I don't know why I didn't do this sooner. There's maybe like ten casting calls a month here. There are ten every hour there! I can't believe how much time I've wasted—"

"So did they offer you a job?"

Sarah blinked. "What?"

"Asylum," Owen said. "Did they offer you a job?"

"Uh, well, um, not yet," Sarah stammered.

"But this guy—your hotshot producer—he's going to get you a gig, right?"

"Well, we didn't really talk about that," Sarah said. "I mean, I'm sure he'll introduce me to people and stuff—"

"Well, that's great and all," Owen said, "but how's that gonna pay the bills?"

Sarah froze, feeling suddenly deflated. "Owen, if I didn't know better, I would say you didn't think I should be going."

"I'm just not sure you've thought this through," he said. "You have to admit, this is incredibly sudden for such a big decision. I mean, you go to L.A. for a weekend, and you come back and immediately decide to move out there when you don't even have a job. Do you even have a place to live?"

"Well, not yet," Sarah said, "but Daniel said I could stay at his sister's apartment until I found my own place."

"Of course he did," Owen snorted.

Sarah frowned. "What is that supposed to mean?"

"Well, it's obvious," her friend replied. "He wants you to be conveniently located for his midnight booty calls."

"Oh, please," Sarah groaned. "Daniel isn't like that at all. He's been so great to me, and he's never asked for a single thing in return. And you know what? If he did call me up for a booty call, I would be more than happy to comply."

"So that's it, huh?" Owen said. "This isn't about moving to L.A. to further your career—this is about moving to L.A. for this guy."

"What?" Sarah couldn't believe she was actually hearing this. "Owen, how can you say that? Ever since you've known me, all I've ever wanted was to be an actress."

"And if you were actually going to L.A. to become an actress, I would be a hundred percent behind you," he responded. "But I don't think you are. I think you're going for this guy."

"That's the stupidest thing I've ever heard," Sarah snapped. "You know I would never do that."

"Then why the rush?" Owen demanded. "Why not wait until you get an apartment, get some job leads, maybe have an actual audition? Why run out there now when you have nothing?"

"Why not?" Sarah retorted. "You're the one who always told me I need to be more spontaneous. You were the one who told me to stop being a tight-ass and live. Well, now I'm doing exactly that. How can you not be supporting me?"

"Because I think you're doing this for all the wrong reasons," he said. "And I can't support that."

Sarah laughed incredulously. "This is rich coming from you. I'm trying to make my dreams happen, and you can't support that? What do you know about making your dreams happen? You've talked about becoming a producer for the past five years. How's that coming along? Have you done anything other than get coffee for the production assistant? How long do you plan on working at Balloon Burger anyway?"

"Well, at least I haven't had to sleep with anyone to get ahead," Owen snapped.

Hot tears sprang to Sarah's eyes. "Well, if that's how you feel, I guess we don't have anything else to say to each other," she said angrily.

"I guess not," he said.

And he hung up. Sarah stared at the phone, stunned. She couldn't believe he had just hung up on her. And she really couldn't believe what he'd said. Owen was supposed to be her best friend. He was supposed to know her better than anyone. How could he say those things to her? How could he not support her?

Suddenly feeling truly alone in the world, Sarah buried her face in her arms and started to cry.

"He really said that?" Chad gasped.

Sarah nodded morosely. "Yes."

They were sitting at the Bryant Park Café the next afternoon, having scored a much-coveted table in the jostling crowd of bankers and editors out to enjoy the unseasonably warm weather. Looking at them, Sarah suddenly thought how she was going to miss all of this. *Stop it*, she told herself. *So you won't have Bryant Park. But you'll have Malibu.*

Chad shook his head. "I can't believe Owen would say those things to you. How could he possibly doubt that you're going to L.A. to pursue your career? I can't believe he would even question it."

"Imagine how I feel." Sarah took a swig of her beer.

"Maybe he's just worried about you," Chad offered. "He's concerned that you'll be all alone out there."

"Well, I'm not going to be alone," Sarah said. "I'll have Daniel helping me."

"Ah, yes, Prince Charming." Chad raised an eyebrow. "How is Mr. Perfect?"

Sarah smiled. "He's been so supportive. He said the apartment is all ready for me to move in. He said he would even pick me up at the airport!"

"Wonderful!" Chad clapped his hands together. "You just make sure you invite me to the wedding."

Sarah laughed. "You know you just want an excuse to party with some soap stars."

"Well, that's a given." He grinned. "Why else would I want come? I'm getting all tingly just thinking about it—you must be so excited."

Sarah exhaled. "More excited than you know."

"So you're moving to L.A., huh?"

Still a bit light-headed from all the cocktails Chad had pressed on her at lunch, Sarah glanced up at the gangly, pimply-faced figure fingering the "Balloon Burger Manager" insignia on his shirt like a talisman.

"Yes, that's right." She turned back to the termination forms she was filling out.

"Are you going to work at In-N-Out?"

Sarah blinked and looked up. "What?"

"I heard they have really good benefits," her manager said wistfully. "Plus, they have these cool uniforms. If you get in there, do you think you could put in a good word for me?"

Sarah sighed. "Uh, yeah, sure."

"Great!" He beamed. "I always did want to move out to the West Coast. It's just that I always thought I'd be competing against all these surfer dudes. . . ."

As he babbled on, Sarah stole a glance around the restaurant. Unfortunately, the only other Balloon Burger employee present seemed to be Earl, the fry guy, who had a propensity for snacking on everything he touched.

"So"—Sarah tried to sound casual—"is Owen on today?"

"No, he called in sick." Her manager fiddled with a napkin holder. "Pain in the ass, too, since that leaves me short-handed, with you quitting and all."

"Bummer." Sarah tried not to look disappointed.

It had been twenty-four hours since the big blowout between her and Owen, and she hadn't heard a peep from him. She'd been sure that he would call her once he came to his senses, but apparently that was not the case. Sure, she could have called him, but something held her back. Maybe it was pride or maybe it was stubbornness; Sarah wasn't sure what it was, but somehow she just couldn't bring herself to contact him. Which was why she'd come to give notice at Balloon Burger with the secret hope that she would run into Owen there. If nothing else, she could say good-bye to him, since she was leaving in two days. Unfortunately, that was not to be . . . apparently, she was really going to L.A. without ever seeing her best friend again.

"So how much money you make?" Kim asked.

Sarah paused in the middle of taking a bite of her soup dumpling. Well, she'd almost made it through an entire dumpling before the question was asked. Glancing around the table, she saw the rest of the family exchange glances. They'd probably all been wondering the same thing, thinking that there was no way a soap opera gig could pay very much, let alone support her room and board.

It was the night before Sarah's big move, and the family had of course insisted on an elaborate farewell dinner of sorts to commemorate the occasion. Well, okay, maybe they hadn't insisted so much as expected it. Without consulting her, they'd showed up on her doorstep, fussed over the packing job she'd done, shoved another box of "necessities" at her (which included such must-haves as a roll of stamps and an apple), and then ushered her into the car to go to dinner.

"Well?" Kim demanded. "How much this soap opera pay?"

"Yes," Amy chimed in. "Is it even enough to pay the rent?"

Sarah chomped down on the rest of her dumpling as she glared at her sister. "Yes, Amy," she said coolly, "it is enough to pay the rent. It's actually pretty good. Three thousand dollars a month."

Her sister raised an eyebrow. "Soap operas pay three thousand dollars a month?"

"That's right." Sarah scooped up another dumpling. "Not bad for some dumb acting job, huh?"

"That's fantastic!" Lin said enthusiastically. "Sarah, I'm so excited for you. It must be so gratifying to know that all that hard work has actually paid off."

"Yeah." Sarah forced a smile. "It's pretty . . . amazing."

"So your apartment safe?" Kim asked. "In good neighborhood?"

"It's a great neighborhood," Sarah lied. "The show helped me find it. Malibu is a very nice area."

"You check locks when you get there," her mother ordered. "Make sure you have chain. And don't open your door for strangers."

Sarah rolled her eyes. "Mom, I do live on my own right now."

"But you here," Kim retorted. "Your family—we take care of you. California too far away for us to help you."

Sarah took a deep breath. "I'll be okay, Mom. Really."

After dinner, they took her home, where they once again fussed over her and her boxes for another hour. Finally, when there was nothing more left for them to dither over, they reluctantly took their leave. Stephen gave her a hug, her father a concerned pat, and Amy a suspicious frown. Kim lingered, handing out some additional tips about eating habits and suspicious strangers lurking in corners before she departed.

Lin was the last to go.

Taking Sarah's hands in hers, she looked her in the eye intently. "Just remember," she said. "If you need anything, call. Whatever it is."

Sarah smiled. "I'll be fine, sis."

"I know you will," her sister said. "And I know you don't need this, but humor me and take it. Think of it as an early birthday present."

She pressed a piece of paper into Sarah's hands. Sarah blinked at the check she was holding.

"Lin . . ." She shook her head. "I can't take this. Besides, I told you I'll be making—"

"I know," Lin said, "three thousand a month. So don't cash it—just keep it. Please."

Sarah hesitated, then nodded. Her sister gave her a fierce hug. "I'm so proud of you, Sarah," Lin whispered.

And then she was gone. Shutting the door slowly behind her, Sarah closed her eyes and sighed. Somehow, her sister's words cut her, more deeply than she could have imagined. Here Lin was, thinking she had finally made it and was on her way to her first big acting gig, when in reality Sarah didn't even know how she was going to pay for her next meal in L.A.

Looking around at the cardboard boxes littering her now empty apartment, she suddenly had a stab of doubt. What was she doing? Should she really be moving to L.A. when she had no job, no apartment, and no actual prospects lined up? Especially when her family thought the opposite was true?

You will be fine, she told herself. She would spend every waking moment trying to land a gig that would make all of this worthwhile. She was going to make this lie come true. She had to.

Two hours later, Sarah sealed her last box of belongings and sat down heavily on the cardboard mass. It was amazing how even the littlest knickknacks could end up taking so much time to pack. And even with all this meticulous packing, it was inevitable that she would end up forgetting something. Looking around, she counted up her boxes—twelve in all. Her entire life . . . all boiling down to a dozen cardboard crates.

The doorbell rang. Sarah frowned and glanced at her watch. It was eleven o'clock. Who would be coming by at this time of night?

Going over to the door, she called out, "Hello?"

"It's me," responded a familiar voice from the other side.

Sarah blinked. She paused for a second, then opened the door. Owen stood there.

"Hey," he said.

"Hey," Sarah said.

For a long moment, they just stood there. Then Owen lowered his head.

"I'm sorry," he said. "I shouldn't have said what I did—"

"No," Sarah said, cutting him off. "I'm sorry for what I said. You were just looking out for me, and I—I just lost it and lashed out at you."

They both fell silent. Then Owen held out a bottle of red wine.

"The two-dollar Chianti you smuggled back in your overweight luggage from Italy?" Sarah asked.

"My very last bottle," he said. "I was saving it for a special occasion."

Sarah smiled and pushed open the door.

"So I'm surprised your family took this all so well," Owen remarked.

They were sitting on lawn chairs on the roof of Sarah's apartment building, sipping the last of Owen's precious contraband wine. Down below, sirens screamed by, but on the roof, it was just background music. Looking out onto the cityscape before her, Sarah wondered if there were even such things as skylines out in L.A.

"I think they're still in shock," she said. "I didn't really give them much time to process, you know. Basically, I told them I was moving, and now I'm packing and subletting this apartment—thank God for Craigslist and summer interns who need a cheap place to live—so, really, I haven't had much of a chance to spend time with the family."

"Makes sense." He took a swig of his wine.

"Besides"—Sarah let her breath out slowly—"they think I'm heading off to fame and fortune. It's kind of hard for them to argue with that. They wouldn't be nearly as cool if they knew the truth." She shuddered at the thought of her family knowing she was jobless, penniless, and homeless.

"It'll work out," Owen assured her. "You'll get there, you'll find a place, and you'll hit the audition circuit. Before you know it, you really will be on *Asylum*, and none of this will matter anymore."

She glanced at him. "You sound almost like you believe it."

Owen's expression was pensive. "I do believe it. I know I didn't sound like it before, but I think I was just . . . scared. Scared of losing you."

Sarah raised an eyebrow. "Why, Owen, I had no idea you felt this way about me."

He chuckled. "I'm serious. When you told me you were leaving, I think my first reaction was . . . that I didn't want you to leave. That's why I said all those crappy things to you. I just couldn't deal, you know? I mean . . . you're my best friend, Sarah."

Sarah swallowed, suddenly feeling a little misty. "I'm going to miss you," she whispered. "I don't know how I'm going to handle not having you around anymore."

He turned to look at her and smiled his familiar crooked grin. Reaching over, he slung an arm around her.

"You're always going to have me, babe," he said. "Do you really think I would've wasted my last bottle of Chianti on you if I was never going to see you again?"

Sarah laughed and leaned back against his shoulder. Gazing out at the New York skyline, she felt—for the first time since she'd decided to do this—that she was really doing the right thing.

Los Angeles

8

This time when Sarah landed at LAX, everything felt peculiar.

She wasn't sure what it was—why it was that just a few weeks seemed to make such a universe of difference. All she knew was that she felt this strange trepidation in her chest, this odd sense of being unsettled and out of place. Maybe it was because she knew she wasn't going to be going home in a few days and that there was no turning back. She had gone all in at the poker table, and she had no choice but to fulfill her dreams—or crawl back to her family as a certified failure.

Deciding that she didn't want to analyze or contemplate her situation any longer, she boarded the shuttle to the rental car place straightaway. As she stood in line in her exceedingly wrinkled yoga pants and T-shirt, she looked longingly at the gold member line and the cars zipping up at a speedy, efficient pace. Even though she would have liked nothing more than to cruise around L.A. in a Mercedes or BMW like all the other twenty-something Paris Hilton wannabes, she was jobless, on a budget, and going to have to settle for a Chrysler Sebring.

"Yes, Mom, I've landed," Sarah said on her cell phone as she shifted from one side to another in her place on line to pick up her car. "I'm fine."

"Please drive carefully," Kim admonished. "Traffic is terrible out there. People drive crazy and they shoot you if you try to fight lanes with them."

Sarah sighed. "Got it. Is there anything else you want to tell me?"

"I have lot to tell you, but you don't listen," Kim said. "I just want you to be careful."

It shouldn't have been a surprise to Sarah that her mother was calling her within moments of her arriving in L.A. She was pretty sure Kim would be calling nonstop now that she was no longer within driving distance. Once, that would have annoyed Sarah, but right now she took some comfort in the thought. Now that she knew she wasn't going back to New York, she felt a certain warmth in the knowledge that her mother was still trying to look out for her.

"I will, Mom," Sarah said, checking her caller ID after hearing a beep. "I'll be fine. My friend is calling on the other line. I'll talk to you later."

She clicked over to the other call. "Hi there, I just landed a little while ago."

"Welcome to L.A., beautiful!" Daniel's voice echoed on the phone.

Sarah blushed. "Thanks. Too bad I don't feel that beautiful at the moment."

"Uh-oh," Daniel said. "I'm sensing some travel stress here. I guess you haven't had a chance to settle in yet."

"Nope." Sarah sighed. "I'm still in the nightmare at Hertz. At this rate, I'll be lucky if I get out while there's still daylight."

Daniel's tone was sympathetic. "Well, hopefully you'll have time to go check out a few of those apartments I found for you on Craigslist."

"I hope so," Sarah responded. "I've got Santa Monica, Burbank, and a beach house by Manhattan Beach on the agenda today." She paused. "I don't mean to be a whiner. I'm really glad to be here, and I'm so excited to see you! Want to grab dinner or should I just meet you back later at your sister's?"

"I'll have to get back to you. We have a couple of tapings, and we're behind schedule," he said. "I'm sorry—I'll call you later. If anything, I'll see you tonight, and we'll celebrate your arrival tomorrow." There was a clatter of voices in the background. "You should probably head to your appointments soon, though, because there's always traffic on the freeway."

"Okay," Sarah said.

After clicking off her phone, she stared at the phone for a moment, not sure how to feel. She was thrilled, of course, to hear from Daniel, and yet . . . it hadn't exactly been what she'd hoped for. She wasn't sure what she'd been looking for. It wasn't as though she thought he'd planned some elaborate, romantic night on the town for them. But she had hoped to at least be greeted by Daniel's handsome face, reassuring her that she had done the right thing.

Finally up at the rental desk, Sarah decided to push aside her thoughts as she started filling out the requisite forms. *Enough of the wishing for something that wasn't going to happen*, she told herself as she grabbed the car key and vowed to focus on her apartment search.

She soon found out that when Daniel had said there would be a lot of traffic, he wasn't exaggerating. Stuck on the 105 freeway, Sarah became increasingly irritated with each passing moment. Sure, she'd been stuck in her fair shares of taxis in New York during rush hour, but this was ridiculous. With only five miles to drive, she'd figured it would be a quick trip, but instead, it was taking her double the time to get to her destination. What was really unfathomable, though, was the complete absence of any reason for the traffic; it wasn't as if there were an accident—the freeway just happened to be one big parking lot in which she was stuck at a standstill.

Finally, after an interminable forty-five minutes on the freeway, Sarah made it to Burbank. Even though she wasn't that familiar with L.A., she did know that Burbank was where the soap opera *Days of Our Lives* was taped. Driving past the NBC Studios, she couldn't help but feel a little starstruck. She'd been too intimidated to talk to *Days* soap legends Deidre Hall and Drake Hogestyn at the *Asylum* party, but if she lived around here, maybe she could conveniently run into them on the street. . . . Shaking her head, Sarah chuckled. Apparently, she was channeling Chad, because that was exactly the kind of ridiculous, harebrained scheme he would have come up with.

Pulling into a large apartment complex, she was instantly impressed by how immaculate and spanking new the condos looked. If she saw a place like this in New York, it would be well over her budget. *See,* she told herself, *here's already one advantage to living in California.*

As she got out of the car, her broker waved at her from the front lobby.

"This is gorgeous." Sarah gazed around the building. "I'm from New York, so I'm used to living in a dingy little shoebox."

Her broker clucked understandingly as he led her to a one-bedroom on the second floor. Walking into the apartment, Sarah couldn't believe how spacious it was. The place had a balcony, a mammoth kitchen, an airy living room, and a bedroom that was at least three times the size of her bedroom at home. All in all, the apartment was ideal, except for the fact that it was late afternoon and sunlight was flooding the apartment. In the back of her mind, she could hear her mother's voice saying it was bad feng shui to have the sun facing west of the house and not east in the morning. Wow, Sarah thought. She couldn't believe how her mother's archaic superstitions had apparently rubbed off on her. Still, she was perturbed by that niggling little thought.

"Thanks," she told the broker. "I'll give you a call soon to let you know."

As she walked back to her Sebring, her phone started to ring.

"How's my Hollywood heroine?" Owen's voice boomed from the phone. "Are you tanning with the babies on the beach or what?"

The familiar intonations in Owen's voice made Sarah smile.

Thank goodness they'd managed to make amends before she left New York. It was hard enough to be away from Owen—she couldn't bear the idea of being estranged from him, especially when he was three thousand miles away.

"Oh, yeah, George Hamilton's oiling me up as we speak," Sarah quipped as she unlocked her car and eased inside. "I'm actually driving around town looking for an apartment. Just checked one out in Burbank, but it just wasn't quite right for me." She pulled out of the driveway and headed toward the freeway. "Now I'm off to spend the next three hours in this town's godforsaken traffic. All these cars! How am I supposed to get anything done sitting in this mess?"

"It'll be fine." Owen's voice was soothing. "You always get like this when you go somewhere new. Remember when we went camping? You were ready to leave after three hours. Then we started a fire, and next thing you know, we're plastered on s'mores and my uncle's moonshine."

Sarah felt her lips turn up at the memory. "If only everything in life happened so easily."

"It'll happen," Owen assured her. "You'll find an apartment, get a job, go on auditions, and become a big-time soap star. I'm trying to get in some overtime now, so I can come see you before your publicist starts blacklisting all your scruffy ruffian friends. Plus, I'm already suffering from my Sarah withdrawal," he drawled. "There's no one here to lecture me when I'm puking and peeing on the street at the same time because I'm so wasted."

Sarah laughed. She knew exactly what Owen was referring to—the night she took him to her friend Frank's wedding. Even though Owen hadn't known a soul at the wedding party, he'd managed to participate fully in the festivities. Indeed, he'd proceeded to fully embarrass Sarah by getting trashed and loudly making a toast to the bride's father for being "the most awesome dad on the planet." After that highlight, he'd taken it upon himself to solicit invitations to each of the bridesmaids' hotel rooms. In the end, Sarah had to physically drag him away from the reception hall and into a cab to the train station. There, while she'd fumed in one corner, Owen had lain down on the station platform and proceeded to serenade the homeless woman camped out next to the trash can. Sarah had been so furious at him that it had taken days before she'd relented enough to answer his calls.

"Yes, well, I hope we're behaving ourselves out east," Sarah said. "And I would love it if you would come visit me."

"Just remember that when you're on the front cover of *People*," Owen said.

Sarah just laughed.

As Sarah drove toward Santa Monica and passed by sign after sign for Beverly Hills, she had to pinch herself. In a way, it was surreal that she was here, actually living out her dream. She couldn't help feeling that she was going to wake up in her old bedroom in New York at any moment. She wondered if this was how Lin felt when she moved to London; while their family had greeted Lin's departure with tears and frowns, Sarah had been swept away by the romance of the whole situation. Who knew that just a year later, she would be following in her sister's footsteps, albeit three thousand miles in the opposite direction from New York?

Getting out of the car, she found herself near the beach at Santa Monica's Third Street Promenade. Sliding on her shades, she took a quick stroll toward the pier to watch the setting sun. The sight was breathtaking. Seeing the vast stretch of white sand before her and listening to the waves crash ashore, Sarah suddenly experienced a moment of pure happiness. It was all going to be okay—she just knew it.

Walking down the street, she realized that the apartment she was going to look at was directly across from the beach. So far, so good, she thought. At least her initial impression was positive. Before crossing the street, she snagged a free magazine from one of the newspaper dispensers on the street. There was page after page of classifieds in the magazine. If she was going to be renting an apartment, it would probably behoove her to start pounding the pavement.

"Hi, I'm Edmund." The broker shook Sarah's hand. "Welcome to the Santa Monica Condos."

"Thanks." Sarah smiled. "This place looks amazing. Love the beachside view!"

"Breathtaking, isn't it?" Edmund beamed with pride. "Looking at this view every morning will make you live a few years longer."

Unlike the apartment in Burbank, the apartment faced east. Immediately upon crossing the threshold, Sarah felt at ease. The place might not be as big as the one in Burbank, but she couldn't have everything. While the kitchen was a tad small, it reminded her pleasantly of the kitchen she'd had when she lived on the Lower East Side. As for the living room and the bedroom, they were just right—perfect for a singleton like her.

"How much are we talking here?" Sarah decided to cut to the chase.

"I can tell you're not from out here, little lady," Edmund drawled. "You get right down to business, don't you? It's fifteen hundred a month, including utilities."

Fifteen hundred a month! That was more than what she'd paid in New York. Of course, Lin had cut her a sweet deal for subletting her apartment, but she'd also had two jobs to defray the rental costs, while she currently had none here.

"Huh." Sarah bit her lip. "That's a little above my budget."

"If that's the case, you can always take on a roommate," Edmund said helpfully. "Lots of kids around here are looking for housing."

Sarah nodded but inwardly recoiled at the suggestion. The mere idea brought back memories of the roommate she'd had her first year out of college. She'd been incorrigible—never cleaning the bathroom, leaving the garbage in a decomposing heap on the kitchen tiles. Sarah had lost count how many times she'd walked out of her room to step on a sticky floor covered in dried beer. How nice it would be not to have to deal with any of that, to have a place all to herself. She could just imagine herself cooking a leisurely dinner for Daniel that they would feast on while watching the sun set over the ocean. . . .

The problem was that she had only two thousand in her bank account, which would be good for little more than one month's rent. Of course, she had Lin's check, but Sarah was determined not to resort to that until she was pretty close to destitute. Sighing, she rubbed her temples. She was already in deep trouble, lying to her parents that she had this amazing career-making job out here when she didn't. Which was funny in a way, because she didn't have a job, period.

But then she thought about Owen and how he had told her just to live. Didn't that mean living in a halfway decent place? Even if Owen himself would never pay fifteen hundred a month for rent? After all, she wouldn't want to scare her mother and tell her that she was living in a shack in Compton.

"I'll take it," Sarah decided, reasoning that if she was going to be able to dig herself out of the morass she was in, it would certainly help to be living nicely while doing it.

"Wow, I wish everyone who came to see apartments were like you," Edmund remarked. "You're quite the decision maker."

Sarah took a deep breath. "Hopefully, I'm making all the right ones. So . . . when should I stop by to sign the lease?"

"Well, we usually do a background check first," Edmund said. "We have to make sure that you're financially stable. May I ask what you do?"

I'm really unemployed and jobless, with two thousand dollars total in my entire bank account, Sarah thought. Again, her thoughts returned to the check that Lin had given her, but Sarah reiterated to herself that she was not going to use it. Not even for a dream apartment.

"Well, I'm an actress . . ." Sarah hesitated. "But I'm a waitress, too, so I do have a steady income."

Edmund paused for a microsecond, then shrugged. "Well, I guess you're like the rest of these townies here. If you pass the credit check, we should be okay, and we'll go from there. Moving day is the first of the month, so you could move in next month—as long as everything is good to go, of course."

"Wonderful." Sarah beamed at him. "Thanks."

Walking out, Sarah couldn't believe how quickly she had just rented an apartment. She'd looked at shoes in Bloomingdale's for longer than this. It was all happening so fast. She had to call and relay to someone her insanity.

"Chad, I've lost my mind—again," Sarah exclaimed. "I just looked at two apartments, and I completely fell in love with the one in Santa Monica. I was literally there for like ten minutes when I told the guy that I would take it—even though the place is überexpensive and I can't afford it. I mean, it's fifteen hundred a month. What in the world am I thinking?"

"First, take a deep breath," Chad advised. "Now, are you letting the smog affect your brain? Sarah, my love, fifteen hundred a month? Are you doing this to impress Daniel?"

First Owen, and now Chad? How could he think she was doing this just for Daniel? While Sarah admitted to herself that her recent actions had been a bit . . . unpredictable, it was ludicrous to think she'd gamble everything for a guy she'd met only a few weeks ago. Everything she'd done had been in pursuit of her lifelong dreams of becoming an actress. She didn't have a sliver of doubt about it.

"No, I'm not," Sarah said firmly. "How could you say that? You're starting to sound like Owen."

"I'm just trying to point out the facts, sweetie," Chad soothed her. "You *are* on a budget *and* you have a lot on your plate right now. You need to think rationally. It's a pivotal time, you know? You've got to always remember the endgame—and that's me watching you on an episode of *Asylum*."

Sarah sighed. "I know you're right. I just want so many things right now. I really do love this apartment, though. Look, I'm going to get a steady job to cover my bills while I go on auditions. And I'm going to call the casting director of *Asylum* and hopefully get the ball rolling on some things."

"Good, just keep your focus," Chad said. "Okay, *Grey's Anatomy* is on right now on the East Coast, so I gotta run. Call me if you need anything."

"Later," Sarah said, smiling.

As she hung up, her Sidekick trilled. She glanced down to see a text message from Daniel:

WILL BE STUCK AT WORK TONIGHT. SORRY WE WON'T BE ABLE TO GO TO DINNER. MIND IF I TAKE A RAIN CHECK? IF NOT TOO LATE, WILL STOP BY MY SISTER'S PLACE TO SAY HI.

Sarah dropped her head, disappointed. She'd been mentally practicing how she was going to relate to Daniel her apartment-hunting adventures, how she'd said yes to an apartment on a whim, how she'd been stuck on the freeway for so long that she'd been this close to becoming a road rage statistic . . .

Calm down, she told herself. Hadn't she just told Chad that she didn't come to California for a guy? And Daniel certainly wasn't her boyfriend or anyone who had even the slightest bit of obligation toward her. She couldn't be having these—or any—expectations of him. After all, he'd already done enough for her, what with the introductions and the roof currently over her head. No, she'd come here to make it on her own, and that was exactly what she was going to do.

She typed him a text back:

NO WORRIES. DO YOUR THING. I HAVE A FUNNY STORY FOR YOU. I'LL PROBABLY BE UP, BUT IF NOT, WE'LL TALK TOMORROW. GOOD LUCK WITH WORK.

Even though she was disappointed that she wouldn't get to see Daniel, Sarah realized that she wasn't devastated about having an evening to herself. There was something strangely liberating about not having anything planned. There were so many things she'd been wanting to do that she wasn't even sure what she wanted to do first. On the one hand, she could go to Chin Chin's on Sunset for a nice dinner. On the other hand, she could grab a quick bite at In-N-Out and spend the evening browsing the classifieds and getting down to the business of putting together her portfolio. In the end, she headed to In-N-Out for an Animal Style burger meal, which she brought back to Daniel's sister's apartment.

After shoving her luggage over to a corner, she plopped herself down on the couch to peruse the classifieds while devouring her fries. There definitely seemed to be job listings galore. Scanning the section, she paused as several ads caught her eye.

HELP WANTED
Make fast $$$.
Upscale restaurant looking for young hostess.
Must have experience and be skinny!
Call now at 310-555-4962

HELP WANTED
Want quick $$$?
Be an extra in a commercial
Up to $450 a day!!
Call 310-555-2379

Hmm, Sarah thought as she immediately circled the two listings, I'm definitely going to call this place. Earning $450 a day as an extra would be good money, and it was always possible it might lead to something; certainly, it would be a nice contribution to her hypercritical rent fund.

Her phone rang. Noticing that it was nine already, she reached for the phone. It's probably Daniel, she thought. Instead, her phone read: Lin.

"Hey, Sarah! How's the new job? Did you find a place yet? Are you settled in?"

A part of Sarah was dying to tell her sister all about her insane day and how she'd taken an apartment in Santa Monica with pennies in her savings account and how she was sitting at that moment in Daniel's sister's apartment circling classifieds. But of course she couldn't.

"I'm great," Sarah said brightly. "I think I found a place today! I said yes to this place in Santa Monica that's across the street from the beach. The apartment even faces east. Mom would be proud of me."

"Nice, Sarah." Lin sounded impressed. "I'm so proud of you! And now you won't have to stay in a hotel anymore. To be honest, I didn't think you could pull it off, but you sure proved me wrong."

Sarah closed her eyes. If only she knew, she thought. It was times like these—times when she came face-to-face with her lies—that made her glad she was three thousand miles from New York so her family wouldn't see the truth in her eyes.

"Thanks." Sarah cleared her throat. "Well, I would really love to chat some more, but I have to run. Got to learn my lines for tomorrow!"

Hanging up the phone, Sarah felt more conscience-stricken than ever. It suddenly hit her how much trouble she could be in if she didn't make her lies come true. How could she ever face her family again? Maybe she should start calling now, in case anyone was there. Zeroing in on the newspaper classifieds she'd circled, she flipped open her phone and started punching in the second number.

"Hi, I'm calling about the ad looking for extras in today's classified section," Sarah said. "When are auditions?"

"You mean the cattle call?" a woman's bored voice droned. "It's tomorrow at nine."

"Oh," Sarah said uncertainly, "sounds good."

Think positive, she told herself as she hung up. Next on the agenda was the hostess position at the restaurant.

"Is the hostess position still open?" Sarah asked the manager of the trendy Clique restaurant.

"It is," responded a snooty pseudo-French accent. "How tall are you?"

Sarah paused. That's a weird question, she thought.

"Umm . . . five seven," she said slowly.

"And how much do you weigh?"

Sarah frowned. "Excuse me? Why is that even relevant?"

"Well," the manager said, "just to let you know, we have a certain standard of attractiveness for the hostesses in our restaurant."

Sarah's jaw dropped. Sure, she knew people in L.A. were shallow when it came to looks, but this was ludicrous!

"Uh, well, I'm about one-twenty," she finally stuttered.

"I'm sorry, but our weight requirement for hostesses at five seven is one ten and under," he announced. "Thank you for your interest, though."

And with that, he hung up. Sarah stared at the phone in disbelief. She couldn't believe it. She'd been turned down for a job and called fat all in a span of thirty seconds. The nerve of the guy—and how rude! But as she stood there looking at the phone, she thought about the manager's words.

Was she actually fat? While she'd never really worried about her weight, it suddenly occurred to her that maybe she should. Sure, she went to the gym and was generally pretty active, but she'd never had to eat carrot sticks or wheatgrass juice like all the other aspiring actresses she knew. Part of it was that she came from an Asian family where eating was a religion. Like the time she'd told her mother she wanted to go on a diet. Her mother had screeched at her for an hour, then proceeded to whip up a three-course meal, which she'd insisted on watching Sarah consume in front of her. With that kind of attitude around her, it was no wonder that Sarah never dieted. She'd always figured that minimal exercise and eating sensibly was all she needed to maintain a Hollywood-acceptable figure . . . until now.

Someone knocked on the door. Opening it, she saw Daniel standing in the doorway, looking like some burnished Hawaiian god. Bursting into a smile, Sarah flung her arms around him.

"I'm so glad you're here!" she cried out. "I've had the craziest day!"

"That makes two of us." Daniel wrapped his arms around her. "What happened today? How was your first day in L.A.?"

Sarah shook her head. "Feels like I've been here for ages—can't believe it's been less than twenty-four hours. The good news is that I found an apartment in Santa Monica that I've absolutely fallen in love with. It's more than I can afford, but it's across from the beach so I decided to take it." She led him into the living room. "Which of course meant that I had to start looking for a job, so I grabbed the classifieds and found these two great listings. One was for a hostess and paid really well, but when I called, the manager asked how tall I was and how much I weighed! Can you believe that?"

Sarah suddenly stopped, realizing that she must sound like a raving lunatic.

"Sorry to babble," she apologized. "It's just been a little crazy for me. I guess I've been feeling a lot of pressure to get everything set up as fast I can."

"No worries." Daniel settled down on the couch. "That's a good story, though. Did he really ask you over the phone how much you weighed?"

"Oh, yeah." Sarah nodded. "And when I told him how much, he basically told me I was too gargantuan to work there."

"What?" Daniel shook his head. "That's ridiculous! Sometimes I think this town has Hollywood on the brain."

"Yup." Sarah sighed. "Now I feel like a big tub of lard."

As she plopped down next to Daniel, he took her feet and placed them on his lap. "Well, you look really good to me," he declared. "I would hire you in a second."

"Thank you." Sarah smiled. "So tell me about your crazy day," she said, scooting closer to him.

"Well, one of our crew members got sick and threw up on the set." Daniel ran a hand through his hair. "As you can imagine, that put a bit of a damper on the taping schedule for the day. All of the scenes got pushed back, the actors were throwing temper tantrums, and I had to appease everyone and change the scheduling. It was a complete shit-show."

Sarah winced. "That does sound terrible. Well, tell you what—if you forget about work for now, I'll forget about my job problems. I'm just happy you're here."

"Same here." Daniel put his arm around her, his expression sincere. "It's nice to be able to come home to you."

Home. Just hearing Daniel's words was enough to wash away the trials and tribulations of her day. Who cared about the traffic and the lack of job prospects and the snooty restaurants? As she nestled her head against Daniel's chest, Sarah felt as if she had everything she could ever want.

9

By the beginning of her second week in Los Angeles, Sarah was still exploring L.A. and no closer to finding a job. Every morning, she would take a leisurely stroll on the beach, watch the waves crash against the shore, and head over to the corner café for a smoothie and a bagel with salmon cream cheese. It was a pretty nice life, if only she had a job to support herself. Still, Sarah reassured herself that something would turn up sooner or later. She'd managed to buy herself some time with her mother by telling her that *Asylum* shot months ahead of schedule and that it would be a while before any of her episodes aired. And she was working as diligently as possible; she'd almost checked off half of her to-do list, and she had a jam-packed schedule of interviews ahead of her, including a few hostess positions that didn't have weight requirements. She'd also left messages for both Lucas Meyer and Clyde Turner, and she was sure it was just a matter of time before they called her back. More important, the much-anticipated casting calls were starting to trickle in. On Monday, she went to her first audition—a tiny role in an independent film where she had one line: "Good day, Mr. Cahill."

The casting call was at a small, nondescript studio in Century

City. By the time Sarah got there, over a dozen women were already lined up to try out for the part. Gazing at them, she was amazed at how many people had shown up to audition for what was essentially a one-liner. Countless women were huddled in corners, saying, "Good day, Mr. Cahill," in about seventeen different intonations. Scoping out the scene, Sarah couldn't help but notice how emaciated all of the women were. It didn't matter if they were Caucasian, Hispanic, African, or Asian—they were all giraffe-thin lookers with flawless makeup and outfits fresh off the pages of *InStyle* magazine. Sarah had glammed herself up for the occasion, but she was hardly dressed to the nines in this company.

Taking a deep breath, she walked up to the casting director. "Hi, I'm Sarah," she said brightly.

"Nice to meet you." The bespectacled man didn't even look up from the stack of head shots he was rifling through. "Okay, so the scene takes place in a living room. Your boss, Mr. Cahill, will be walking down the stairs. You will be playing Molly, the woman watering the plants."

"Okay," Sarah said.

"Anytime you're ready." He drummed his pencil against his clipboard.

Sarah suddenly felt a little flutter of nerves. It was ridiculous how four little words would determine whether or not she would get the part.

"Good day, Mr. Cahill," Sarah said in her most professional tone.

"Thank you." The casting director was already looking at the next head shot. "We'll contact you for callbacks in a few days if you're chosen."

Not even sure what had just happened, Sarah walked out. She couldn't believe she'd woken up at dawn and gotten herself all primped up just to read four words. Yet she clearly wasn't the only one—all these other people had shown up for this as well. It just showed how ravenous people were in L.A. to get into acting.

As she walked to her car, she shook her hair out of the updo she'd painstakingly put it in and smoothed down the vintage black crepe dress she'd donned to try to look like a maid. Once she was inside the car, she picked up her phone to call Daniel. It had been a few days since she'd seen him, and he'd been too preoccupied at work to talk when she called. But she knew he would want to know how her audition went. She sighed as she got his voice mail.

"Hey, Daniel," she said. "I had a crazy audition—can't wait to tell you about it later."

Hanging up, she mulled over who would appreciate hearing about her latest acting adventure. Smiling, she called Chad.

"I just went on the most bizarre audition," Sarah complained. "The whole thing lasted ten seconds, and all I said was, 'Good day, Mr. Cahill.' The casting director looked bored beyond belief and barely even looked at me. I don't know if I can deal with it if they're all like him."

"Sounds heinous," Chad said. "I'm sorry, sweetie, just forget about it. The show must go on, right? What's next on the agenda?"

Sarah sighed. "Well, I have an interview later for a hostess position."

"That sounds fun," Chad remarked. "Now, is there a weight and height requirement for this place, too?"

"Don't remind me," Sarah snorted. "Have you ever heard of something so ridiculous?"

"You'll get something eventually," Chad soothed. "Remember what they say—patience is a virtue. Now, how are things going with Mr. Daniel?"

Sarah smiled. "They're good. We saw each other a couple of nights ago. Work is keeping him so busy, though—he was working twelve-hour days all last week. I just tried calling him, but he didn't pick up."

"Well, he's Mr. Hollywood," Chad said. "And you're going to be, too—real soon."

"Thanks, Chad." Sarah fiddled with her phone. "How are things going back home?"

"Oh, like always," Chad replied. "My boss is working my last nerve, I spilled Merlot on my new Armani shirt, and my mother's been leaving me messages about how she's still waiting for her first grandchild."

Sarah laughed. "Classic. So what did you tell her?"

"What I always tell her—that she needs a new hobby," Chad responded. "By the way, good luck on that interview today."

"Thanks." Sarah sighed. "I better head off to the Stinking Rose now."

"Yummy!" Chad commented. "The garlic place? I heard that the dishes there are delicious and full of gahhhlic, as Emeril would say. Good luck!"

Sarah smiled and hung up. As she drove down Sunset Boulevard, she thought how surreal it was to be doing that. She'd been in Los Angeles for only a short while, but for some reason, it felt like aeons. Part of it was that she hadn't talked to her family in what felt like an eternity. Kim had called every day for the first five days, but she'd been mysteriously silent the past day or two. Lin had called once or twice, but Sarah had made sure to keep those calls short and succinct, lest her sister start delving into her supposed employment on *Asylum*. And while Sarah didn't miss her sister Amy's snide comments, she did miss the weekly family dinners—especially after a week of Animal Style burgers, which was pretty much all she could afford to eat at the moment.

When she arrived at the restaurant, she walked in and was immediately greeted by the pungent aroma of garlic, the restaurant's signature taste. Inhaling deeply, Sarah was reminded of her own house and how her mother was always making their family favorite garlic ginger chicken accompanied by minced vermicelli and sautéed bok choy.

As she strolled farther inside, Sarah had to sidestep several fast-moving, food-laden servers. Apparently, business was booming; the lively, cavernous restaurant was a whirlwind of activity and chattering customers. Speaking to one of the waitresses, Sarah asked to see the manager. As the waitress bustled off, a woman came and intercepted Sarah.

"Excuse me," the woman said. "My husband and I are visiting from out of town. Have you ever eaten here before?"

Sarah smiled. "I have—it's very good. If you like garlic, this is your place. They're famous for having these really inventive garlic dishes."

"Mmm," the woman remarked, "sounds tasty. Well, my husband is already parking the car outside, so I guess we'll try it out. I hope we don't need reservations," she said as she checked the restaurant's menu.

"I think they're suggested, but I'm pretty sure they take walk-ins . . . well, that's what their Web site says, anyway," Sarah explained, mentally running through the site she'd studied earlier in the day on Daniel's sister's computer.

Someone behind her cleared his throat. Turning, she saw a guy with the name tag "Manager—E.J." pinned to his shirt.

"This young lady is absolutely correct," E.J. said. "We do accept walk-ins."

"Great," the woman exclaimed. "I'll go tell my husband."

As she hurried off, Sarah swallowed, wondering how much of her exchange with the woman had been witnessed by E.J.

"You must be Sarah." The Stinking Rose manager held out his hand. "I'm E.J. Thanks for convincing that lady to come eat here."

"Oh, that was nothing." Sarah shook his hand. "I do like the food here very much, which is why I wanted to work here."

"Well, that will score you some points immediately," E.J. said. "It's good to interview a candidate that eats."

Sarah couldn't believe it. Finally, a place that wasn't looking to hire anorexic waifs! She also couldn't help but notice how cute E.J. was—tall, athletic, with that perfect, sun-kissed California glow that was apparently omnipresent in L.A. residents.

"I'm glad you think that," Sarah said. "Thanks for giving me the opportunity to interview for this position. Here's my résumé."

E.J. took her résumé and scanned it. "Balloon Burger?" He glanced up at her.

"Yes, it's actually one of the best burger joints in New York," Sarah replied. "They have these absolutely enormous burgers. It's a little hectic at times because they have nineteen different toppings, and you wouldn't believe some of the combinations that people come up with."

E.J. chuckled. "Yes, I'm familiar with Balloon Burger. The chef here is quite the slider connoisseur, and he told me he had a great burger there, even if the place is a little Chuck E. Cheese's in ambience."

"Wow, there are burger connoisseurs out here in L.A.?" Sarah grinned. "I'm impressed."

"So I guess you're a New Yorker, then. Did you just move here?" E.J. asked.

"Yes, born and raised," Sarah declared. "I've been here a week, and so far, I've been pretty busy running around L.A.—you know, looking for a job while going on auditions and everything."

"Ahhh . . . yes." E.J. nodded. "That is the Hollywood story. Well, as you know, the position here is for a hostess. It's three days a week—Thursday to Saturday from six P.M. until midnight. Dress is all black, but that shouldn't be a problem since you're from New York. We pay by the hour, but you get pretty good tips. A good hostess can make up to eight hundred a week—that is, depending on tips and performance."

Eight hundred dollars? That sounded like a fortune to Sarah. She would definitely be able to pay her rent if she got this job. Then she would at least feel she had something under control; plus, not having to worry about paying for housing would allow her to concentrate more on her acting.

"That sounds great," Sarah said. "How soon are you looking to fill the position?"

"The old hostess is leaving in a few weeks, so you can start next month," E.J. said. "I started the process early because I usually have a hard time finding people I like. But you may prove the exception. I've interviewed three people already today, and I can already tell you're the best of the lot. Like your background, and I was pretty impressed with your sales pitch." He made a sweeping gesture toward the restaurant. "We here at the Stinking Rose are looking for someone who can make our customers feel welcome, and you certainly seem to be able to do that." He paused. "I usually never hire people on the spot . . . but the position's yours if you want it."

Sarah gasped, not sure what to say. Yes, there was excitement and surprise, but the overwhelming emotion flooding her was relief. Now she could live in her Santa Monica apartment without constant fears of eviction hovering over her. Plus, it would be nice to finally tuck away Lin's check in some hidden corner of her sock drawer.

"Thank you so much!" Sarah squealed. "I really appreciate your taking a chance on me. I can't tell you how thrilled I am."

"Great." E.J. grinned. "Don't prove me wrong."

The minute she left the restaurant, Sarah tried calling Daniel, but her call headed straight into voice mail again. Feeling a little disappointed that he couldn't be the first one to hear her good news, she trudged over to her car.

That was when Owen called her.

"So, I'm coming to visit!" Owen announced. "I'll be there real soon."

"Owen," Sarah yelped, "that's fabulous! Did you get an extra shift at our favorite burger place?"

"Way better than that," he scoffed. "I got a freelancing gig this week. The guy who usually does the graphics for *NFL on FOX* is out, so they needed someone to fill in."

"That's awesome," Sarah exclaimed. "Do you think they might have more work for you?"

"Keep your fingers crossed," Owen said. "There isn't anything permanent, but hey, I'll be happy to fill in for them anytime."

"I'll definitely keep my fingers crossed," Sarah promised. "And I'm so glad you're coming. You can help me settle into my new place. I won't have too much time to do that anymore because I just got a job five minutes ago!"

"Awesome, baby," Owen exclaimed. "Where at?"

"The Stinking Rose restaurant—I'm going to be a hostess," Sarah said. "They apparently loved me so much that they hired me on the spot."

"What does the big-time Hollywood producer have to say?" Owen asked. "Did he help you lock this one down?"

Sarah paused. She hadn't thought about this before, but Daniel had never really put in his two cents when it came to finding a job for Sarah. It had all been up to her own pavement pounding and cold calling.

"No . . ." Sarah licked her lips. "I haven't even told him yet. I haven't seen him in a couple of days, and he's not answering his phone right now."

"Whatever, that's fine," Owen said. "I'm just really happy for you."

"Thanks." Sarah smiled. "I think everything is finally falling into place."

It was eight in the evening, and Sarah still hadn't heard from Daniel.

Telling herself that he was probably dealing with some prima donna on the set or perhaps yet another ailing crew member, she tried to relax with a glass of Chardonnay on the patio. But even though the sunset was breathtaking and the wine soothing, Sarah couldn't relax; she was still too wired from her nonstop day. If she were in New York, she would either be regaling Owen or Chad with stories about her whirlwind day over drinks or laughing with Lin about her latest adventures. But she'd already spoken on the phone to both of her friends, and as for Lin . . . it was times like these that Sarah fervently wished there weren't this fortress of lies separating her from her sister. When they were growing up, Lin had always understood Sarah best. Like Sarah, Lin had striven to break free of their family's antiquated conventions, even when it meant the inevitable explosive confrontation with their mother. Sarah had happily skipped along the path paved before her by Lin, and she'd always taken comfort in her sister's counsel and hard-earned wisdom as to what her crucial next steps should be. But that was before Sarah's current predicament—before she told so many lies that there was no turning to her sister anymore.

With that thought in mind, Sarah resolved to focus on the here and now. Hauling out one of the many books she'd collected on how to become a soap actress, she tried to concentrate on processing all the assorted wisdom on casting directors and on-set protocol. But it wasn't long before her thoughts strayed to her roller-coaster day, and all she could think about was how she couldn't wait to tell Daniel all about it. Which was probably why she practically besieged him the minute he strolled through the door an hour later.

"Daniel! I've been waiting all day to talk to you!" she greeted him. "You won't believe the crazy day I've had."

Daniel walked past her, tossing his jacket on the sofa. "Yeah?" he said.

"Yes, it was insane," Sarah continued. "But it all worked out in the end because I finally got a job. It's only a hostess gig at the Stinking Rose, but I'm actually kind of psyched about it. Plus, I'm just so relieved that I'm finally employed. I tried calling you to tell you afterwards, but you weren't around. Busy day, huh?"

She looked at him expectantly, but Daniel said nothing as he stared out the window.

"But, um, enough about me . . ." Sarah cleared her throat. "How was your day?"

"Fine," he muttered.

He lapsed into silence. Suddenly feeling out of her element, Sarah tried to think of something to fill the quiet . . . except that she had no idea what had prompted this bout of moodiness in the first place. Sure, she knew that he'd had a long day, but was that all there was to this? Or was he getting tired of listening to her prattle on childishly about getting an apartment and a job? Maybe he was finally realizing that she was just some unemployed little wannabe actress—or maybe he was just in a bad mood.

"Okay," she mumbled. "Maybe I should just leave you alone." Her tone immediately snapped him out of whatever funk he was in.

"I'm sorry." Daniel touched her arm. "I've just had a really long day. I didn't mean to take it out on you. Come here—please." Despite her hesitation, Sarah felt her resolve weaken in the face of Daniel's imploring smile. She reluctantly allowed him to slip his arms around her.

"I'm sorry you had a bad day," she said. "I have this tendency to keep babbling on about myself, and I'm sure that's the last thing you want to hear."

"No, no, no." Daniel sighed. "I'm the one who's sorry. I just had a really aggravating shoot today, but I should never have taken out my frustrations on you. How about a peace offering?" He reached for her hands. "Maybe we can grab a bite? There's some great sushi down the road."

Sarah broke into a grin. "You know that's one thing I can never resist."

As she followed Daniel out to the car, she tried to clear her head. Even though there was still a tiny bit of annoyance lingering from their disagreement, she knew she had to let it go. After all, what was there to complain about, really? She'd just gotten a job, and she was with this wonderful, handsome man whom she adored. So what if he'd had a bad day? This was just a day in the life of an average couple. Of course, that was assuming that she and Daniel actually were a couple. Which Sarah wasn't quite ready to bet the house on. . . .

It was times like these that Sarah wished she could talk to her sister—or that she had the girlfriends Lin had, girlfriends who could dissect her every word and action. But since she didn't, Sarah chose the next best thing.

"Have you guys said 'I love you' yet?" Chad interrogated her several days later.

Sarah shuddered. "Hell, no. I don't even know if he thinks of me as his girlfriend. We're so far from exchanging those three words. I mean, I don't even know how to ask him what our relationship is or whether we're even a couple. And every time I think about saying something, I feel like I'll just sound like a complete idiot." She exhaled heavily. "I mean, why doesn't he say something? He's ten years older than me! Shouldn't he be the one moving these conversations along?"

Chad chuckled. "One would think, but that's not always the case. Okay," he concluded, "here are my thoughts. I think you two definitely need to have the 'talk' soon—but you have to be cool about it. Don't be all smothery or obsessive or clingy. And don't let him think you're one of those crazy girls who wants to move their stuff into a guy's apartment after a week together."

Sarah groaned. "Ugh, I hate having these talks. I never know when's a good time to bring this stuff up. I think the last time I tried was with the druggie I dated in college, and he just shrugged his shoulders anytime I brought up anything serious. Believe me, it wasn't hard breaking up with him."

"Oh"—Chad burst out laughing—"you're talking about fun Bobby, right? I remember him. He was really dreamy—for someone who could only read at a kindergarten level. Ah, so cute, but so dumb, as they say."

Sarah chewed her lip. "How about this? I'll plan a nice dinner for us, and then I'll . . . slowly broach the subject. We'll have had a couple glasses of wine, and he'll be feeling mellow. Plus, it'll be all nice and romantic. Maybe he'll be in the mood to talk then?"

"That's a good idea," Chad agreed. "Sarah Cho, your brain's still working even if you're trying to become a soap star," he said as Sarah stuck her tongue out at the receiver. "Speaking of—did you meet with the casting director of *Asylum* yet?"

"I left him a couple messages, but I haven't heard back." Sarah twisted a strand of her hair. "I'm sure he's just busy and he'll get back to me soon, though. I still haven't heard back from that agent I met, either." She checked her voice mail. "Anyway, I have another audition coming up in a few weeks, so that should keep me busy."

"What's the audition?" Chad asked.

"Some commercial," Sarah replied. "It's kind of embarrassing, actually. There are two lines in it, and basically, I have to say, 'What do you do when you're constipated?' "

That left Chad roaring with laughter. "If only your mother knew—or Amy! Amy would flip in her panties."

"I know." Sarah sighed. "I can't tell you how glad I am they're three thousand miles away. The funny thing is, I actually haven't heard from them that much. I mean, my mom called a lot when I first got here, but now I only hear from them every couple of days. I mean, it's a good thing, but . . ."

She trailed off as a fresh wave of homesickness washed over her. She never would have thought this possible, but she actually missed hearing her mother's voice—even if it was in full lecture mode. And she certainly missed her confabs with Lin; more than anyone, Lin always got a kick out of her stories, probably because she had a history of engaging in harebrained schemes herself. A part of Sarah wished she could jump on a train and be home in time for dinner. But then she would remember why she was in L.A. and how forging her own path here was the only way she'd be able to chase her dream.

Chad picked up on her tone right away. "Are you feeling a little misty about the Big Apple? I know I miss you every time I hoist a margarita."

Sarah smiled. "Just a little. I know I need to do this, and most of the time, I'm fine. But . . . it can be lonely sometimes."

"But you have Daniel, right? How can you be lonely when you've got that luscious hunk of a man?"

Yes indeed, how could she? Wasn't it every girl's dream to meet a devastatingly handsome Hollywood player who would sweep her off her feet like some Harlequin novel hero? So what if Daniel wasn't Mr. Dependable Every Day Guy? Sarah wouldn't have been drawn to him in the first place if he were a clock-punching, nine-to-five homebody, so how could she penalize him for not being that person now?

Sarah took a deep breath. "Right. Okay, well, thanks for the pep talk." She gazed out the window. "I'm thinking I'll make oysters. Don't you always say that oysters are the food of love?"

"Yes, that's so Nicholas Sparks!" Chad said approvingly. "I want details—call and tell me how it goes!"

Now that she had a game plan in mind for her budding relationship with Daniel, Sarah turned her attention to the other most pressing concern in her life: her career. Her morning bagel runs were now accompanied by a perusal of *Variety* and *Hollywood Reporter* for any projects that she could submit herself for, as well as potentially useful articles on casting directors that she came across. After digesting any fascinating factoids contained in the articles, Sarah would studiously organize her notes in her Rolodex so that she would have them handy in case she ever came across one of these directors. She would then cap off her morning with an intense weekly combing of the popular actors' resource periodical *Backstage West* and the Web site lacasting.com for any potential audition opportunities.

After completing her morning homework and throwing together some mixed greens for lunch on Monday, Sarah headed out for the acting class she'd signed up for on her second day in L.A. Even though it took another chunk out of her fast-disappearing reserve of cash, she had decided that this was one necessary expense. How else was she going to learn about scene studies and cold readings and camera techniques? Besides, her shift at the restaurant wouldn't start until six, and there weren't any auditions yet to occupy those precious daytime hours every day until then.

"Have you taken any of these classes before?"

Startled, Sarah looked up from the notes that she'd been poring over during the break in her audition techniques class. A striking woman with creamy, café-au-lait skin, flashing tortoiseshell eyes, and a long, lustrous mane of chocolate ringlets leaned toward her from an adjacent chair.

"Uh, no." Sarah cleared her throat. "I just started taking these classes last week."

"I thought so." The girl nodded. "After a while, you start to recognize the regulars—and notice any new faces." She held out a hand. "I'm Giselle."

Sarah shook it. "Sarah."

"Nice to meet you, Sarah." Giselle smiled. "Are you from around here?"

"Actually, no," Sarah responded. "I'm from New York. How about you?"

"Born and bred in the O.C.," Giselle said. "I've always wanted to live in New York, though."

Sarah shrugged. "It's got some appeal, but I love being in L.A. Have you been taking these classes a long time?"

"Off and on for about two years." Giselle ruffled her hair. "The classes here are pretty good, and you have to learn this stuff somewhere. How else are you going to be ready for auditions?"

"Yeah." Sarah sighed. "Wish I had that problem. The auditions have been pretty scarce so far."

"That happens," Giselle reassured her. "Sometimes, when things are a bit tight, you have to try some different approaches. Have you worked on any student films?"

Sarah paused. "No, I haven't thought about that."

"Look, no one says you're going to become a superstar doing them," Giselle said, "but you can build some tape for your reel and expand your credits. I don't know what you've done before, but if you need to beef up the résumé, that's one way to do it."

"Huh, what a great idea," Sarah said. "Thanks for the tip!"

"No problem." Giselle smiled. "We can all use an ear to the grapevine—and I'm a big believer in sharing the info." She paused. "Want to grab a Jamba Juice after class? I just heard about this independent film that's looking for actors, if you're interested."

Sarah beamed. "I would love that."

That night, Sarah hummed to herself as she fixed a tortilla salad. She'd been in such a good mood after her Jamba Juice outing with Giselle that she'd decided to take a walk to the farmer's market and actually try to make herself a dinner for once that didn't consist of a burger and fries. Unlike Lin, who subsisted on takeout and expense-account Bouley dinners, Sarah had been forced early on by monetary constraints to sustain herself with her own cooking. Not that this was such a hardship; she'd always found the mechanical process of combining ingredients a perfect accompaniment when she was trying to learn lines.

Since she didn't have any lines to learn at the moment, Sarah seized the opportunity to reflect on her day as she sautéed some baby spinach in olive oil and garlic cloves. It was amazing what a difference meeting a friendly face made. Yes, of course she had Daniel, but he was like an absentee father—present only for brief pockets of happiness and then gone as quickly as he'd shown up. Which was why, sitting in the juice bar with Giselle and laughing at all her making-it-in-Hollywood exploits, Sarah had felt a new lightness. For a minute, it was as if she were back in New York, sharing stories with her friends or Lin.

Salad in hand, she snagged her glass of Chardonnay and headed out to the dining table, which was littered with post-cards she'd picked up on the way home from the farmer's market. Another tip Giselle had given her was to mail out postcards with her picture on them to casting directors around town. As Giselle had explained, the more familiar she looked to a casting director, the better the chances were that they would call her in for auditions.

Three hours later, the postcards were all labeled and stamped, the wine was long consumed, and Sarah was tuckered out on the couch. She reluctantly got up from her nook to open the door when Daniel knocked.

"Hey there"—he leaned down to give her a kiss—"how's my sleeping princess?"

Sarah flashed him a blissful, if sleepy, smile. "I had a great day. I met this really cool girl named Giselle in my class . . ."

"Wow," Daniel said after she'd chattered on for an eternity. "You seem really excited to have met this girl."

Sarah gave him a self-conscious shrug. "I guess I've been feeling a little isolated. It's kind of nice to have someone to hang out with—I mean, when I'm not hanging out with you, that is."

Daniel furrowed his brow. "You feeling a little lonely out here?"

Sarah looked down. "Maybe a little," she admitted.

"Well, that's no good." He shook his head. "I can introduce you to some people. Maybe we can do a lunch thing tomorrow."

"I would love that—" Sarah broke off, then looked up at Daniel uncertainly. "Except I just made an appointment with Giselle's photographer for noon tomorrow. Giselle said it's important that I get a really good photographer to take great head shots of me, and the ones I have are kind of generic and not really unique or standout."

"That's true," Daniel acknowledged. "Head shots are key in this business. I've seen hundreds of bad photos, and I can tell you that your head shot is really your calling card."

It was times like these when Daniel would say things that would catch Sarah and give her pause. So head shots were that important? If that was the case, why hadn't he told her so before? Why was it left to some girl she had just met to impart this wisdom to her?

"I'm actually going to this dinner next month," Daniel said slowly. "It's being hosted by one of the producers on *Asylum*. Why don't you come with me? Maybe you can meet some people there."

And that was the thing with Daniel. Just as the doubts and the questions were starting to gather in her mind, he would suddenly turn around and morph into her Prince Charming again before her eyes.

"I would love to!" Sarah exclaimed.

She threw her arms around him, and just like that, all was forgotten.

"Arigato! Sayonara!" Sarah smiled brightly through her bright red lips and white pancake makeup a week later. She adjusted

her obi sash and waved to the businessmen weaving drunkenly out of the downtown L.A. restaurant.

"Looking good, geisha girl," Giselle drawled as she ambled over in her white-aproned French maid costume.

"Same to you, Fifi." Sarah sighed and wriggled around uncomfortably in her kimono. "I feel so . . . tawdry."

"Oh, come on." Giselle rolled her eyes. "All you did was pour some tea, giggle a little, and throw out a couple of Japanese phrases. Not exactly *Debbie Does Dallas*. Besides, you have to admit—the money's pretty good for being a glorified waitress."

Sarah chuckled as she wet a napkin and tried to wipe off some of the makeup. "True. And I did become an actress because I loved dressing up as a kid. I guess even though it's kind of degrading to have to dress up like this, two hundred dollars to host a lunch party for a couple of drunk businessmen is not a bad gig."

Giselle smiled. "Stick with me, kid, and you'll find that this is just the tip of the iceberg."

"Oh, really?" Sarah turned around to face her friend. "What else is in your repertoire?"

"Hmm, let me think . . ." Giselle yanked her hair free of her lace headpiece. "I've had so many random jobs over the years to make ends meet. There's the usual, of course—office jobs, cashier, bagger at a supermarket. But I've also sold fitness clothes on a traveling fitness cart, been a tape dubber for Catholic Conventions, and was a professional eBayer for the rich. Oh, and I was also a desk beautifier."

Sarah just stared at her. "Okay," she said finally, "I'll bite. What's a desk beautifier?"

"Exactly what you think it is," Giselle said. "I made desks pretty for closet-slob executives who needed to impress their colleagues." She paused. "It's a long story."

Sarah raised an eyebrow. "I'll bet."

"Worst job hands down, though?" Giselle said. "Being an envelope licker and stamper. Yeah, that was as hellish as it sounds."

"Ugh," Sarah said, cringing. "I feel a paper cut forming on my tongue just thinking about it!"

"Oh, yeah." Giselle laughed. "There were a lot of those." She shook her head as she yanked off her apron. "But I'm going to need a drink before any more trips down memory lane. What do you say we grab margaritas, then go shopping on the Promenade with some of our hard-earned money?"

Sarah broke into a grin. "That sounds fabulous."

That night, Sarah sailed blissfully into the apartment, arms laden with shopping bags. After downing a couple of frozen pomegranate margaritas, she and Giselle had gone power shopping for an outfit for the big dinner with Daniel's friends. Despite the allure of a gorgeous five-hundred-dollar DVF dress, she had sensibly rejected that enticing little item for a knockoff that was less than half the price. Sarah had been so proud of herself that she'd decided to splurge on a pair of discount Marc Jacobs pumps.

As she dropped her bags on the floor, her phone rang. Sarah snatched up her cell and checked the caller ID: Owen.

"Owen!" she shrieked. "I feel like I haven't talked to you in ages!"

"That's because you haven't," Owen said with a sniff. "I've been feeling kind of neglected."

"I'm sorry, sweetie." Sarah smiled. "Any more football?"

"Not lately," Owen said. "But hey, at least I got another entry for the résumé."

"True," Sarah said slowly. "So how's Balloon Burger?"

"Well, I haven't deep-fried the boss man yet, so I guess things are pretty good," Owen responded. "He sends his love, by the way."

Sarah snorted. "Tell him I'm keeping my eye out for him for openings at In-N-Out."

That got a laugh out of Owen. "So what's been going on with you, babe? What's been keeping you so busy?"

"Oh, it's been pretty crazy." Sarah collapsed onto the couch. She proceeded to detail her geisha girl adventures with Giselle.

"And tomorrow I'm going to be an official sake taster," she exclaimed. "Can you believe I'm going to get paid to get drunk?"

"That is a really sweet gig," Owen remarked. "So who is this Giselle chick?"

"Oh, she's fabulous!" Sarah gushed. "She's totally cool and so much fun. I met her in acting class—she's given me a ton of great tips. It's been a blast hanging out with her."

"I can tell," Owen said dryly. "No wonder you haven't been calling—I feel like I've been supplanted. Either I'm going to marry this girl or I'm going to hate her."

"She's great," Sarah assured him. "You would love her. It's been really wonderful to have her around."

"What about your boy toy?" Owen asked. "Don't you have him to hang out with?"

"Yeah . . ." Sarah gazed out the window. "I do, but he's busy a lot."

"Uh-oh," Owen said. "Do I hear trouble in paradise?"

"Don't be ridiculous." Sarah tossed her head. "Everything's perfect. Just perfect."

10

After five weeks in L.A., Sarah was finally moving into her own apartment.

There had been times—especially when she'd had to share an apartment fresh out of college—when she'd dreamed of having her own place on the beach, especially after another night of being kept awake by the bedroom gymnastics of her roommate and her deadbeat drummer boyfriend. It was such a surreal feeling to think that she would be able to move into an enormous space entirely her own, one that she could outfit and adorn as she liked. She wished Lin could see her new apartment; after all the years of mooching off her sister, it would have been nice to show Lin that she had finally managed to get her own place. And that she was finally growing up. . . .

Certainly she felt very grown up as she was buying furniture for her apartment. Thanks to a tip from Giselle, she'd picked up enough cash being a spokesmodel for Kia and Daewoo over the past two days to afford some accoutrements for her new home. Maybe it wasn't much, but Sarah was more than thrilled with the functional bed, futon, and tiny dinner table that she picked up at Ikea with Daniel. After she'd painted the walls a warm sienna, touched up the crown moldings, and hung black-and-white framed prints of her favorite Tinseltown actresses of yore—Katharine Hepburn and Bette Davis were particularly prominent—in cozy clusters around the rooms, the once Spartan apartment felt perfectly lived in and uniquely hers.

"I'm so excited that this is finally happening," Sarah said, glowing. "This is my place—my very own place."

"It sure is," Daniel said. "You're a definite rock star. Now you can tell your parents you're not a loser."

Sarah paused. A loser? Was that what Daniel thought she was? Well, who could blame him when she didn't have a job and had been mooching off his sister all this time?

"So you thought I was a loser?" Sarah raised an eyebrow. "Thanks!"

Daniel winced, realizing that he'd stepped in a minefield.

"Of course not. I was just thinking about what your parents said. What I meant was that you've finally done it," he said hastily. "You have a job and don't have to worry about rent anymore, which means that you can concentrate on your career now."

Sarah hesitated, still not quite sure what Daniel really thought of her. In the end, though, she decided that not reading too much into his words was the best course of action.

"That's true," she relented. "Well, you'll have to help me christen the bedroom later."

"I would love to." Daniel smiled as he kissed her.

"On the other hand, we could stop decorating for a minute and go check out the bedroom right now." Sarah mock batted her eyelashes at him.

"I love that idea even more," Daniel whispered.

Thursday morning was Sarah's commercial audition.

She'd woken up feeling particularly downtrodden, because she still hadn't heard back from her other audition—which no doubt meant that she hadn't gotten the role. Not that a one-liner as Mr. Cahill's maid was exactly the role of a lifetime, but still . . .

Forget about that, she ordered herself as she brushed her teeth and tried to rev herself up for showtime. She needed to concentrate on the audition today. There was no time to obsess about past failures.

As she pulled into the parking lot of the production company, she noticed that this casting studio was vastly more expansive than the previous one. The casting call itself was taking place on the second floor of the huge triangular building off of La Cienega Boulevard. Smoothing back her hair, Sarah took the elevator to the second floor and got in line, all the while rehearsing in her head: "What do you do when you're constipated?"

Just thinking about the line made Sarah want to crack up. It was hard to keep a straight face while saying something so inane. If only Owen were here, she thought. The thought of her best friend brought back memories of the two of them having French-fry-eating contests at Balloon Burger after store hours. Of course, this probably showed how immature she actually was, despite her attempts to seem otherwise with Daniel. If Daniel ever heard about some of her exploits, he would no doubt think her childish and uncouth, not to mention a gluttonous pig.

With that in mind, she decided to text Owen:

AUDITIONING NOW FOR A CONSTIPATION COMMERCIAL. WISH YOU WERE HERE! I'M DYING THINKING OF HOW WE WOULD PIG OUT ON FRIES.

At that moment, Sarah's name was called. Quickly pocketing her Sidekick, she hurried over to the casting director. He looked up at her with an encouraging nod; Sarah flashed her most charming smile at him. He might just be trying to be friendly, but she was pretty sure he was the type with a roving eye.

"Hello, Sarah," he said. "I'm Kendall Stein. It's a pleasure to meet you. You're looking very nice today."

If there was something that Sarah could do in spades, it was flirt. The talent ran in the Cho family—certainly from Lin to

Sarah, and even in Amy to some extent (well, at least when it came to pharmaceutical sales).

"Thank you." Sarah flashed him a dazzling smile as she smoothed out her boho-chic black lace sundress. "Like it? I picked it out at this vintage store in NoLita."

"Well, it looks stunning on you," Kendall commented. "And you wear it well. I see on your résumé here that you're a native New Yorker. One of my favorite cities in the world."

"Yes, I really miss it sometimes," Sarah admitted.

"Well, who wouldn't?" Kendall said. "I was just there last weekend—"

One of the production assistants behind them cleared his throat.

"Uh-oh, I think I'm going to get a call from Legal." Kendall winked at Sarah. "So, are you ready?"

"As ready as can be," Sarah responded.

Kendall slipped on his glasses and glanced down at the sheet in front of him. "I'm having one of those days. I woke up this morning with a queasy stomach and felt so uneasy. I don't think I'm eating enough fiber or fruits and vegetables," he said.

Sarah was on the verge of bursting out laughing at what she was about to say, but she managed to contain herself.

"What do you do when you're constipated?" she said with a straight face.

"Thank you very much." Kendall looked up and smiled. "We'll give you a call back if you make it to the next round. I do want you to know that it was a pleasure meeting such a beautiful girl."

Without thinking, Sarah winked at him and sashayed out of the studio. Once outside, she doubled over, giggling. Sometimes she surprised even herself. She couldn't believe she'd just flirted so outrageously with a casting director! Who was she?

Feeling her phone vibrate, she yanked it from her bag. A text from Owen read:

I STILL HOLD THE WORLD RECORD FOR EATING FRENCH FRIES. I AM AWESOME! MISS YOU, BABE.

Sarah laughed as she strolled into the parking lot. Crazy Owen—he had the maturity of a kindergartner. And yet, somehow she missed him. . . .

Flashing back to her audition, she wondered what her chances were of getting the role. Would flirting with the casting director score her any points? After all, casting directors were supposed to like coquettish girls, right? Of course, the same could be said for producers, she thought, her mood darkening a bit. *Stop it, Sarah,* she told herself, *don't start letting your insecurities get the best of you.*

She decided to give Daniel a call to make plans for dinner. Once again, though, the phone rang for an eternity and then went into voice mail. Sarah sighed. She was trying really hard to be understanding, but she couldn't help being a little peeved at how Daniel never answered his phone calls. Sure, she knew he was probably putting out fires left and right at work, but still . . . Having no other recourse, she texted him:

HEY THERE. ME, YOU—DINNER TONIGHT? I'LL EVEN COOK AT MY PLACE.

Tucking away her phone, Sarah felt an anticipatory burst of excitement. Tonight was the night she was going to put Chad's advice into action and talk to Daniel about the "status" of their relationship. Even though she and Daniel were ostensibly together, Sarah felt she needed some clarity on certain things. Like were they dating? Were they boyfriend and girlfriend? Were they "exclusive"? A part of her hated having even to broach the subject. She'd always hated labels, and she particularly hated the word *exclusive*. It was so stereotypically female to have these conversations, but for the first time, Sarah understood the need for them—the need to have definition to her relationship with Daniel. In the beginning, all she'd cared about was living this fantasy where she would get to go out with a big-time Hollywood producer. Now, though, Sarah found she wanted more. Maybe it was because she'd moved to

L.A. and was actually seeing him all the time, but the idea of being Daniel Wong's girlfriend no longer seemed so out of reach. She felt ready to take that next step—and what better way to do it than being Daniel Wong's significant other? Even though she'd been in L.A. for only about a microsecond, Sarah was feeling aeons more mature already.

Her phone beeped. It was a text from Daniel:

WOULD LOVE TO HAVE DINNER. WHAT AM I IN FOR? IS THIS PUNISHMENT OR A TREAT? ☺

Smiling, Sarah texted back:

A TREAT YOU WON'T REGRET! ☺

Back in her car, Sarah headed straight to the closest Whole Foods. She'd never been so excited to go grocery shopping before. Then again, she'd never cooked for a guy before. Oh sure, she'd made meals with Owen. Owen was a great cook, and whenever Sarah offered to help, he would allow her to cook only the one dish he grudgingly admitted she did well—her chicken cutlet with rice pilaf. Even though Sarah had that dish on her menu, she felt something above and beyond was called for on this momentous occasion. Perhaps like oysters, which Chad was always telling her was the perfect dinner/"big talk" food. Shaking her head, Sarah couldn't believe that she was actually going to listen to Chad for romantic dinner advice.

After finding a spot in the Whole Foods parking lot, she took her pen out of her bag and jotted down her checklist:

Chicken cutlets
Rice pilaf
Fresh oysters
Chocolate cupcakes
Candles
A bottle of Chianti

Twenty minutes later, she'd picked up all her items and was speeding home. Originally, she'd planned to go running and then head over to the Third Street Promenade to purchase some new work clothes, but those tasks would have to wait for another day.

In her apartment, she tossed her bag to one side and headed straight for the kitchen, determined to put on her Martha Stewart face. After yanking on the apron that her mother had given her to inspire her to cook—and which she had never used until now—she pulled out all her assorted cookery items and started to dice away.

Sarah was so immersed in her culinary preparations that she didn't even notice the hours roll by. It was six o'clock already when she heard her phone ring.

"How's it going, Rachael Ray?" Daniel said. "I was planning to come by around eight—is that cool? I can't wait to see what you've got going in the kitchen."

"Come over and see." Sarah brushed back a stray tendril. "I'll see you at eight!"

After breading the cutlets, adding a potpourri of spices, and frying the chicken in a skillet, Sarah placed everything in the oven and hurried off to the shower. Daniel was going to be over soon, and she wanted to look ravishing—not like she'd spent the whole day slaving away for him. She didn't know how Donna Reed had done it; the whole domestic goddess thing was a hard act to pull off when one had to look like a Victoria's Secret model at the same time. Which was probably why Victoria's Secret models never ate, let alone cooked. Deciding to wear a lace tank top under her apron—she had to try to look as if she'd been cooking—she greeted Daniel at the door with a bright smile.

"You're the hottest chef I know," Daniel said as he kissed her. "Something smells great. I can't wait to sample your culinary skills!"

"Well, there's a lot of food, so I hope you're hungry," Sarah replied. "Have a seat, and I'll serve you."

"I like the sound of that." He grinned. "Thanks for making dinner tonight. Is there a special occasion? You seem to have something new up your sleeve every time I see you."

"No, no, there's no occasion," Sarah said, flushing. "I just wanted to do something nice for you."

"Well, thank you," Daniel said. "How was your audition today? How constipated were you?"

Sarah slapped Daniel playfully on the arm. "Very funny," she said as she checked the oven. "I do think I'm getting the hang of these auditions. I mean, doesn't everyone in L.A. have to go through this? I'm hoping that by the tenth try, something will work out, right?"

"Yes, and no." Daniel started pouring the wine. "It's a tough business out there, and not everyone succeeds. But people who really work for it usually get to where they want to be."

"And how do they work for it? Give blow jobs?" Sarah said, arching an eyebrow.

"What are you trying to say about 'Jenny from the Block'?" Daniel grinned.

Sarah laughed. Everything felt calm and relaxed and comfortable; it was a good start to their evening—and to their "discussion" later.

"So . . ." Daniel handed Sarah a wineglass. "What's the first course?"

"Baked oysters," Sarah announced as she set the dish carefully on the dinner table.

"Hmm, oysters." Daniel raised an eyebrow. "Trying to seduce me, eh? Not that I think I'll be needing any aphrodisiacs tonight. . . ."

Sarah blushed, thinking about Chad's advice for surefire dinner seduction tips. Apparently, Daniel was on to her.

"Oh, believe me, if I wanted to get you into bed, I wouldn't need to feed you oysters," she said with a toss of her head.

"True," Daniel acknowledged.

Sarah scooped up a spoonful of the oysters. "Here, try."

He took a bite as Sarah hovered over him nervously. She'd

copied the recipe off the Internet. It had sounded pretty good on paper, but since this was her first time making it, she just hoped it was edible. After what seemed an eternity, Daniel smiled.

"It's delicious," he said. "I'm very impressed. You can come cook for me anytime."

"Really? You like?" Sarah exhaled inwardly. "Let me try."

She took a bite of her dish and nodded to herself slowly. Not bad. Apparently, she was a better cook than she knew. Definitely not bad. She couldn't wait to tell Owen—she was no one-trick pony. Forget about the chicken cutlets!

After they gorged themselves on her meal, Sarah and Daniel retired to the couch, sated.

"Thanks again for cooking," Daniel said as Sarah rested her head on his lap.

"I'm glad you enjoyed it," Sarah said happily. "I was actually thinking of cooking Chinese food, but there were too many ingredients I didn't have. I guess we'll just have to go back to NBC Seafood for Chinese. Actually, maybe we can go there for dinner next time. What do you think?"

"Sure," Daniel said absently.

"How about Sunday?" Sarah suggested. "We can have Sunday night Chinese. That's what my family does at home."

"Hmm," Daniel said noncommittally.

Sarah paused. Well, that wasn't quite the response she'd been hoping for. She'd certainly expected a more enthusiastic reaction—at the very least, some excitement, even a sliver of appreciation. After all, wasn't he the one who'd said he wanted to get in touch with his Chinese roots? When Sarah had first arrived in L.A., she'd had visions of the two of them doing weekend dim sum and Daniel being ever so grateful to her for helping him get in touch with his Chinese roots. It would be something that none of the other blond Hollywood bimbettes could possibly ever offer him. So far, though, her master plan hadn't panned out, and she couldn't figure out why the Orient seemed to have lost its lure for Daniel.

The next moment, though, her concerns quickly dissipated

as he leaned down to kiss her while *Larry King Live* blared in the background.

"Do you want to go to the bedroom?" he said.

Sarah smiled. "Are you trying to get me into bed with you again?"

"Absolutely," Daniel said.

Even though Sarah had been replaying in her mind what she would say to Daniel in their "discussion," she decided it would be better if she waited. After all, there was no point in ruining the moment right then. Besides, he would no doubt be in a much better frame of mind later. Who wouldn't after a night of great sex? He would be feeling calm, relaxed—not to mention he would be lying next to her in bed, naked. Not exactly conducive to running away; he would have no choice but to answer her question then. It was a brilliant plan, Sarah concluded. Yet at the back of her mind was the specter of all those stories about actresses sleeping with producers to get themselves roles in movies. Was this how those stories unfolded? But this was completely different, of course. Daniel wasn't some gross, lecherous producer, and they weren't on the casting couch right now. She and Daniel were in an actual relationship, and that made all the difference.

Afterward, Sarah lay in bed beside Daniel, wondering how long she had to wait before she started the "discussion." Glancing at her alarm clock, she decided that ten minutes would be a sufficient amount of time so that what she was doing wouldn't be completely obvious. *Come on, Sarah,* she urged herself, *no more procrastinating!*

"That was nice," Daniel said.

"It sure was." Sarah turned over to face him. "So did I rock your world?"

"Without a doubt." He leaned over to kiss her.

They fell silent. Looking at him, Sarah could tell that he was ready to drift off to sleep. It was now or never.

"So, Dan . . ." She took a deep breath. "Can I ask you a question?"

As the words left her lips, Sarah's fists clenched involuntarily beneath the covers. For some reason, she was suddenly a mass of nerves—heart pounding, clammy palms, and all. So much for taking comfort in the dark.

"Sure," he said on a yawn.

"Are you dating anyone else?" Sarah blurted out.

There was an interminable pause. Sarah swallowed, uncertainty suddenly enveloping her. Ideally he would say no, but suddenly the possibility that he would say yes was enormously real. . . .

"No, I'm not," Daniel said carefully.

Sarah exhaled. She waited—in fact, she was prepared for him to ask her the same question—but Daniel remained strangely quiet. Finally, she decided someone had to break the silence.

"Well, that's good. Neither am I," she volunteered. "So what's going on between us?"

There. She'd finally said it.

Another long pause from Daniel. Sarah was starting to detest the omnipresent dead air between them. And her heart was beating double time again.

"Well, I like you," he said finally. "I would say we're dating, right?"

Sarah pinched her forehead. Was that it? Was that all he was going to say? After all the stress and anxiety she'd suffered over asking that question, his response was anticlimactic, to say the least.

"Yes," she said as nonchalantly as she could. "So I guess since you're not seeing anyone else and I'm not either . . . does that make us boyfriend/girlfriend?"

The minute she uttered the words, Sarah was seized with regret. Now she sounded like a sixth-grade schoolgirl pining after the coolest boy in class.

"I don't really like labels," Daniel replied.

Once again, Sarah was at a loss for words, not knowing whether she should be offended or not at Daniel's non-answer.

"I don't like them either," she mumbled, not knowing what else to say.

Dumb-ass! Even the darkness probably couldn't hide her embarrassment. How could she say that she didn't like labels when she was the one who'd brought them up in the first place! She was really winning brownie points for brilliance today.

"I mean, I don't like them either," she backtracked, "but we have been dating for a few weeks now, and I guess I just wanted to see if we were moving forward. I kind of thought it was time for this conversation, no?"

Okay, that was a good recovery.

"No, you're right," Daniel agreed. "It is. I just don't like to talk about my feelings that much. You know guys don't like talking about this kind of stuff, right?"

"I know," Sarah said. "But I'm still glad we did."

Or was she? And had they actually talked about anything? In her mind, she'd been expecting some dramatic declaration as to how much she meant to Daniel and what their future was going to be like, not a mere "Yeah, I like you." But maybe this was what older guys were like—silent and taciturn, not like some green, wet-behind-the-ears teenage boy. After all, what did she know? More than once, she'd felt young and naïve with Daniel. Maybe this was what older men said in relationships. Maybe this was what adult relationships were like, period. All Sarah knew was that she wasn't going to press Daniel anymore. Knowing that he liked her was enough—at least for now.

11

Sarah started her first day as hostess at the Stinking Rose a nervous wreck.

First off was the outfit. Not having time to shop for work outfits, she'd tried on about seventeen ensembles before deciding on a classic black wrap dress. She wasn't sure if that was the appropriate attire for a hostess—after all, her previous employment had always been as a bartender or waitress—but she figured this couldn't be that different.

"Welcome to the Stinking Rose," Sarah greeted a customer. "The waiting time will be about twenty minutes. Can I have your name and your party number, please?"

After ushering the customers to the bar, Sarah hurried back to the front of the restaurant, where E.J. soon showed up at her elbow. "How's it going? Things look like they're running pretty smoothly."

"Thanks." Sarah shuffled together some menus. "Things are going okay. But they say you always get one bad customer eventually."

"Don't say that." E.J. sidestepped a waitress bearing three precariously loaded plates. "You're sounding like a pessimist."

"I'm just saying . . ." Sarah paused as a couple wandered over to gaze at the menu by the door. "I've dealt with enough in New York to know how many lunatics are out there."

"Tell me about it." E.J. shook his head. "I once had to throw this guy out because he started smearing his face with garlic and running around the restaurant, harassing people to kiss him."

Sarah cringed. "Ew."

"Well, I'm sure that won't happen today." E.J. chuckled as he studied his clipboard. "By the way, we're catering a huge party in a few weeks. This production company is holding their annual dinner here, so if you don't mind, we might ask you to help out and wait some tables—if that's okay."

"Of course," Sarah said. "Count me in."

As she hurried off to greet some newly arrived customers, Sarah reflected that this job wasn't a bad one, as day jobs went. After all, she'd learned early on that trying to be an actress meant getting a day job that was extremely flexible, non-time-consuming, and relatively well paying. Between this and all the random gigs that Giselle was helping her find, Sarah was hopeful that she would earn enough to make ends meet—at least until that big break finally appeared on the horizon.

"Okay, so I was right—I'm never going to be on Broadway," Sarah declared as she collapsed onto the seat next to Giselle in the palatial art deco interior of the Pantages Theatre at Hollywood and Vine.

Giselle giggled. It was Tuesday, and the girls were at open call auditions for the L.A. version of *Spring Awakening*. Sarah had been dubious of the likelihood of success from the start—especially since she couldn't sing *or* dance—but Giselle had convinced her that it would be good practice nevertheless.

"Oh, come on," she said, "it wasn't so bad. Besides, what else were you going to do this morning?"

"Nothing," Sarah admitted, "but maybe that may have been

better than letting all those people hear me sing. My people aren't exactly known for their great singing voices."

Giselle rolled her eyes. "Hello? *Miss Saigon?*"

"Hello? William Hung?" Sarah countered.

Her friend laughed. "Okay, but you were really much better than you think. Besides, it's not a bad idea to try some theater auditions. It's similar to soaps in that you don't have a million takes to do the scenes. You basically have one take and that's it."

Sarah nodded slowly. "That's a really good point."

"That's what I'm here for"—Giselle tossed her curls over her shoulder—"to be Yoda to your Luke."

Sarah laughed. It *was* true. In the short time that she'd known Giselle, she'd already learned a treasure trove of information from her friend. From the moment she'd arrived in California, her ignorance—at least relative to the five billion wannabe actors and actresses in Hollywood—had been quickly made all too apparent to her. She'd hoped that Daniel would be the one to guide her through the Tinseltown maze, but given how rarely she saw him these days . . . well, it was a good thing that she'd met Giselle.

"You *are* my Yoda—and boy, do I need one," Sarah said. "When I first decided to do soaps, I had no idea there was so much involved."

"How *did* you decide that?" Giselle asked curiously. "Out here, the entertainment industry is so in your face that you can't really get away from it . . . but I would have figured that things would be different in New York."

"They are," Sarah admitted. "In fact, I'm probably the only one I know who ever wanted to be an actress. I'm the youngest in my family, and growing up, all I wanted was to get my family's attention, so I used to stage these little plays with my dolls." Sarah thought back to her ever-adoring childhood Care Bears audience. "My mom wanted to be an actress when she was young and encouraged me at first. I don't think she ever expected me to take it seriously, though. When she finally got the picture, she did her best to steer me toward the kind of nine-to-five job my sisters had, but by then it was too late."

"I take it your sisters aren't actors," Giselle surmised.

Sarah shook her head. "Definitely not. Amy's a pharmacist and the most conventional, bourgeois person you can imagine—she's a stereotypical Asian who only cares about stockpiling Coach bags. Lin, on the other hand, could be an actress. She's incredibly gorgeous, but her looks are wasted in I-Banking. Let's face it, you don't have to be beautiful to be a banker." Sarah sighed wistfully. "I've always wished that I had even a fraction of her looks."

"Oh, come on," Giselle said loyally, "what are you talking about? You're stunning!"

Sarah snorted. "I think I can make myself look pretty cute, but I'm nothing compared to Lin. She was always the star of the family. I'd be lucky just to share the spotlight with her. Sometimes, I think that's why I decided to be an actress—"

"Giselle Beaumont!" yelled the director's assistant.

"Oh, I'm up." Giselle jumped to her feet. "Wish me luck!"

"Break a leg," Sarah called after her friend as Giselle sprinted down to the stage. Talking about Lin inevitably evoked memories of her childhood, when she would watch her sister sail in and out of the house in a cloud of perfumed glamour. She would sneak into her sister's wardrobe and finger the Armani suits and Versace party dresses while imagining herself among the guests at the Black and White Ball on *General Hospital*. The men would be dashing in their tuxes and the women resplendent in their snowy-colored gowns as they floated around the ballroom with their champagne flutes. Sarah would of course be the lowly, no-body housekeeper/nanny, who would be revealed as the heiress to the Quartermaine fortune at the climax of the ball. . . .

Shaking her head, Sarah smiled ruefully as she smoothed down the folds of her kelly green vintage halter sundress. While her childhood fantasies were certainly entertaining, it was now time to make those dreams reality. From inside her bag she pulled out some brochures about a filmmaking class that Giselle had told her about. The professor in her audition class had talked about how increasing numbers of actors were making their own short films to promote their work. With all the digital technology available, it didn't cost a lot, and most actors who did it said it helped them learn about every aspect of the filmmaking process. Plus, the film could be submitted to film festivals, where there was always a chance some producer or director might take notice of the actor in the starring role. . . .

Suddenly, Sarah's attention was caught by a beautiful, haunting soprano. Glancing toward the stage, she realized that the owner of this amazing voice was none other than her friend Giselle. As she gaped, Giselle clasped her hands, tossed back her long, lustrous dark curls, and sang a passionate, lilting aria that left Sarah spellbound. When she was done, Sarah burst into completely spontaneous—and completely unprofessional— applause. But even though a few faces turned to look at her, Sarah noticed that no one in the theater seemed to disagree with her fan-girl reaction.

"Omigosh!" Sarah exclaimed when Giselle came back over to her seat. "Giselle, I can't believe you've been holding out on me! You have the most amazing voice!"

"Thanks," Giselle said, laughing. "I'm just glad there's not much dancing in this role. I once fell off the stage because the buckle on one of my tap shoes came loose. Talk about embarrassing!"

"Well, you definitely shouldn't feel embarrassed today," Sarah said. "I was looking around, and everyone was completely enthralled by you."

Her friend smiled. "Hopefully, I'll have a shot at getting cast in the chorus. Let's get some lunch! I think we deserve a *doner kebab* after this morning."

Sarah jumped up. "Now, you're speaking my language. Spitz, here we come!"

After lunching on their Turkish gyros and splitting a green tea gelato, Sarah and Giselle headed to a casting director workshop in West Hollywood.

"Thanks for telling me about this," Sarah remarked as they got in line with their scripts. "I had no idea these things even existed!"

"It's definitely a good thing to do if you're interested in being on a soap," Giselle said. "For most actors, the only way to get to know these casting directors is to do a scene at one of these workshops. Otherwise, you're just one of a gazillion head shots that these directors have sitting on their table."

"Wow," Sarah said, "that is so true—"

At that moment, someone knocked into Sarah, and it was only Giselle's fortuitous grab that kept her from a dominolike toppling. Turning, Sarah saw that her assaulter—an Amazonian blonde in a spandex minidress with a plunging neckline obviously geared to showcase her double-D cups—hadn't even bothered to stop after the collision.

"Are you okay?" Giselle looked worried.

Sarah shook herself off. "I'm fine. Can you believe her nerve? She didn't even stop to say sorry. And if there ever was someone who fit the word *skank*, she'd be it! Did you see that dress? She might as well be naked."

"That's Trishelle Kent for you," Giselle said.

Sarah blinked. "You know her?"

"Everybody knows Trishelle," Giselle said. "She's one of those women that you always hear about. The kind that goes on reality TV shows as the 'kitten' or the 'cougar.' Or has bit parts in movies where her only line is to scream and run around in her skivvies. She's the type who comes to workshops like these so she can try to sleep with the casting director."

Sarah gasped. "Really?"

Giselle pointed toward the front of the room, where Trishelle was talking to the casting director.

"Look," Giselle instructed. "There she's flirting and laughing with him. Toss of the bad-weave hair, batting of the fake eyelashes." The blonde leaned forward. "Now she's giving him a good look at the best silicone that money can buy." Lots of animated talking. "She's telling him how she's always been a fan of his work and how she's always dreamed of meeting him. Now she's pretending to listen to him and act like he's god's gift to women—and acting." Trishelle scribbled something on a piece of paper. "Oh, and now she's going in for the kill—she's writing down her phone number for him and promising him the best blow job he's ever had if he calls her."

Sarah clapped a hand to her mouth as she doubled over laughing.

"I'm not kidding," Giselle said. "Trishelle's a legend."

"That's so pathetic." Sarah shook her head. "You hear these stories about actresses sleeping their way to stardom, but you don't believe it's true."

"Of course it's true," Giselle said. "Girls in this town will do anything to get a gig. What's fifteen minutes in the sack if it means a chance at stardom? Believe me, no one gets laid more than these casting directors, gay or straight."

Sara turned her gaze toward the casting director ahead of them. "You think that's what Ross Lane is thinking? That he's watching these actresses do their scenes and expecting them to sleep with him?"

Giselle shrugged. "Who knows? I wouldn't stress about it. Whatever he may be thinking, you just need to focus on your craft. Besides, you're already shagging your gorgeous hunk of a meal ticket. Who needs Ross Lane?"

Her friend was smiling at her in a way that Sarah knew she didn't mean any malice. But however innocent the intent, Giselle's words still stung. Was that what people thought of her? That she was sleeping with Daniel to get ahead? Never mind that that was the farthest thing from the truth; not only had being with Daniel not gotten her some big Hollywood role, she couldn't remember the last time they'd even discussed her acting. If anything, he seemed to go out of his way to not offer her even the slightest bit of advice, wisdom, or guidance. All of Sarah's combined industry knowledge had come from either Giselle or *The Idiot's Guide to Being a Soap Star*.

Sarah swallowed as she fingered the script in her hands. Too bad none of that mattered. Even though Daniel had had absolutely no effect on her acting career, the rest of the world would see their relationship as nothing more than a glorified casting couch.

"Sarah?" Giselle poked her. "They just called your name."

Sarah shook herself out of her reverie and forced a smile for her friend. "Wish me luck," she said.

Giselle gave her a quick hug. "Break a leg!"

Taking a deep breath, Sarah hurried up onto the stage. She flashed the casting director of *One Life to Live* her most dazzling smile.

"Hi," she said. "I'm Sarah Cho."

Ross Lane lowered his glasses. Sarah wondered if he was assessing her for shagging possibilities, but his eyes were kindly, not lecherous. Either he was actually interested in her acting or she was just being naïve again.

"I'm Ross Lane," he said. "It's a pleasure to meet you. Are you ready for your scene?"

Sarah took a deep breath. "I'm ready."

Saturday was a blur of angst and activity for Sarah.

The day started off with an eight A.M. shoot on the beach for an ad that required just the right amount of windswept surf in the background. After Giselle had hooked her up with a print and modeling agent, Sarah had started getting a few gigs—none of which paid that much, but given her current uncertain employment status, they were at least something to chip away at the blizzard of bills she kept finding in her mailbox.

Once the shoot was over, she zipped off to a meeting of the East West Players, a networking group for Asian talent that she'd read about in *Backstage*. Sitting in the meeting, Sarah felt a conflicting mix of emotions. On the one hand, it was nice to be around her fellow Asian actors, to hear their half-hilarious, half-ludicrous stories of trying to convince some Hollywood bigwig to take a chance on a non-Caucasian no-name. On the other hand, the experience also depressed her, sapping the hope and optimism from her. Seeing so many of these Asian actors and actresses competing for so few roles and knowing that only a handful would ever get cast inevitably made her question her own chances.

Once the meeting was over, Sarah all but fled home. There, back in the soothing silence of her apartment in Santa Monica, she felt her anxiety ebbing away. It didn't matter that the odds were radically stacked against her or that she was just one of a sea of struggling Asian actors trying to break the cultural glass ceiling. She would beat the phylogenetic odds and make it . . . she was sure of it.

Besides, she had a much more pressing source of angst: the much-awaited dinner with Daniel's Hollywood friends that night for which she'd had to switch her shift at the Stinking Rose. As she bustled around the apartment, pressing her DVF knockoff, laying out her shoes, trying on myriad pairs of earrings, all she could think about was how much she wished she could talk to someone in preparation for the momentous event. At home, she would have chatted up Lin, who could not only pull together a knockout ensemble in her sleep, but could reel off ten surefire cocktail banter topics that were sure to charm. But here . . . Giselle would have been ideal, of course, if only Sarah weren't afraid that Giselle might attribute some stardom-seeking motive to her relationship with Daniel. Which was ludicrous, of course, because being with Daniel had netted her absolutely nothing in the acting department; clearly, Trishelle Kent she was not.

Maybe it was time to channel Trishelle, Sarah thought as she blew out her hair. She couldn't afford to mess up this evening now that Daniel was finally willing to grant her entry into his world. Even though she had seen him several times that week, their time together never seemed to bring her the satisfaction she was seeking. Despite their "discussion" more than a month ago, Sarah still had no idea how committed Daniel was to their relationship. Things that had once seemed to connect them— their Asian background, for instance—now no longer seemed applicable; indeed, Daniel had brushed aside her last few invitations to go to dim sum or Chinatown in favor of more ritzy Hollywood fare. It was almost as if his claimed desire to get in touch with his Asian roots were nothing more than warm and fuzzy morning-after conversation. . . . Then there was the fact that after three months, she had yet to meet any of his friends, let alone the sister whose apartment she'd been staying at. She had only a handful of friends in L.A. and the rest back home; it would have been nice if Daniel had introduced her to a few more friendly faces. Which was why, even though she was happy to be with Daniel, Sarah couldn't help but feel the weight of discontentment with how things were progressing.

Feeling a wave of anxiety sweep over her, she reached over and snatched up the phone. She started to punch in Owen's digits, then stopped. No, this was boy trouble. Chad.

"Girl, you need to chill," Chad said when she was finally done with her diatribe about how she was going to get through the evening with her sanity and relationship intact.

"I know, I know . . ." Sarah sighed as she smoothed hair wax through her bangs. "It's just that this is my chance to really be a part of Daniel's world, and I don't want to fuck it up."

"Then don't fuck it up," Chad said calmly. "Just be yourself and they'll have to love you."

Sarah paused in mid–hair prep to gaze out the window. The sun was starting its descent into the Pacific, which meant she had a scant hour or so left before dinner. Her commercial notwithstanding, she couldn't help thinking how not much had worked out as planned. Even though she was diligently logging in the hours and the effort, she was no closer to attaining her *Asylum* dream than she had been in New York. And even though she and Daniel were ostensibly together, there were times when she felt she didn't know him any better than when she'd met him at the Waldorf a lifetime ago. . . .

"Yes," she said finally, "they'll have to love me."

* * *

Alessandro Martelli's mansion was everything Sarah imagined it would be: large sprawling columns, polished marble tiles, palm fronds in every corner.

Sarah strolled into the house on Daniel's arm like a figure from one of her dreams. In those dreams, she was beautiful, glamorous, a celluloid goddess mingling with the rich and famous on the arm of George Clooney. And here she was, the fantasy made into reality . . . well, except for the part where she was actually a star.

"Daniel!" A very blond, very tanned vision in persimmon chiffon ran toward them and enveloped Daniel in a cloud of Chanel No. 5.

"Hilary!" Daniel laughed and clasped her to him. "It's so good to see you. It's been too long."

"I'll say," Hilary said pertly. "But the time has done you good. You still know how to rock an Armani suit, I see."

"Valentino," Daniel corrected her. "You're slipping, Hil."

She batted her eyelashes at him. "Trust me, Daniel. I'm still the best."

As they traded their innuendo-laced Hollywood-speak, Sarah watched, spellbound, knowing there were undercurrents there that she didn't get but wanted desperately to understand.

After what seemed like an eternity of banter, Daniel cleared his throat and turned toward Sarah.

"Hilary James," he said, "this is Sarah Cho. Sarah, Hilary and I are . . . old friends."

Hilary held out her hand to Sarah, her smile gleaming and bright. "Hi there," she said. "It's nice to meet you, Sarah."

Sarah shook the proffered hand, all the while searching the other woman's eyes for something—a smirk, a glare, some evidence of malicious intent. But Hilary's eyes were guileless and friendly, and somehow that was worse than anything. Because if Hilary didn't view her as a threat, how significant was Sarah in Daniel's life?

"Come on . . ." Daniel caught her elbow. "Let's get a drink."

Dinner was a feast of foie gras tarts, black truffle quiche, and escargot puff pastry—delicacies Sarah had heard of but had never actually sampled. Alessandro, a larger-than-life half-Italian, half-Parisian producer whom Daniel credited with mentoring him in the soap opera business, had kissed Sarah's hand and immediately pressed a caviar-laced piece of toast into it upon learning of her dearth of epicurean experience.

Now he was presiding over the table, regaling them all with tales of his days in the soap trenches while waiters poured glass after glass of Cabernet. As she sipped her third glass of wine, Sarah gazed around the table and wondered how she'd gotten there. All around her, the conversation flew fast and furious about married *Asylum* actresses having torrid affairs with co-stars, *Asylum* actors caught snorting coke in some club in West Hollywood, *Asylum* writers being axed because of the latest dip in the ratings . . . Ever since Sarah could remember, she'd dreamed about being a fly on the wall in this type of gathering, being an insider privy to all the exclusive goings-on behind the scenes.

But now that she was actually here . . . all she felt was this strange isolation. Maybe she was drunk from the Cabernet, but the conversation seemed to whisk around her at warp speed without ever actually coming in contact with her. Everyone was too preoccupied with chasing the latest rumor to pay any attention to her, even Daniel. In fact, he hadn't spoken to her in the past twenty minutes, so absorbed was he in some story of an up-and-coming producer whom everyone was projecting to be the second coming of Bill Bell, the legendary creator of *The Young and the Restless*. And Sarah certainly didn't want to intrude on the conversation that had him so enraptured; after all, he'd promised to bring her to one of these gatherings only because she'd practically thrown herself at his feet and begged him to. The last thing she wanted was for him to think that he needed to babysit her at the dinner as well.

"So you're Daniel's friend?"

Glancing up from the wine she'd been steadily imbibing, Sarah realized that the couple next to her was looking at her.

"Uh, yes . . ." Sarah cleared her throat. "I'm Sarah."

"It's a pleasure to meet you," fluttered the peroxide blonde with the perfectly symmetrical breasts. "I'm Santana, and this is my husband, Jared."

"We've been wanting to meet you." Jared flashed a blindingly white smile at Sarah. "You're an actress, right?"

Sarah nodded. "Yes, well, I'm kind of just starting out. I–I only moved here a few months ago, and so I'm still learning the ropes, I guess."

"What have you been in so far?" Santana asked.

"Oh, well . . ." Sarah blushed. "I've been in some commercials, but in terms of acting jobs, I've mostly been going to auditions. I'm still waiting for my big break."

"Well, we all have to start somewhere, right?" Jared said.

"That's right," Santana agreed. "I auditioned forever before I got a role on a soap. What kinds of auditions have you been going on?"

Sarah rolled her eyes. "Oh, the craziest auditions." She took another swig of her wine, even though she was already feeling a little light-headed. "Yesterday, I had an audition to be a dominatrix—there was a lot of man spanking there."

"Been there, done that," Santana said. "What else?"

Sarah chewed her lip. "Well, last week, I was auditioning to be an Asian milkmaid. Who knew there were such things? I don't think I got it, though—I had no idea how to milk the cow's udders."

Santana and Jared roared with laughter.

"That's great," Jared said. "Only in Hollywood would there be an Asian milkmaid."

Santana prodded one of the women beside her. "You've got to hear this—Sarah's telling us all about her auditions."

As all eyes turned toward her, Sarah felt herself warm to the subject, emboldened by the pleasant feel of Cabernet swirling in her bloodstream. "Well, being an Asian milkmaid was still better than when I was a tap-dancing chicken. Or when I had to give this really sad, sentimental monologue about dying young while I had my arms and legs ripped off by rabid wolves!"

Her audience laughed uproariously as Sarah continued to regale them with her audition tales—so much so that Daniel's attention was finally caught.

"So what's so funny?" Daniel furrowed his brow.

"Your girl," Jared said. "She's a riot."

"Yes," Santana said. "She's such a hoot. Where'd you find her?"

"We met in New York," Daniel said.

"Finally ran out of women here in L.A., huh?" Jared cracked.

As they all laughed, Sarah felt her smile falter a little. But then she took another sip of her Cab, and the ensuing warmth quickly made her insecurities melt away.

"It must have been tough for you to move out here, Sarah," Santana remarked.

"Not at all." Sarah shrugged. "I love L.A. What's not to love? The weather, the beach, the In-N-Out burgers."

Santana and Jared exchanged glances. Watching them, Sarah was seized with a sudden wicked urge.

"Yes," she said, "I have In-N-Out burgers for dinner pretty much every night. On the weekends, though, I treat myself to some really authentic Chinese food."

"Oh?" Santana said. "What kind of authentic Chinese food?"

"Beef tripe," Sarah responded as Santana wrinkled her nose, "sea cucumber, bird's-nest soup, thousand-year-old egg."

Jared furrowed his brow. "Bird's-nest soup?"

"Yes," Sarah said, warming to the subject, "it's a soup of a bird's nest made entirely of the bird's saliva—"

"Uh, Sarah," Daniel interrupted, snatching the wineglass from Sarah's hand, "here, why don't you have something to eat?"

There was a strain in his voice that stopped Sarah. As his hand brushed hers, Sarah noticed the tautness in his neck, the tightly wound tension in his shoulders.

"Well, you have quite a find here, Daniel," Santana drawled. "Sarah here has quite a repertoire. Darling, what was that audition you went to last week again?"

Sarah licked her lips, the thrill over being the center of attention fading fast. "Office worker by day, ninja princess by night," she mumbled.

That set off another round of laughter. Daniel laughed, too, but his smile was thin and he evaded her eyes. Sitting beside him, Sarah thought about how much she'd looked forward to this night, how she'd dreamed of being closer to him, how she'd envisioned being able to bridge the invisible gap between them by becoming part of his world. But now that she was finally here with him among all these Hollywood talking heads, the chasm between them seemed insurmountable, the distance between them greater than ever.

12

When she was in high school, Sarah would obsessively dissect her dates. Every word, gaze, and facial tic would be combed over in her efforts to ascertain the thoughts behind the inscrutable male façade. After Saturday's disastrous outing, it took everything in her to resist the urge to spend every waking moment fixating on what Daniel was thinking. What if he thought she was immature, déclassé, and FOB-ish beyond repair? What if he was so embarrassed by what a hot, drunken mess she'd been that he wanted never to see her again?

In the end, though, Sarah didn't have that much time to obsess over Daniel—because she landed her first commercial that Tuesday.

Still hesitant about the state of things with Daniel, Sarah called Owen, then Chad when Owen didn't answer. Chad picked up almost immediately.

"That's fabulous, darling," Chad cheered. "Your first commercial—how momentous!"

Sarah laughed. "Thanks, but you haven't heard what commercial it is. It's that awful constipation commercial! I'm going to be the face of constipation to America!"

"But you'll be an absolutely darling face of constipation!" Chad countered after he stopped chortling. "If everyone could look like you, who wouldn't want to be constipated?"

Sarah snorted. "Good one, Chad. Whatever—it's still a commercial. All these famous actors have started with commercials. This can be my milestone."

"Well, I think it's great," Chad declared. "And if I was there, I would take you out for a martini and a laxative."

"Very funny," Sarah said, chuckling. "I'm just happy the check will take care of that mountain of bills sitting on my kitchen table."

"Speaking of momentous . . ." Chad cleared his throat. "I have something to announce on that front, too."

"Oh, really?" Sarah raised a curious eyebrow. "And what would that be?"

"Well, it's kind of tough to say this." Her friend hesitated. "I—I guess I'm not really sure how exactly to tell you this."

"Chad . . ." Sarah frowned. "I've never heard you like this. You're starting to stress me out. What's going on?"

"Okay, well . . ." Chad took a deep breath. "This is going to sound very after-school special . . . but I've been going out with someone. And his name is Davis."

Pause. Then Sarah squealed.

"Omigosh," she gasped. "Chad, I'm so happy for you! More importantly, I'm so glad you told me about this!"

"Really?" There was palpable relief in her friend's voice. "I wasn't sure how you would react—"

"Are you kidding me?" Sarah demanded. "How could I be anything but thrilled for you? I just don't know why it took you so long to tell me."

"You're right," Chad admitted. "I always knew you'd be happy for me, but it was still hard to take the step and actually say it. How long have you known?"

"Oh, I don't know," Sarah said. "Since we were nineteen?"

He chuckled. "Point taken."

"Have you told your family yet?" Sarah asked.

"Are you kidding me?" Chad said incredulously. "It took me how many years to tell you? Multiply that by three."

"I'm sure they would be cool." Sarah tried to sound reassuring. "They just want you to be happy in the end, right?"

"Tell you what," Chad said. "I'll tell my folks about Davis as soon as you tell your family about L.A."

Sarah smiled ruefully. "Point taken."

"It's really sad when you think about it," Sarah said to Daniel later. "Chad has made this amazing, life-altering decision, and he can't share it with his family."

"Sometimes, it's hard to be honest with your family," Daniel remarked. "Especially when you're hiding something from them that they just can't understand."

They were lying in bed that night. Daniel had showed up after work, and they had had an amiable dinner at a local French bistro. Neither of them had uttered a word about dinner Saturday night, and Sarah was more than happy to suppress any discussion of the episode.

Now Sarah was silent, thinking about her own secret. "That's true," she said quietly. "But hopefully, there'll come a day when you can be straight with your family. Chad said he doesn't know if he'll ever be able to tell his parents he's gay."

"It's a big revelation," Daniel commented. "Especially when you have parents with high expectations for their only son."

Sarah glanced at him. "Did your parents have high expectations for you?"

"Of course they did," he responded. "Like every other Asian parents, they wanted me to be the prototypical doctor or lawyer. They didn't really understand when I told them I wanted to be a producer. In fact, my father must have told me a hundred times that there was no job security in Hollywood—which he's absolutely right about."

Sarah sat up on one elbow. "Well, now that you're so successful, they must have come around, right?"

He gazed up at the ceiling. "Maybe. I'm not sure if they'll ever completely come around. Oh, they're not worried about me moving home anymore, but they still don't completely understand me—and they probably never will." He paused. "When I decided that I was going to be a producer, I knew I had to forge my own path. Not only was I doing something my parents didn't understand, but I was entering a world they could never be a part of. Hollywood is like its own little universe, and if you want to have a life in it, you have to follow the rules."

Sarah frowned. "Like what to wear or who to know?"

"Yes, but it goes far beyond that," Daniel said. "So much about succeeding in Hollywood is looking and sounding and acting like you belong there. It's hard for anyone who wasn't born into Hollywood royalty, but it's even harder for someone who's Asian, because we clearly don't look like we belong there. Which means that people like us have to try three times as hard to make it there."

It was strange, hearing Daniel talk like this, speaking so openly about his fears and insecurities. While on the one hand it was comforting to hear him reveal this aspect of himself to her, Sarah wasn't sure how she felt about the revelation itself.

"Well, you don't feel that way anymore, do you?" she said finally. "I mean, at this stage in your career, you can do whatever you want, right?"

He folded his arms behind his head. "I don't know. I've spent so long disassociating myself from anything that wasn't mainstream Hollywood that I'm not sure if I can ever reconnect with my family—at least in the way they would want. I don't remember a shred of Mandarin, and the last time I set foot in Chinatown was with you." He turned and flashed her a crooked smile. "Good thing I have you."

Sarah smiled back, but it was all reflex.

"Do you think we spend our whole lives trying to live up to our parents' expectations for us?" Sarah asked.

It was the next day, and Sarah had finally managed to connect with Owen to relay her good news about the audition.

"What do you mean?" Owen asked.

"I mean, Chad can't tell his parents about Davis, and I can't tell my parents the truth about my life here." Sarah chewed her lip. "Sometimes, it seems like we're living our lives more for our parents than for ourselves."

"Maybe," Owen said. "But hopefully, there's a point where it all converges. I can tell you that both my parents and I will be very happy the day I get a bona fide producer gig. And I'm pretty sure that your folks will be as thrilled as you will be the day they see you on TV—even if you're constipated."

Sarah laughed. "You're never going to let me live that down, are you? But you're right about that. I guess hearing Chad and Daniel talk about their families made me think about mine. I mean, I've always wanted to be an actress—probably because there was nothing I liked more as a kid than dressing up and being the center of attention. But maybe I wanted to prove a point to my parents, too. Ever since I can remember, they always talked about how amazing Lin was. And I totally agree that she is. I just wanted them to think I was amazing, too."

"And they will," Owen reassured her. "But on your own terms—as an actress, not an I-banker. Isn't that enough to show that you're living your life for yourself and not for your family?"

"Yeah," Sarah said slowly. "I guess so."

Giselle got the call three weeks later.

"Omigosh!" Giselle raced around her bedroom that Monday, yanking clothes from her closet and flinging them into one of three gargantuan suitcases lying on the ground. "I still can't believe it! I never thought I would even get cast as an understudy, let alone Wendla!"

"Well, believe it!" Sarah cheered from her perch on Giselle's bed. "You're not only going to be the lead female star of *Spring Awakening*, but you're going to be on Broadway!"

"I know!" Giselle dropped down on the bed beside Sarah. "You know, when I was a kid, I used to dream of being on the Great White Way, but I always figured I wasn't a good enough singer or dancer. Who would've thought that a girl from the O.C. would end up on Broadway?"

Sarah shook her head. "Well, I'm not surprised. Anyone who's heard you sing would know that's where you belong. And obviously, the producers agree with me. Why else would they decide that you should be in the original instead of the production out here?"

Giselle broke into a beatific smile. "Isn't that amazing? I keep asking myself every five minutes if this is all a dream."

"I'm so happy for you," Sarah said. "I really am."

And she was. She really, truly was. Even though she'd known Giselle for only a short time, she couldn't think of anyone more deserving. Giselle was practically ethereal in her beauty, with her chestnut ringlets and flawless café-au-lait complexion. When she'd first met Giselle, Sarah had been keenly reminded of Lin— not because Lin was a Tyra Banks–type stunner, but because both women carried themselves with such effortless grace, almost as if they were born to be goddesses. What was incredible about Giselle was that not only was she overwhelmingly beautiful and talented, but she'd also been impossibly kind to a girl who had no friends and not much to offer in return. Sometimes, Sarah felt as if she'd known Giselle forever; she would dream about some escapade she'd had with Owen and Chad, or some childhood memory with Lin, and it often seemed like Giselle was there on the canvas, too.

No, if there was any other emotion that Sarah felt other than happiness for Giselle, it wasn't envy or jealousy—it was sadness. Because she was losing her only friend in L.A. and soon she would be alone all over again.

Giselle suddenly enveloped her in a hug.

"You're going to have to come back to New York to visit now," she said. "Otherwise, who's going to show me the ropes there?"

And of course that was the irony of the whole situation.

Wasn't it enough that her friends and Lin and the rest of her family were in New York? Did the city have to claim the one uniquely Californian friend she'd made, too?

"Yes." Sarah hugged her friend back. "I guess I'll have to come back now."

"You look like you've lost your best friend."

Sarah straightened up wearily from her draped position at the front desk. It was only a day after Giselle's departure, and she was still feeling in the doldrums, as evidenced by the sloppy updo she'd resorted to in lieu of making any effort with her hair. Giselle would have been mortified, Sarah thought. Her friend had preached endlessly about how every minute in public was a potential minute one could be discovered, which made looking one's best at all times an absolute must.

"I have." She sighed. "I've certainly lost my only friend here in L.A."

"What am I?" E.J. demanded. "Chopped liver?"

"Only the highest-grade pâté, my friend," Sarah said, smiling. "Seriously, it's just . . . it hasn't been that easy adjusting to life out here. All my friends and family are back in New York, and I really didn't know anyone out here. When I met Giselle, she was so sweet and fun and cool . . . it was kind of like I was back home again."

"Yeah," E.J. said. "I get it. But aren't you living with your boyfriend here? What about him?"

What indeed about Daniel? Sarah fingered her stack of menus reflectively. It had been almost two weeks since the dinner with Daniel's friends—and more than a month after that revelatory conversation they'd had in bed—and still nary a word had been said between them about the party. Daniel had come over to the apartment several more times, and they'd smiled and drunk wine and acted for all the world as though everything were fine. Yet there still hadn't been a single mention of the dinner or what his friends had thought about her.

"Yes," Sarah said. "There's Daniel."

By the time Sarah got home, she was exhausted. Before her shift at the Stinking Rose, she'd done a three-hour gig in the morning as a rice cooker saleswoman—as if she had the faintest clue how to use one. Fortunately, the only prerequisite appeared to be her Asian features, and at least the stint had netted her an extra two Benjamins. Still, following that job with her shift at the restaurant wasn't easy. It had been a while since she'd been on her feet all day, so she'd forgotten what it was like—and it wasn't a great feeling. Trading in her black wrap dress for sweats, she plopped down on the couch, where she suddenly remembered that she had another audition in the morning. She'd gone on five auditions already in the past month, and she hadn't heard back from any of them—not even one callback. Speaking to Daniel the night before, she'd tentatively broached the subject of helping her get some more auditions, but he hadn't been very responsive.

At any rate, her next audition was going to be her biggest one so far. It was at least for a real character on a real production, even if it was for a character in a Lifetime TV-movie. It was thanks to a tip from Giselle (who had a conflict) that she even knew about the audition. Of course, if Giselle were here, she would tell Sarah that she was a classic example of how reading for a minor role could turn into a gold mine. And she would be right.

Wondering what Giselle was doing at that moment, Sarah picked up her phone and quickly dialed her friend's number. Giselle's voice mail greeted her.

Sighing, Sarah hung up. She lay on the couch for several minutes, phone still in hand. Finally, she sat up and dialed again.

"Hello?" Lin's melodious voice trilled through the phone.

"Hey, Lin," Sarah said. "How are things going?"

"Sarah!" Lin sounded genuinely happy to hear from her. "It's so good to hear your voice! How are you doing?"

"I'm okay," Sarah said. "Busy. You know."

Something in her tone must have caught her sister's attention, because concern suddenly tinged Lin's voice.

"Is everything okay?" Lin asked. "How's the job?"

"Oh, that's good," Sarah said quickly. "It was just a tough day at work, and I'm beat. How's the family doing?"

"Everyone's fine," Lin said. "Mom is having us over for dinner tomorrow, so it's a toss-up whether the topic du jour will be Amy's wedding or my nonexistent children."

Sarah laughed. She could picture the scene vividly—her mother lecturing her daughters over bok choy and sea bass, Lin rolling her eyes, her father oblivious to it all, and Stephen focusing intensely on folding and refolding his napkin.

"Sarah?" Lin said. "Are you sure you're okay?"

Sarah shook herself out of her reverie. "Absolutely. I'm just tired. I'll talk to you later. Say hi to the family for me."

After hanging up, Sarah gazed at the ceiling from the couch. Much as she and Lin liked to mock the inevitable Cho family dinner rituals, Sarah felt a sudden yearning to be part of it all— even Mama Kim's lectures.

Enough of this pointless self-pitying, Sarah. Stop wasting time thinking about New York and start focusing on your audition tomorrow.

Taking a deep breath, she reached for her script from her bag. As she settled down to practice her lines, she checked her phone to see if Daniel had called her. Alas, no calls or text messages from him. He must be busy again, she thought. Wondering when he would call, she continued reading her lines . . . all the way until she fell asleep on the couch.

The next morning was Sarah's audition.

After waking up on the couch, she stumbled into her bathroom. Staring at her reflection in the mirror, she was aghast to find herself looking like some wasted college girl. She still had her clothes on from the night before, and there was day-old mascara crusted on her eyelids. Plus, she had the imprint of her phone on her left cheek because she'd fallen asleep while clutching it in hopes that Daniel would call her—which he never had.

Taking a look at her clock, she decided that she didn't have time to obsess about her annoyance with Daniel. She jumped into the shower and barely rinsed herself off before racing through a three-minute makeup job and shrugging into a turquoise sundress she'd picked up at Echo Park.

How did she end up being so late? Sarah shook her head as she sped off toward Burbank. Ever since she'd moved to L.A., she'd felt as if she'd been living on a treadmill. Between auditions, her new hostess gig, all her other assorted jobs to make ends meet, and squeezing in every opportunity to see Daniel, she hadn't had much opportunity to ponder the 180-degree arc her life had taken since she'd gotten to L.A. Overall, she liked the changes. It was empowering to feel like she'd finally taken charge of her life. But she still desperately missed not having her family and friends around her—being able to throw back a pint with Owen and Chad or chattering with Lin on the LIRR en route to their Sunday night family dinners. And now with Giselle gone . . .

Of course, Sarah told herself that none of that mattered because she had Daniel—the guy she'd fallen head over heels for. Unfortunately, at the moment he was also the guy who'd been completely unresponsive to numerous invitations she'd extended to him, including a return visit to the NBC Seafood for dim sum. Sometimes, it seemed as if she spent every waking moment trying to see Daniel, while he didn't seem to make much of an effort at all. And when he did make an effort—by inviting her to that dinner, for example—well, the results were disastrous.

"Are you ready, Ms. Cho?" asked Noah, the Lifetime casting director.

"Absolutely." Sarah nodded.

"Okay, you know the scene. Let's do it." Noah started reading from the script. "Monica, you say you're happy and that you're on cloud nine, but every day when I see you, you look miserable. What's the matter with you?"

"No one gets it. Not even my shrink gets it," Sarah complained. "It's not all black and white. Sometimes, you have to sacrifice a little for the things you want. We all have to give something in a relationship."

"Why do you have to be so dramatic?" Noah said. "Just let it be."

"I'm not being dramatic. I give you everything that you want, including the space that you say you need. I just need to know that you love me, too. Is that so hard? I guess if you can't see that, we're just not meant to be together," Sarah said.

As she recited the lines, Sarah could feel the dialogue resonate. This was one time that she didn't have to worry about not understanding her character's motivation.

"Thank you, Sarah," Noah said. "Callbacks are tomorrow. You'll know by the end of the day if we're going to call you back."

"Great, thanks," Sarah said.

As she headed out, Sarah thought about how tedious the words *callbacks are tomorrow* were becoming. There was a sinking feeling in her stomach that this was yet another audition down the drain. The only difference between this audition and all her other failed ones was that a text message from Daniel greeted her as she walked out of this one:

HOW ABOUT WE GO TO CATALINA ISLAND OVER THE LABOR DAY WEEKEND?

Reading those words, Sarah had to squelch a shriek of happiness right there in the Lifetime Studios parking lot. If only she could shout out loud: "Daniel wants to go away with me! Be jealous, world!" Maybe the dinner hadn't been the travesty that she thought it had been. Maybe Chad was right after all—maybe her momentous talk with Daniel had made a difference, and it had just taken him a while to truly process it. Maybe he was finally, finally coming around to the realization that their relationship was a two-way street.

I WOULD LOVE TO.

Heading over to her car, Sarah did a little skip of joy. She couldn't help it. All those years of watching soap operas had inevitably molded her into a hopeless romantic. Which reminded her that she'd been so hectic since coming to L.A. that she hadn't been keeping up with her beloved soaps. She didn't even know what the latest plotlines on *General Hospital* were anymore. It just went to show how her priorities had changed. But that could be easily remedied.

"So what's been going on with *General Hospital*?" Sarah asked Chad.

"Oh, a ton. Pick up a copy of *Soap Opera Digest*, and you'll see. Besides, why are you asking me? Isn't your boyfriend the soap expert?" Chad demanded.

"He's a little busy right now—busy planning a trip for us to go to Catalina Island!" Sarah screamed.

"What?" Chad exclaimed. "That's fabulous! So, I'm assuming your little talk with him worked."

"Apparently," Sarah said. "Who said that men don't listen?"

"Certainly not I," Chad said. "I'm thrilled for you! But hey, wasn't your Lifetime audition today?"

"Yes, and it actually went decent," Sarah said. "For once, I actually felt like I was the character. Not to be overly optimistic, but I think I have a fighting chance of at least getting a callback."

"You know who to call when that happens," Chad said. "I'll be keeping my fingers crossed for you."

"So how was dinner with Mom?" Sarah asked. "I take it there was no discussion of Davis?"

"You take right. And dinner was abysmal," Chad groaned. "She foisted another one of her friends' spinster daughters on me."

"Eek." Sarah winced. "That must have been a riot."

"Almost as bad as my second root canal." Chad sighed. "But I'm just tingling with excitement for you. Lifetime's a big deal. Those movies are basically two-hour soap operas on a bigger budget."

"True," Sarah agreed. "Hopefully, my soap obsession will help me. In the meantime, at least I don't have to worry about rent with my Stinking Rose gig."

"I can sense things coming together for Sarah Cho," Chad exclaimed. "I can feel it all the way down to my Ferragamos! We'll have to make sure it all gets included in your *E! True Hollywood* story."

Sarah laughed. "Cross your fingers."

For the first time in weeks, Sarah felt truly happy.

It was amazing how a mere invitation to Catalina Island from Daniel made the sun brighter, the sky bluer, and everything just plain more blissful. Deciding to go for a run on the beach Thursday morning, she zipped off with more energy than she'd had in ages, the Shins playing on her iPod. After jogging for a bit, she took a break on a bench near the beach to watch the sunset, her lululemon tank drenched with sweat. She could already envision her and Daniel on a boat in Catalina Island, swigging champagne and feasting on chocolate-dipped strawberries . . .

Her phone rang.

"Is this Sarah Cho?" a voice asked.

"Speaking," Sarah responded. "Who's this?"

"This is Nick Chase from the Lifetime network," her caller said. "I'm one of the producers for a new show called *Matches Made*, and we'd like to have you come in for a callback."

A callback! So was this what it was like to get a callback? Because sheer euphoria did not even come close to describing it. *What a phenomenal day!* Sarah thought.

"Of course," Sarah said with as much calm as she could manufacture. "Just tell me when and where!"

"Ten o' clock tomorrow at the Lifetime Studios in Burbank," Nick replied. "We look forward to meeting you."

The minute she got off the phone with Nick, Sarah speed-dialed Daniel to relay the good news. Of course, he didn't answer his phone, so she was forced to text him again:

I GOT A CALLBACK! CAN WE CELEBRATE AFTER WORK TONIGHT?

She then quickly texted Chad:

CALLBACK BABY!!!

And then there was Owen:

WHO'S YOUR DADDY NOW!! LIFETIME CALLBACK!

The first person to text her back was Owen, whose response was almost instantaneous.

FUCK YEA! YOU'RE IT BABE! I GOT A SURPRISE FOR YOU TOO. I'LL HOLLA SOON.

Looking at his text, Sarah furrowed her brow. She was curious what surprise Owen could have in store for her, but then visions of her callback and Catalina Island quickly co-opted her thoughts. The monumental move to L.A. was finally paying dividends, she thought happily. After what seemed like forever, she was finally getting somewhere.

13

Sarah was in a euphoric mood at the Stinking Rose.

As she chatted with customers, she couldn't help pondering how things were finally coming together. She and Daniel were getting over their relationship growing pains and going on their first trip together. And now she was even getting callbacks!

"You're happy today," E.J. remarked. "Any particular reason why you're in such a good mood?"

"There is, actually," Sarah said, beaming. "I got a callback today from Lifetime!"

E.J. immediately swamped her in a hug. "That's great news!" he cheered. "That doesn't mean you're going to quit on me soon, though, does it?"

"No, no . . ." Sarah laughed. "Nothing like that. Who knows if I'm even going to get it?"

"Is that it?" E.J. asked. "Not that that isn't great news, but it seems like there's something else. You're practically glowing."

"Oh, come on." Sarah blushed as she twisted a fold in her black tunic dress. "Well, actually, my boyfriend and I are in a really good place right now."

The minute the words left her lips, Sarah stopped. Could she call Daniel her boyfriend? It certainly seemed she could. After all, boyfriends asked their girlfriends to go on trips. And didn't Daniel say that they were dating? Even if he had an aversion to labels, this didn't seem like such a stretch.

"Your boyfriend is one lucky guy," E.J. remarked. "He better hold on to you—he's not going to find another one of you out here."

"Ain't that the truth." Sarah smiled. "Thanks, E.J. So have all the logistics for the big party next week been ironed out?"

"We're all set," E.J. responded. "The production company signed the contract and we have commitments from a bunch of their potential sponsors. Oh, and by the way, there's a surprise for you."

"There is?" Sarah blinked. "What?"

E.J. nodded toward the bar. At first, Sarah wasn't sure what he was directing her to because of the scads of people walking back and forth that blocked her view of the bar. But then as the crowd parted, one of the bar stools swung around—and there was Owen with a Guinness in hand and a wink.

"Owen!" Sarah gasped. "What in the world are you doing here?"

"I'm here to see my best friend," Owen said, grinning. "You look great—and you don't even smell like garlic."

Sarah laughed and threw her arms around Owen, who enveloped her in one of his trademark bear hugs.

"How did you know I was here?" Sarah asked as she pulled away.

"Well, you told me you got a gig here," Owen explained. "So all I had to do was call the Stinking Rose to see when you were working and have them keep their mouth shut—and voilà! E.J. over here is a great co-conspirator."

Sarah turned to E.J. "I can't believe you were in on this."

E.J. shrugged. "I think it's great he flew out here for you. I couldn't stand in the way of your reunion. Anyhow, I'll let you guys talk. See you later."

"Thanks again," Sarah said.

Turning back to Owen, Sarah suddenly thought how long it had been since she had seen him—or any of her friends.

"You must be my lucky charm, because I got the callback today!" Sarah remarked. "And where the hell were you, by the way, when I texted you?"

"Connecting on a flight from Dallas." Owen grinned. "I didn't want to tell you and ruin the surprise."

"Awww . . ." Sarah smiled. "So how long are you staying here?"

"I'm thinking three days," Owen said. "Is it all right if I crash at your place, or are you getting so much action every night that no visitors are allowed?"

"Shhh!" Sarah shushed him. "Of course you can stay with me! Actually, Daniel invited me to go to Catalina Island with him over Labor Day, and we were going to talk about it and my callback tonight, but I haven't heard back from him. But I'm sure the three of us will go to dinner together before you leave. I can't wait! I really want you two to meet."

"I don't need to meet another Asian," Owen joked. "I only have room for one in my life."

"Shut up." Sarah punched his arm. "I'm going to text him that you're here."

"Don't tell him that I'm here," Owen said. "Let it be a surprise; I want to see how this guy handles pressure. And by the way, why are you texting him? Isn't he like fifty-seven years old? Does he even know how to use text? Why can't you just pick up the phone and call him?"

Even though she knew this was just one of Owen's quips, his words hit a sore spot with Sarah. How many times had she wished that Daniel would answer her phone calls? Did anyone think that she liked talking to his voice mail more than him? Or that she wanted to be texting him like a twelve-year-old?

"Daniel's really busy," she said to excuse Daniel's actions. "Texting is better."

"Since when for you?" Owen demanded. "You practically sleep with the phone glued to you. Besides, since you two are so lovey-dovey, isn't it a little impersonal to be texting each other all the time?"

Sarah mumbled some other excuse, but as she ushered Owen away, her words sounded hollow even to herself. And suddenly, Catalina didn't seem so special after all.

After Sarah finished her shift (which E.J. was kind enough to cut short), they drove to Manhattan Beach for dinner. On the way, Sarah checked her phone for messages, but there were none. She couldn't believe she still hadn't spoken to Daniel about her callback, not to mention about Owen being in town. But since Daniel wasn't responding to her, there wasn't much she could do.

"Okay, where are we going for dinner?" Owen clapped his hands together in anticipation.

Sarah gestured down the palm tree–lined street leading to the boardwalk. "There are a ton of good places here. What are you in the mood for? Sushi?"

"Sounds good to me," Owen said. "Just remember, not all of us are big-time actresses. Some of us are still on a budget."

Sarah rolled her eyes. "Please! You're talking to the queen of budgets. I think I'm going to get an award from In-N-Out for being their best customer, because that's all I can afford to eat. If I hadn't gotten that job at the Stinking Rose, I'd probably be living in a cardboard box in West Hollywood by now!"

Owen laughed. "Well, you heard about your callback today, so I have a feeling that there won't be any cardboard boxes in your future. Besides, I'm sure your family would help you out if you were really in such dire straits."

Sarah sighed. "I don't know about that. I don't even want to imagine what they would say if they found out I lied about having a role on *Asylum*. I keep telling them that soaps film months in advance, but sooner or later, they're going to start wondering why I'm not showing up on the screen." She chewed her lip. "Actually, I haven't talked to my family in a while. Part of it is that

I've been ducking their calls because I'm afraid to talk to them before I get a gig. But the other part is that they haven't been calling me, either."

"Well, maybe they just don't want to bug you," Owen suggested.

Sarah snorted. "That's never stopped them before. No, this has only been since I moved out here."

Even though she would never have admitted it, her family's silence bothered Sarah. She didn't really care about hearing from Amy, but her mom? Her dad? Lin? She couldn't believe they weren't wondering what she was up to. And even though she dreaded talking to them, a part of her couldn't help feeling that they had forgotten about her already.

"Hey, hey . . ." Owen slung his arm around her. "You know your mom and your sisters are chomping at the bit to know what's going on with you. They're just trying to give you time to get settled in—kind of like when parents try to let go of their kids when they go off to college."

Sarah looked up at him and smiled. She knew he was trying to make her feel better, and even though she didn't believe him, she appreciated the effort.

"Okay." She nodded toward a nearby restaurant. "This place here has great soft-shell crab rolls."

"Sounds good to me," Owen said. "Hey, look, they even have a special. Twenty dollars off each table."

"That is a good deal," Sarah agreed. "Too bad it's not twenty dollars off for each person. I think I could eat a lot more than twenty bucks' worth of sushi."

"Yeah," Owen said. Then a slow grin crept across his face.

"Uh-oh." Sarah frowned. "What are you thinking?"

He flashed her his familiar rakish smile. "I've got an idea."

"I can't believe we're doing this," Sarah said.

"Why not?" Owen asked. "This is perfectly legit."

"But it's so crazy!" Sarah exclaimed.

"Not at all," he responded. "It's . . . what do they call it? Fiscally sound."

Sarah rolled her eyes as she looked at Owen—all the way at a table across the restaurant from her. He waved at her as he leaned into his cell phone.

"Look, this way you get what you wanted—twenty dollars off each of our meals. Basically, we double our savings," Owen said. "What's so bad about that?"

"It's just ridiculous," Sarah protested. "We're supposed to be having dinner together!"

"And we are," Owen replied. "We're seeing each other, we're eating, and we're having a lovely conversation. Plus, we could even have phone sex if we wanted."

Sarah snorted as she shoveled some *edamame* into her mouth. "Right."

"Seriously"—Owen popped a dragon roll into his mouth—"what are you wearing right now?"

Sarah glanced down at her plain white T-shirt and jeans. "Black bustier and fishnet stockings."

"That's hot," Owen said. "But not as hot as me. I'm wearing gold tassels and crotchless panties."

Sarah laughed so hard that she nearly choked on a soybean.

Afterward, they headed over to Eddie J.'s Karaoke House.

"I read about this place back when I was in New York," Sarah said as they strolled into the dark, Bon Jovi–blaring, packed-to-the-rafters establishment. "I've been dying to come ever since I moved here."

"Yeah?" Owen said. "Why didn't you bring your man here? I bet they got some Sinatra for him."

Sarah punched him in the arm. "Very funny. Karaoke's not really Daniel's thing."

"Really?" Owen frowned. "Who doesn't love karaoke? Maybe you need to bring him out of his shell, Sar—he sounds kind of boring."

Sarah cleared her throat. "Anyway, I'm feeling very Avril Lavigne tonight."

"None of that bubblegum pop for me," Owen declared. "I've been practicing some new genres. Wait until you hear me rap."

Sarah rolled her eyes. "Last week, I auditioned for the role of 'African-American ghetto girl who raps.'"

"Really?" Owen chortled. "How'd that go?"

Sarah just shook her head.

Three hours later, they finally stumbled back to Sarah's apartment. After Sarah had finished her teen queen renditions of Britney, Christina, and Michelle Branch, Owen had insisted on singing every single 50 Cent song the karaoke place had. Which was probably why both were in serious danger of losing their voices now.

They plopped down on the couch in an exhausted heap.

"If I can't speak tomorrow, I'm going to kill you," Sarah muttered.

"You'll be okay," Owen said, yawning. "If I didn't think I was going to set your apartment on fire, I'd get up and make you some lemon tea."

"That's a nice thought," Sarah croaked. "You just better hope I get this job, or else you'll be supporting me with monthly rent checks."

"No problem," Owen responded. "Now that you're gone from Balloon Burger, I'm the apple of our wunderkind manager's eye. Heck, I might even make an extra fifty cents an hour next year!"

Sarah chuckled as she dropped her head onto his shoulder and closed her eyes.

Despite her late night shenanigans, Sarah woke up early for her big callback with Lifetime.

Fortunately, she had weathered the evening with few ill effects. Her voice seemed to be in good working order, and she'd apparently managed to ward off a hangover with the aspirin Owen has insisted she take before going to bed. Maybe this callback wouldn't be a complete travesty.

As Owen snored away on her couch, Sarah straightened her hair, perfected her makeup, and generally made sure she looked ravishing in her latest find—a vintage tangerine chiffon dress she'd managed to get at bargain basement prices—or as ravishing as was possible with four hours of sleep. After she'd finally gotten up from the couch the night before to make some tea, she'd discovered a script for the callback waiting for her in her e-mail in-box. Despite their non-optimal state, she and Owen had managed to run through her lines together, even though the script was a little longer than what she was used to and had the added challenge of a kissing scene. Still, after practicing all night with Owen—sans kiss, of course—Sarah was feeling pretty confident about the audition. It was going to be another dramatic scene, and she felt prepared to impress. Even though she had yet to land any real gigs, she felt the tide was finally turning. No doubt having Owen here to boost her spirits helped.

"Sarah, good to see you again," Noah greeted her as she walked onto the stage. "This is our senior producer, Ralph Hillman."

Sarah smiled at him. "Great to meet you."

"Good job on the audition." Ralph shook her hand.

"Thank you." Sarah glowed at the approval. "I'm glad you liked it."

"I sure did." Ralph nodded. "Well, you're going to be reading today with an actor we just cast."

As Sarah glanced around the room, she saw a Latino man with smoldering good looks stroll in. Was this her prospective co-star? How cool was this? It was like a scene out of *People* magazine, she thought. Would she have to kiss him? Did she have to use tongue?

"Sarah, this is Enrique," Ralph introduced them. "Enrique will be playing your lover in this scene."

"Pleasure to meet you." Sarah tried to sound cool and composed. Inwardly, though, she was a jumble of nerves and adrenaline. Enrique sure looked like the only other Enrique she had ever heard about—Enrique Iglesias! With a megawatt smile and beautiful chocolate eyes, this Enrique was definitely someone Sarah had no qualms locking lips with. At that moment, it was hard to remember she even had a boyfriend.

"Why is this good-bye again?" Enrique demanded passionately.

"Because you and I are in different places. We may be in the same relationship, but we're continents away from each other," Sarah declared. "It's best if we just let go of each other."

"So all the time we've spent together? Just gone with a snap of a finger? What about everything we've been through?" Enrique demanded.

They locked eyes. Sarah couldn't believe she was actually doing this. Where had that piece of gum been that she'd stashed in her purse for these occasions?

"Don't do this," Sarah implored. "This is what's best for us. Even though there's a part of me that will always be in love with you, we can't be together anymore—"

"Stop," Enrique interrupted.

He yanked her toward him and kissed her. For a second, Sarah felt paralyzed. Based on all the *Soap Opera Digest* magazines she'd devoured over the years, she'd always thought that soap actors didn't use tongue, so she didn't. Still, she couldn't help but think how crazy it was even to be pondering the question. So *this* was how Brad and Angelina got it on at the set!

"Don't!" Sarah pushed Enrique away. "You're just making this harder. I told you this is good-bye."

Enrique stared at her angrily as Sarah gazed back at him sadly, her eyes moist.

"Cut!" Ralph called. "Thank you. Nice job, both of you."

Nice job? This was the first time that Sarah had been on an audition where the casting director hadn't given her the automatic "Thank you, we'll call you for callbacks!" Sarah resolved to take this as a positive sign.

"Thanks," she said.

"Nice to meet you." Enrique smiled at her. "That was fun. You're a good kisser. Was this your first on-screen kiss?"

Uh-oh. Could Enrique tell that she was a newbie? Talk about humiliating!

"It is," Sarah admitted. She leaned over and whispered jokingly, "Could you tell?"

He chuckled. "No, you just seemed a little nervous, that's all."

Despite his words, Sarah was worried. Could everyone tell she was an amateur? How could Enrique tell she was nervous? After all, she'd kissed her share of men in real life. She wondered if Daniel thought she was a poor kisser, too.

"All right, kids," Ralph said. "Thanks for coming. Sarah, we'll be in touch!"

Walking out of the studio, Sarah suddenly felt overcome with uncertainty. Overall, she felt that her performance had been pretty good. But now this whole kissing incident had somehow marred it.

She took out her phone to check voice mail and found a message from her mother to call her. Frowning, Sarah quickly dialed her mother's number.

"Hi, Mom," she said. "How are you?"

It was more difficult than usual to focus on her conversation with her mother. All Sarah could think about was her audition. But of course, she couldn't tell her mother that she had been on an audition.

"I have not heard from you in a while," Kim said. "How come you don't call me?"

"Things have been busy, Mom," Sarah mumbled.

"Amy tell me that she tape *Asylum* soap opera, and she not see you on," Kim declared.

Shit! Leave it to evil sister Amy to go DVR *Asylum* and tell her mother that she wasn't on it!

"What are you talking about?" Sarah did her best Oscar impression of sounding shocked. "Of course I am! I told you it takes months to film, and at first, I'm just an extra, so you won't see me front and center right away."

"No, she said that she tried to look for you in the credits and didn't see your name," Kim said.

Sarah's jaw dropped. What in the world had she ever done to Amy to make her hate her so much?

"Like I said, I'm an extra, Mom." Sarah swallowed. "So you just don't see me that often. Also, I might be getting other jobs."

"Other job?" Kim's tone immediately shifted from accusatory to concerned. "Why? You get fired?"

"No, no, no." Sarah sighed. "In this business, people jump around and do other projects. You have to try to get as much exposure as you can."

"I don't know what you do there." Kim didn't sound convinced. "I'm just glad you are okay with money and support yourself. Start save some money, too. Amy bought house recently."

Sarah suppressed a groan. Save money? She could barely buy three meals a day. Between paying for rent and her car, she was eating In-N-Out burgers half the time and counting her lucky stars that she hadn't gained any weight. Otherwise, she'd have to worry about paying for a gym membership, too.

"I have to go work now." Sarah sighed. "Talk to you later, Mom."

Daniel showed up at Sarah's apartment that afternoon.

Sarah and Owen had just returned from a surfing lesson at Hermosa Beach. Sarah had always wanted to learn, but somehow she'd never gotten around to doing it on her own. The great thing about Owen was that all she had to do was mention how she had a yen to do something, and he would immediately take charge and make her put her words into action.

"I'm so hungry now," Sarah declared as she shook the sand from her flip-flops. "Surfing really takes it out of you!"

"I'm pretty hungry for that instructor of ours," Owen remarked. "What a babe."

"Yeah, she was really jonesing you, too," Sarah countered with a smirk. "Especially when you almost drowned because she was making goo-goo eyes at that other guy!"

"O ye of little faith." Owen shook his head as he toweled off.

"She was just playing hard to get. But for that comment, I get dibs on the shower."

He dashed off before she could say anything.

Sarah shook her head, smiling. There was a certain comfort to having Owen around, especially because he hadn't changed one iota since she'd last seen him. A tiny part of her that she would never admit to worried that everyone back home was moving on with their lives and forgetting about her—like her mysteriously silent family. Even though Sarah knew that things couldn't stay the same forever, she couldn't help hoping that some things were as immutable as granite—

The doorbell rang. Wondering if this might be another script, Sarah hurried over to the door—and found Daniel standing there.

"Oh—hey," Sarah said, momentarily startled. Looking at him, she suddenly realized that she hadn't really thought about him over the past twenty-four hours. But how could she be thinking about him when she was so busy singing karaoke and surfing?

Daniel gave her a quizzical smile. "Expecting someone else?"

"No, I just thought that maybe it was someone delivering a script." Sarah broke into a smile. "I had my first callback today!"

"That's great!" Daniel hugged her. "Why didn't you tell me?"

"I tried," Sarah said. "Your phone was off."

"Yeah," he said. "Things have been pretty crazy on the set. I haven't even had time to check my messages. Sorry I wasn't able to celebrate with you—"

As if on cue, Owen walked in, clad only in Sarah's purple towel. "Hey, Sarah," he called out, "I like how this shampoo of yours smells like strawberries—"

Daniel stared at Owen. Sarah clapped a hand to her mouth in disbelief. This was the stuff of soap operas—or *Three's Company*. It never happened in real life, but apparently, out here in Hollywood, fiction and reality had a funny way of blending into each other.

"So . . ." Sarah cleared her throat. "Guess what? Not only did I hear about my callback yesterday, but I also got a visit from an old friend."

*   *   *

They had dinner that night (made possible by Sarah's new switch to the lunch shift) at a nearby Mediterranean bistro that Daniel liked to frequent.

After she'd managed to explain to Daniel who Owen was—and how Owen was most definitely a platonic friend—Daniel had suggested they get to know each other over some drinks. Even though he seemed to believe her explanation and was thoroughly polite to Owen, Sarah was pretty sure he had some further reconnaissance in mind. For his part, Owen had been more than happy to comply once he heard that alcohol was involved.

"So," Daniel said as he poured all of them some Pinot Grigio, "how do you two know each other?"

"Balloon Burger." Owen dug into his penne à la vodka. "I flip the patties, and Sarah rings it all up on the register."

"Huh," Daniel said. "That sounds charming. So are you an actor, too?"

Owen snorted. "Me? No, I'm strictly behind the camera."

"Owen's a freelance producer," Sarah explained.

"Really?" Daniel said. "Where have you worked?"

"Nowhere big," Owen said. "Unless you're into porn."

Sarah groaned inwardly. Of course Owen had to say that!

Daniel blinked at him. "Excuse me?"

"Owen answered an ad for a freelance producer, and it turned out to be for some porn movie," Sarah interjected hurriedly. "It was pretty crazy."

"I'm sure it was." Daniel rubbed his chin.

"Well, I wasn't complaining," Owen said. "It's not too often that I get paid to watch two chicks get it on. Kind of made me think that I should consider adult entertainment as a profession a little more seriously."

Even though Sarah knew this was just Owen being his usual outrageous self, she was pretty sure Daniel wasn't going to view him with the same amused tolerance that she did. Indeed, Daniel was regarding Owen with a mixture of revulsion and confusion.

"Very funny, Owen," she said quickly. "You're always such a comedian."

Owen gave her a raised-eyebrow look. Sarah shot him a look right back, one that told him he better start behaving stat.

"Well, if you need any pointers, I'd be more than happy to help," Daniel said. "After all, you can't work at Buffoon Burgers forever."

Owen paused. "You mean Balloon Burger."

Daniel shrugged. "Yeah, whatever. Point is, you're not going to get very far working there."

"I do okay," Owen said a little defensively. "There's nothing wrong with Balloon Burger. It helps pay the bills."

"I'm sure it does," Daniel said in a way that left little question as to what he thought about the professional possibilities of working at Balloon Burger.

When Owen narrowed his eyes, Sarah could tell he wasn't thrilled with Daniel's tone. As for Daniel, he was gazing at Owen as if he were barely a rung above some homeless person on Santa Monica Boulevard. Sarah couldn't believe how rapidly things were degenerating.

Owen pushed himself away from the table. "Excuse me," he said coolly as he headed off toward the restroom.

Sarah whirled around toward Daniel.

"That wasn't very nice," she admonished him. "Why did you have to act like he was a loser for working at Balloon Burger?"

"I just call it like I see it." Daniel shrugged. "No wonder you weren't able to get very far with your career when you were in New York. It's important that you hang out with people who are similarly motivated, or else you won't have the proper mind-set for success."

Sarah gaped at him. Was he really trying to say that Owen was a loser? And that she was never going to make it if she surrounded herself with losers?

"Daniel . . ." She shook her head. "I can't believe you think that. That's so . . . so—"

"Elitist?" Owen said from her elbow.

Looking up, Sarah realized that he must have heard her entire exchange with Daniel.

"Owen," she began.

"It's okay." He shook his head. "I think it's time for the check."

"You don't have to do this," Sarah protested.

Owen zipped his duffel bag shut. "I think this is for the best, Sar."

They were in Sarah's living room. Daniel was out on the patio, ostensibly talking on the phone but more likely trying to steer clear of Owen.

Sarah closed her eyes. "I'm sorry about what happened at dinner. Daniel's not usually like this. It's just . . ." She trailed off.

"I don't care about him," Owen said. "I only care about you. I want you to get everything you want, Sarah, because you deserve it."

Sarah stared down at the carpet. "Owen . . ."

He reached over and tilted up her chin. "Sarah, look at me. Are you happy here? Are you really happy?"

She looked into his familiar blue eyes, now clouded over with concern. It was strange seeing him so serious—no longer the jester, only the protector.

"Yes," she said finally. "I really am."

For a long moment, he didn't say anything. Then he nodded.

"Okay," he said. He pulled her to him and kissed her on the forehead. "Take care of yourself, okay?"

Sarah hugged him tightly. "I will."

14

It was Friday morning, and Sarah was trudging down the beach, alone. It had been several weeks since Owen left, and she still missed him. Being with Owen even for such a short time had alleviated some of the emptiness that had been filled briefly by Giselle but had now returned in force. She hadn't realized how much she missed his silly jokes, his easy manner, the way he made her feel it was okay to just be herself, immature or not. Even if it was an illusion, she'd felt almost as if she were back home—mellow, relaxed, centered. And now that he was gone, she felt as though the edges had become frayed again. And then there was the disastrous dinner with Daniel. Sure, Owen had repeatedly assured her that he wasn't upset about it, and everything with Daniel had returned to the status quo, but Sarah continued to feel unsettled. She wondered how her sister had dealt with being with her infamous ex-boyfriend whom her friends had universally despised. Then again, maybe that was why Lin was no longer with him.

It's okay, Sarah told herself as she yanked at the sweat-soaked T-shirt clinging to her back, *things are going to get better*. Glancing down at her watch, she groaned. She was going to be late for her next audition—again.

"Now, remember, Sarah," Ed, the casting director, exhorted from his chair, "think delicious. Sizzling! Temptation!"

Sarah nodded earnestly. "Will do," she chirped as she turned—and almost tripped in her gigantic plastic-and-felt hamburger costume.

"Sorry," she gasped as she righted herself and attempted to look as fetching as a plastic hamburger could look.

Taking a deep breath, she tried to channel the Balloon Burger. After all, shouldn't she have ample experience to draw on for this role? After all the patties she'd flipped in her day, who knew better the essence of a dancing hamburger?

Unfortunately, while Sarah was sure she'd cornered the market on emoting a hamburger, she had a little more trouble with the "dancing" part of the "dancing hamburger" role. Specifically, it wasn't easy tap dancing in this costume. And who still tap-danced, anyway?

"Next!" the casting director yelled the minute Sarah was done with her ten-second routine.

Sighing, Sarah stomped off the stage. As she shucked her costume, she thought how pathetic it was that her acting career had spiraled to where she was competing to be a dancing hamburger. Could things possibly get any worse?

Telling herself to think of serene, calming waters, she somehow sleepwalked her way to her car. Given her current career situation, she really didn't have a choice of auditions. Lucas hadn't returned any of her calls, and Clyde had left only a perfunctory message on her voice mail; though they'd appeared anxious to help her at first, they seemed to have gone MIA once she actually got in touch. Which was a good reason she shouldn't start thinking she was above any audition, even one that involved dancing as a greasy slab of meat.

As she drove back to her apartment, though, the ludicrousness of the situation hit her. Whoever had thought up the commercial in the first place had clearly never eaten a burger. Otherwise, they would know tap dancing really didn't add to the appeal. Turning off the freeway, she had a sudden yearning to pick up the phone and call Owen to tell him about this. More than anyone, he would love this story, and he would completely understand what she was feeling. But after his fiasco of a visit, Sarah didn't know if their first conversation should revolve around some ridiculous dancing hamburger.

As she turned into her apartment complex, she noticed that Daniel's car was already parked downstairs. He'd promised to take her out to dinner so he could hear about her audition, although Sarah had a sneaking suspicion that he was doing so only out of guilt about the whole debacle with Owen. Then Sarah noticed an unfamiliar car parked beside Daniel's Porsche. Not that it was strange to see another car here, but Sarah had lived in the complex long enough to know that the car wasn't her neighbor's.

As she walked up to the door of her apartment, she paused as she heard laughter coming from within. It was a light, feminine chuckle, intermingled with Daniel's familiar baritone. Who was inside with him? Frowning, Sarah told herself not to jump to conclusions. After all, it could just be the TV.

The minute she stepped over the threshold, Daniel sprang up from the couch to greet her. He was all smiles, but Sarah barely noticed because as she gazed past him to the living room, her stomach lurched at the sight of a familiar figure coming toward her—Lin.

When Sarah had first moved out to L.A., she was plagued with nightmares almost every night. Sometimes, it was about a botched audition; other times, it was about not being able to pay her bills. Most of the time, though, it involved some elaborate scenario where her family showed up unannounced in California, and she was revealed as the fraud that she was. Each time, Sarah woke up ramrod straight in the middle of the night, drenched in sweat and practically prostrate with relief that none of it was real.

"Sarah!" Lin squealed as she rushed over to envelop Sarah in her arms.

"Lin!" Sarah choked out, fighting equal parts shock and horror. What was Lin doing here? How could she be in L.A., in her Santa Monica apartment—with Daniel? A tiny burst of panic bubbled up in her throat, threatening to engulf her, and it was all Sarah could do to hold on to her rapidly disintegrating composure. "What—why are you here?"

"I came to visit you, of course," Lin said as if it were the most obvious thing in the world. "I had a business meeting in town, and I had to seize the opportunity to see my little sister! I would have told you, but the trip was so last minute that I figured I would just surprise you."

"Oh . . ." Sarah tried to form a coherent thought as a torrent of conflicting emotions assaulted her. "Yes—yes, this is certainly a surprise."

The words came out all stilted and awkward, and none of it was lost on her audience. Lin's eyes flickered in the way they did when she sensed something was amiss, and Daniel furrowed his brow in confusion.

"Sarah's probably beat from her audition," he jumped in. "Those things can be unbelievably draining."

"Audition?" Lin said.

Sarah closed her eyes briefly.

"Yes," Daniel continued, oblivious, "Sarah's been a real trooper. She's been hitting the audition circuit really hard—and believe me, it's not easy to stand in line all day waiting your turn in these cattle calls. Especially when they have you doing all these crazy things. What was the audition today, Sarah?" He turned to her. "A dancing chicken?"

Sarah swallowed. "Hamburger," she mumbled.

"Yes, that's right!" Daniel turned back to Lin. "Can you believe that? But Sarah's tough, and I couldn't be prouder of how she's really stuck with this."

Lin turned toward Sarah. "That's my sister—tough."

Daniel clapped his hands together. "Well, Sarah and I were

going to have dinner in the neighborhood, but since you're in town, I think this calls for something a little special. Have you been to Joan's on Third?"

"No," Lin said. "But I can't wait to try it."

Sarah looked away.

Dinner was unmitigated torture.

Sitting at the table, Sarah listlessly chewed a strand of spaghetti as Daniel regaled her sister with stories of making it in Hollywood and how he knew, just knew, that one day, Sarah would make it, too. In that first minute when she'd walked into her apartment, Sarah had wondered what would be worse: Lin finding out she was a fraud from Daniel or Daniel finding out her lies from Lin. Now, thanks to Daniel's endless, nonstop chatter, she no longer had to worry about which was the bigger nightmare.

It could be worse, she told herself. *It could have been Amy who showed up at the apartment.*

". . . getting onto a soap isn't easy," Daniel was saying. "Half the time, it's hard work and perseverance, but the other half of the time, it's a total crapshoot. You just have to hope you're in the right place, at the right time, and the right casting director happens to notice you."

"Hmm," Lin said. "What happens if the right casting director doesn't come along?"

Daniel shrugged. "Well, there's a million Hollywood stories of starlets crashing and burning. Sad thought, but it's true."

Sarah took a quick swig of her wine. She could feel her sister's gaze, but she steadfastly concentrated on the rim of her glass.

"Well, I'm glad my sister met you," Lin said. "I was so worried when I heard that she was moving out here without knowing anyone in L.A."

"Oh, Sarah had me way before she ever moved out here." Daniel cast a smile in Sarah's direction. "After her first visit out here, I was pretty much hoping she would decide to come out here for good."

"Huh," Lin said. Despite her misery, Sarah couldn't help thinking that Daniel's comment was news to her, too.

Several minutes later, Daniel excused himself to take a call. Sarah looked up at her sister. Alone at last.

"Okay." Sarah took a deep breath. "Just go ahead and say it."

Lin sipped her wine. "What am I supposed to say?"

"That I'm a failure and a fraud and a terrible daughter and sister," Sarah cried out. "That I looked all of you in the eyes and lied about how I had landed this wonderful job. And all the while . . . none of it was true."

As the last words left her lips, Sarah felt her composure crumble. She covered her face with her hands, not sure what was worse—speaking the truth to her sister or the truth itself.

Lin reached over to take one of her hands. At first, Sarah resisted, but finally, she relented. When she looked up at her sister's face, Lin's eyes were sad.

"I just want to know why," Lin said. "Why did you feel like you had to make all of this up? Why did you tell us you had this job when you didn't?"

Sarah shook her head. "I don't know. It was just—I was sitting there, Amy was laughing at me, Mom was looking so disappointed, and I was feeling like such a failure . . . it just came out. And once it did, I couldn't take it back." She looked up at her sister. "And then there was only one thing I could do—I had to make the lie real."

"Oh, Sarah . . ." Lin sighed. "I know you felt like you were backed into a corner, but to move all the way across the country—isn't that taking it just a little far?"

"You moved to London before," Sarah said. "You said it was the best experience of your life, that it changed you and made you who you are today. Lin, that's all I want, too—to be as successful at acting as you are in what you do."

Her sister was silent. Finally, after a long moment, she stirred.

"I just wish you had told me," Lin said. "I'm worried about you, Sarah. This is a tough business, and there are so many pitfalls waiting out there—"

"It's okay," Sarah said quickly. "I know what I'm doing. Besides, I have Daniel to look out for me."

"Yes, Daniel," Lin said slowly. "He seems like a nice guy. And he's certainly handsome."

"It's not what you think," Sarah said quickly. "Daniel really does care for me. He's made it so much easier to be here."

Lin's eyes were troubled. "Sarah—," she began, but at that moment, Daniel appeared at the table.

He rubbed his hands cheerfully. "Who's ready for dessert?"

The rest of the dinner went by in a blur of Daniel-dominated patter. Finally, it was time to say good-bye to Lin as she headed to the airport for the red-eye back to New York. Standing with Lin beside her rental car, Sarah was suddenly at a loss for words.

"Sarah"—her sister broke the silence—"I can't say I agree with what you've done, but I understand it. Will you at least let me help you and give you some money? I know you haven't cashed the check I gave you, and you must have so many expenses to pay—"

"Lin," Sarah interrupted, "you know there's only one thing I want from you."

Lin stopped. She glanced away, then down at the ground, then back at Sarah.

"Okay," she said as Sarah hugged her. "I won't tell them. I promise."

Sarah came down with the flu the next day.

Or at least it was a psychological flu. As Owen would say back when they were at Balloon Burger, she needed a "mental health day." All Sarah knew was that she was exhausted: physically exhausted from her shifts at the Stinking Rose, her various one-off gigs, and her daily auditions—and mentally exhausted from her confrontation with her sister. It wasn't even what Lin had said or did—indeed, Lin had barely said anything—so much as the expression in her eyes. So utterly disappointed in her little sister. . . .

It didn't help that Daniel had raved nonstop about Lin on the drive back to her apartment.

"She's great," he'd said as he drove them home. "So friendly and nice. And she's obviously really intelligent. Never would have guessed she was an I-banker."

Sarah gazed out the passenger-side window in silence.

"She's beautiful, too," Daniel continued. "Has that elegant, Gong Li quality. Delicate, but strong—flawless skin, too. Too bad she's an I-banker—could have made a great actress—"

"Then go make her an actress," Sarah snapped.

That stopped him. A moment passed, then another.

"Sarah"—Daniel's voice was conciliatory—"you know I didn't mean anything by that. Your sister's great and all, but you know you're my girl, right?"

Sarah turned back toward the window.

"Yeah," she said, "I know."

Thinking back to the episode, Sarah buried herself further under her comforter as *General Hospital* blared in the background. It wasn't that she seriously felt threatened by Lin in any way. It was just that hearing Daniel talk about Lin, seeing the sadness in Lin's eyes, being forced to admit the truth—it all served only to remind Sarah of all her shortcomings.

Her phone rang. Groaning, Sarah snaked a hand out from under the covers to grab her cell. "Hello?"

Noah's voice boomed through the phone.

"Sarah," he said, "I have great news for you. We'd like to offer you the part in our Lifetime movie."

Sarah almost dropped her phone. She couldn't believe her ears. After telling Noah to hold on, she quickly hit "Mute" and let out a loud, somewhat phlegmy yelp. Then she unmuted the phone.

"Really?" She tried to sound composed. "That's fantastic. I'm so excited! Thank you so much."

"Well, congratulations again," Noah said. "We'll start negotiations with your agent, and assuming everything works out, we'll start production next week, and we'll wrap in a week."

A week? Was shooting a Lifetime movie that warp speed? Regardless, she could at least call her mother now and tell her that she was going to be able to see her daughter on television. But first she had to call Daniel.

For once, Daniel answered his phone. Sarah immediately poured out her news to him.

"Can you believe I got the job?" Sarah exclaimed as she fell back onto her pillow, all symptoms of her "flu" gone. "I keep feeling like I'm being punk'd or something. Is this really, truly happening?"

"Of course it is," Daniel said. "That's very exciting! Congratulations."

"I can't wait to get my script," Sarah continued. "I feel like I must be hallucinating from too much NyQuil."

Daniel grinned. "You're a rock star, Sarah. I told you that you had it in you. Now don't forget the little people when you're up there getting your Emmy."

Sarah laughed.

That night, they had dinner in Venice Beach.

Miraculously recovered from her flu, Sarah had spent the afternoon celebrating her first acting gig by shopping at all the boutiques she'd been able only to ogle longingly before. Even though she was technically still on a budget, she decided that she could afford to splurge this once on some DKNY, given the occasion.

"I think I want the lobster tonight!" Sarah announced, still giddy from the news.

"Well, we're happy tonight, aren't we?" Daniel said.

Sarah pursed her lips at the slight condescending tinge to his voice. What had happened since this afternoon? Why did he no longer sound happy for her? After all, this was a huge day for her. She'd just gotten her first big break, and her boyfriend did not seem anywhere as excited as he should be.

"What's that supposed to mean?" Sarah said.

"Nothing." Daniel looked down at his menu. "Sorry . . . I didn't mean anything by it. I just had a rough afternoon—another crisis at work."

Sarah frowned. Even though she adored Daniel, she couldn't help feel irritation creeping into her blissful state. Here she was in such a wonderful mood, and now she was suddenly anything but celebratory. This was the thing about her and Daniel. Sure, there were some aspects about their relationship that were great. Whenever they saw each other, they usually had a good time— and the sex was certainly amazing. But then there were moments like this one where she realized how diametrically opposed their personalities were. Daniel's dry and reserved manner was a direct contrast to her rose-colored outlook on life. Maybe Owen wasn't being so outlandish when he called Daniel boring.

Owen. Thinking about him, Sarah felt a pang. She missed him terribly. . . .

"Well, that was just kind of unnecessary." Sarah wrinkled her napkin. "You of all people should know how much this means to me. And you could try to sound a little more excited about my news."

Even Daniel could tell that Sarah was not a happy camper.

"I'm sorry." He took her hand. "I wasn't thinking. I do know how much this means to you—and I'm really happy for you."

Sarah gazed at him over the rim of her glass. She wanted to believe him, she really did. But she couldn't help thinking that if he truly did understand, he would be ordering them a bottle of champagne and getting all celebratory drunk with her. Instead, he was once again making her feel insignificant. *Calm down, you'll feel better after some wine and food,* Sarah told herself.

"I'm hungry," she said, changing the subject. "Let's just order."

"Okay," Daniel said. "Oh, by the way, I got you a gift."

Sarah looked up. He had a gift for her? Maybe she was wrong after all. Maybe he'd just been waiting for the perfect moment to celebrate her success with a gift!

"What is it?" she said eagerly.

He whipped out a DVD—of *Asylum*'s twenty-five years of highlights.

"Here's a hot-off-the-press copy," Daniel said proudly.

"Thanks!" Sarah wasn't sure what else to say. "This is great."

Despite her avowed devotion to the show, Sarah had been envisioning something a little different from Daniel, maybe something more like flowers or even a congratulatory card. Sure, the *Asylum* video was something she would have once loved to get, but it didn't seem to fit the current occasion. Clutching the DVD, Sarah tried to sort out her conflicting emotions. So what if Daniel wasn't great in these occasions? She wasn't perfect, either, so could she really fault him? They'd been in this relationship for long enough that they were way past the honeymoon phase of roses and wine. Maybe she just had to learn to be an adult and accept certain things.

"You're welcome," Daniel said, beaming. "I thought you would enjoy it."

"I will," Sarah pasted on a smile. "By the way, did you ever ask your casting director if they're looking to cast anyone?"

"I did." Daniel sipped his wine. "I mentioned it to him in passing, and he said he would call you if there was anything."

"Okay . . ." Sarah took a deep breath. "Thanks! Maybe I'll give him a call too one of these days."

"Yeah," Daniel said, "go for it. Anyway, so what are we getting with the lobster?"

Sarah looked up at him and smiled.

Monday was Sarah's first big day of production.

Her script for the day was ten pages long, and she'd spent the night before poring over her lines. Once she was on the set, though, the script disappeared from her thoughts. The studio—and all fifteen sets on it—was abuzz with activity. Sarah had never been on a TV show or a movie set, and it was a thrill just to actually be working on one.

"The makeup room is to the right," Casey, one of the production assistants, directed her.

Makeup room? Suddenly, everything seemed to come into focus, as if her dreams were finally coalescing into reality. Savoring every moment of it, Sarah couldn't wait to be in the action.

"Cool," she bubbled.

"Our dressing room is on the left," Casey continued. "What size are you?"

"I usually wear a four or a six," Sarah said.

Casey frowned. "Most of our clothes are a two or a four."

Sarah was speechless. Was Casey suggesting that she was too fat for the outfits in wardrobe? Suddenly feeling self-conscious, Sarah sucked in her stomach as much as she could. As she stood there looking around the dressing room full of Lilliputian-sized ensembles, Noah strolled in.

"Ready to rock and roll?" he asked.

"You bet," Sarah said as perkily as she could.

"I printed out schedules for the cast and crew," Noah announced. "You'll be reporting in at seven A.M."

Seven A.M.? That was awfully early, Sarah thought. But she was a professional now, and these were apparently the hours that actors worked.

"Enrique just got here." Noah gestured toward Enrique, who was following close behind. "We should get ready. Today we're going to try and tape three scenes. We're running a little behind schedule today, so we'll have to hustle and get things moving along."

"Good to see you again," Sarah greeted Enrique.

"Likewise." Enrique flashed her a grin. "Ready for that kissing scene?"

Sarah's cheeks reddened. "Always," she said, smiling back. "Let's do it."

Deciding to forget about her wardrobe challenges for the moment, Sarah followed Noah and Enrique out onto the set. She paused and watched as the crew flicked on all the lights, wanting to fully absorb the moment—the first "Lights, camera, action!"

she'd dreamed about all her life. Standing there, letting it all sink in, Sarah decided then that it was all worth it—this moment alone was worth all the lies and loneliness.

After twelve long, grueling hours, Sarah finally finished taping her three scenes.

She couldn't believe how exhausted she was. Even worse, she was feeling completely frustrated at how they'd had to tape her first scene seven times because she kept screwing up one of the lines.

"I'm sorry it took so long," Sarah apologized afterward to Enrique.

"No worries. It happens to everyone." Enrique gave her a kind smile. "It was your first time. You did well."

"Thanks." Sarah smiled, feeling just a tad better.

Glancing at her watch, she realized that it was evening already. She'd been completely out of touch with everything and everyone all day. She hadn't even checked any of the messages on her phone. The surprising thing was that she hadn't really wanted to. She'd been so into her acting that she'd forgotten about everything else. Maybe this was why Daniel was always so hard to reach.

"See you tomorrow!" Enrique called as they headed out of the studio.

"I better." Sarah waved good-bye to him.

As she strolled through the parking lot, she hummed to herself a little. It was already late, and the perpetual L.A. haze had dissipated into a breezy evening. Despite the exhaustion factor, she was feeling pretty content about her first day on the job, and she couldn't wait to share all her stories with somebody—like Daniel. She took out her phone and started to dial, then stopped. He probably wouldn't answer, and she didn't feel like leaving a voice mail. She decided to call someone she knew would pick up.

"Can I tell you how fantastic my first day on set was?" Sarah exclaimed.

"You better!" Chad sounded excited for her. "You know I want to hear all about your first love scene."

Sarah snorted. "You're so hilarious, Chad. Actually, we didn't get to the love scene until late. I spent most of the day trying to figure out the layout of the studio. There were fifteen minisets, and they all looked minuscule. But it didn't really matter once we started shooting, you know? I was only focused on the scenes we were doing."

"Sounds swell." Chad chuckled. "I knew you'd be a natural the minute you stepped onto the set."

Sarah smiled. "Thanks, Chad. So how have things been with Davis?"

"They've been going swimmingly." Chad's tone was breezy. "Well, at least in this kindergarten stage we're in right now. The only thing I'm sure of is that he's a good kisser. Which reminds me—we haven't gotten to the good stuff about your first day on the job. How was the kissing scene?"

"It was easier than I thought it would be." Sarah got into her car. "Enrique and I have great chemistry."

"Does that mean he was really happy to see you, if you know what I mean?" Chad joked.

That got a chuckle out of Sarah. "I have a feeling Enrique is a pro when it comes to love scenes."

"Speaking of great chemistry, how's Danny boy?" Chad asked.

Sarah turned on the ignition. "He's fine. I'm looking forward to Catalina Island."

"Ah, yes, very romantic!" Chad sighed. "So I take it that things are going well."

"Yeah . . . they're fine," Sarah said. "Things were a little tense after Owen's visit—*and* Lin's." She pulled out of the parking lot. "Then Daniel and I got into this tiff the other night because I thought he didn't seem very excited when I told him about my gig."

"Really?" Chad sounded incredulous. "I'd think he'd be over

the moon. Wouldn't he know better than anyone how hard it is to break in?" He paused. "Maybe he's jealous? You know, because his acting days are over."

Sarah frowned. Jealous? Why would Daniel be jealous of her? She was the one who looked up to him—he was the one who was a big-time soap opera producer in Hollywood. If there anyone here should be jealous, it would be Sarah, not the other way around.

"I don't think so, Chad." Sarah adjusted her earpiece. "Dan and I have been dating for six months now, and I still feel like I don't know him after all this time. I know that sounds weird, but I feel like I pour my heart out to him about everything, and he won't even let me in a little."

"Well, that's a problem," Chad declared. "It's important that your relationship deepen over time. If he's shutting you out already, it's not a good sign. Do you think he's cheating on you like Carly cheated on Jason with Sonny on *General Hospital?*"

Chad and his soap opera analogies. Sarah rolled her eyes. "I don't think he's cheating on me. I just . . . don't know how he feels about me. I mean, that night when I finally asked him about us, the most he could say was that he really liked me."

Chad tsked. "I'm seeing red flags. Be careful, Sar. I know you're trying to play it off, but I think you're way more head over heels for this guy than you're admitting. The last thing you want to do is fall in love with him."

That stopped Sarah. Was Chad right? Could she be falling in love with Daniel and not even know it? Thinking back to all her past relationships, she realized that she'd never put as much sweat and angst into any of them as she had with this one. Was that because she was falling in love? She wasn't sure. All she knew was that she cared a lot about Daniel, and being with him had elicited fantasies of the future for the first time—him, her, their 2.5 kids, and the whole white picket fence deal.

She took a deep breath. "I'll let you know about our little excursion. Hopefully, it'll be good for us."

"Well, keep on kicking ass," Chad urged. "When are you coming home to visit? I feel like we haven't seen each other in decades!"

"I know," Sarah said. "Hopefully, I'll come home when it's the right time."

The week flew by for Sarah.

Even though she hadn't had a moment to do anything all week but work, Sarah enjoyed every minute of her acting gig. She loved being on the set, cultivating her craft, working with other actors—and most of all, feeling like a professional. Still, she hadn't seen Daniel in days, and she was definitely missing him. As she tidied up the menus at the Stinking Rose the next week, Sarah wondered if Daniel was missing her, too.

"So, superstar, tell me about your experience as a Lifetime actress." E.J. appeared at Sarah's elbow.

"Words can't begin to describe how great it's been," Sarah said, beaming. "I've had such a blast, E.J. I just can't believe it's already over."

"That's the way this acting stuff goes." E.J. sighed. "Believe me, I've seen it before. Until you catch that break, you're always struggling. In the meantime, though, you've just gotta live life and not lose sight of the prize—or who you are."

"How profound of you." Sarah raised an eyebrow. "That was really touching."

"Hey, don't mock—it's true." E.J. smiled. "There's nothing more important than finding true happiness within yourself."

Sarah stared after E.J. as he strolled off. Was she happy? More or less, she supposed. Of course she would be even happier if she was actually a soap star—or if things were better between her and Daniel. Glancing over at a couple sitting in a nearby booth, she couldn't help noticing how blissful they seemed. She'd felt like that in the beginning with Daniel, when everything had seemed covered in magical fairy dust, but now . . . things were taking on an alarmingly routine flavor. It wasn't as though the spark between them had been lost, exactly; it just wasn't that picture-perfect, fairy-tale romance she'd envisioned. *Come on,* Sarah told herself, *you know relationships are never perfect—having ups and downs is supposed to be a sign of a normal relationship.*

"Sarah, there's a phone call for you," called Beatrice, one of the waitresses.

"Me? Here?" Sarah frowned as she hurried over.

Beatrice shrugged as she handed Sarah the phone.

"This is Sarah," she said hesitantly.

"Hi, Sarah, it's Clyde, the casting director of *Asylum,*" said a familiar voice.

Sarah stifled a gasp. *Asylum!* Why were they calling her? Had Daniel said something to them? And how did they know she was working at the Stinking Rose?

"Oh, hi!" Sarah said brightly. "How are you?"

"I'm great," Clyde replied. "Anyway, I'll get right down to business—we're casting for a recurring doctor role on the show, and I'd like you to come in and read with me. Are you free? Dan mentioned that you'd been working on a project for Lifetime, but he thought that you might be available."

"I'm definitely available," Sarah said quickly. "I'd love to come in and read with you."

"Fantastic!" Clyde said. "I'm going to send you a script. Why don't you come next week? I'll put you in touch with my assistant, and she'll schedule a time with you."

"That sounds great!" Sarah said happily.

As soon as she got off the phone, she pulled out her cell and speed-dialed Daniel. Thankfully, he answered.

"Guess what?" Sarah exclaimed. "I'm coming in to audition with you guys!"

"You are?" Daniel said.

Sarah blinked. He was supposed to congratulate her, tell her how thrilled he was for her and how he'd always said it was just a matter of time. He wasn't supposed to act like this was a surprise—or be surprised at all. So much for her thinking that he'd had something to do with Clyde calling her.

"Yes," Sarah said slowly, "Clyde just called me and said they were casting for a recurring doctor role. He wants me to read with him next week."

"That's fantastic!" Daniel said. "I usually know when we're casting a major role, but Clyde generally takes care of the recurring roles on his own. But you're certainly knocking them down— I'm so proud of you."

Well, that was more like it, Sarah thought. At least he was sounding a shade more like a supportive boyfriend! Score two points for him.

"Are you at work?" Daniel asked as Sarah heard a flurry of conversation in the background.

"Yes," she replied.

"Let's meet up after work and have a celebratory drink," he said.

Sarah paused, more than a little surprised at his enthusiastic response. Still, while she hadn't expected this, she was more than happy to accept the invitation.

"I would love to," she exclaimed. "How about I come by your place after work? Then we can really celebrate *Asylum*, baby!"

Daniel chuckled. "No way I can turn that invite down," he said. "Don't run away to stardom yet, though. You and I have a nice weekend together planned for Catalina Island."

How could she forget? Maybe Daniel was finally coming around, Sarah thought. He clearly was looking forward to this trip as much as she was. Add to that the possibility of the two of them working together on the same show—wouldn't that be amazing? They could be the Deidre Hall and Drake Hogestyn of *Asylum*. She could envision the headlines already in *Soap Opera Digest*. . . .

"Sounds like a plan," Sarah said, beaming. "I'll see you tonight with bells on!"

Sarah had never been to Catalina Island before. Then again, she'd never gone away on a grown-up romantic trip with a guy, either, so in a way, all of this was novel to her.

Wearing her Prada sunglasses and white DKNY miniskirt, she stood on the deck of the gleaming white, high-speed catamaran that Daniel had chartered as they headed toward the island. The Pacific Ocean looked blue and serene as they cut a swath through the crystal-clear waters. Rocked by the gentle rhythm of the waves, Sarah felt as if she were being lulled into a dreamworld of white sand and salt-tinged breezes. It was exactly the kind of romantic, glamorous thing that she pictured other women—like her sister Lin—doing on a regular basis. Who would have thought it would be her doing this now?

"How picturesque this all is!" Sarah beamed at Daniel.

"Gorgeous, right?" Daniel said. "Wait until we get to the island. It's even more scenic there."

"Really? How many times have you been there?" Sarah asked.

"A ton. My friends and I used to have a time-share out here in the summer," Daniel explained. "It was like the West Coast version of the Jersey shore."

Sarah chuckled at the image. "So you were a preppy frat-boy drunk singing Bon Jovi in the middle of the night?"

"Something like that." Daniel laughed.

Sarah gazed at him. "I'd like to see that side sometime."

Daniel wagged his head. "Oh no, I have long retired that side of me."

"Oh, come on," Sarah wheedled. "What happened to living a little?"

"Believe me, I've lived—and I've also had things kick me in the ass as a result," Daniel said.

Sarah paused. For as long as she'd known Daniel, that was probably the most honest statement he'd ever made to her.

"What do you mean?" she asked.

"Nothing." Daniel turned away. "Just that sometimes things in life don't pan out the way you want them to."

Sarah chewed her lip. She might not be psychic, but she was pretty sure one of those things was his ex-girlfriend.

"Are you talking about your ex?" she said carefully.

"Not just her." Daniel shrugged. "But yes, I learned a big lesson with that, too. Ever since she and I broke up, I haven't had a long-term relationship."

Sarah bit her lip, not sure what to say. Was Daniel trying to tell her that she was the first real relationship he'd had since his ex-girlfriend? She couldn't help wondering about this mysterious woman who'd apparently had such a traumatic effect on him. Without thinking, she blurted out, "So are you over her?"

As soon as the words were out, she wanted to kick herself. What kind of question was that? And what if he said he was still hung up on her?

"I am over her," Daniel said. "There was nothing left in that relationship by the end. Still, I guess I've been cautious and a little hesitant to open myself up to someone ever since."

Looking at him, Sarah wondered if Daniel was trying to tell her that he wanted to be in a relationship with her but was just gun-shy because of what had happened to him before. If that was the case, she didn't quite know what to do about the situation. After all, it wasn't as if she were licensed in any kind of psychotherapy. And she certainly was no expert when it came to matters of the heart. Still, even though she didn't feel prepared to delve into these shark-infested waters, Sarah felt she had to listen. If she'd learned anything from her time in L.A., it was that she couldn't run away from problems.

"Are you comfortable being with me?" Sarah asked finally.

Daniel turned around to gaze at her. "I think so." He smiled at her. "I like you."

Well, at least he hadn't said that he didn't like her. Still, Sarah was disappointed that he couldn't say more. Although she knew that he did care for her on some level, she wished he could actively express those feelings. His inability to communicate the way she wanted him to—to show her the affection she longed for—automatically erected a barrier that made it hard for her to open up to him as well.

"I like you, too." Sarah gave him a quick kiss on the lips.

As the boat neared the dock, Sarah tried to focus on having a great weekend and to stop her psychoanalysis of Daniel. After all, she technically had everything she'd ever wanted in her life, right? She and Daniel were on their first trip together, and she had an audition with *Asylum* coming up. Things were as perfect as they could be. . . .

After dropping off their luggage at the hotel, Sarah and Daniel headed for a beach picnic by the water. She had changed into an aquamarine sundress she'd bought in Venice Beach, and as Daniel spread out a blanket on the sand, she opened their picnic basket and began to arrange their feast.

"Thanks," Sarah said as Daniel poured her some Pinot Grigio. She took a sip and smiled at him appreciatively. "Wow. I'm not a big Pinot person, but this is delicious."

"It's one of Catalina's best-kept secrets," Daniel said. "It's dirt cheap because they bottle it here—only about five dollars—but it's actually an excellent wine."

Sarah raised an eyebrow. "Five dollars? Remind me to pick up a crate before we leave!"

Daniel laughed. "Will do."

"This is such a perfect moment." Sarah sighed as she leaned back and reclined on the blanket. "Spending the weekend here with you is just heaven. And then next week, I've got the audition for *Asylum*." She paused. "So tell me—what should I be looking out for?"

"Well, you're going to read with Clyde, whom you already met." Daniel took a sip of his wine. "There are probably going to be a lot of people there, so be prepared to wait. Did he send you the audition sides yet?"

"Yes, as a matter of fact, I have them right here." Sarah pulled out the script from her bag.

"Do you want me to read with you?" Daniel asked.

In the entire time they'd been dating, this was the first time Daniel had ever offered to read lines with her. Sarah was thrilled about this first crack in the wall—maybe he really did care about her doing well.

"I'd love to," she said quickly. "I play a doctor who comes between Angela and David."

"Ahhh . . . yes." Daniel nodded. "David's quite the man whore. He's slept with half the staff at the hospital."

"Lovely," Sarah remarked. "I guess I'm auditioning to be one of his hos. Let's start with the part where they're in the hospital."

"Okay." Daniel flipped to the right page.

Sarah took a deep breath. "David, are you working the late shift Tuesday night?"

"I'll be here," Daniel said.

"Good, room 143 is going into surgery, and you'll be in charge of that room that night," Sarah said.

"Well, since you're the rookie on the floor, I'm going to ask you to do it," Daniel read.

"Excuse me?" Sarah whirled around. "And what will you be doing?"

"You don't need to worry about me," Daniel said. "I've got a lot of important things to deal with the staff about, especially since I'm in charge."

"You mean you'll be in some janitor's closet 'dealing' with one of your staff members, don't you?" Sarah sneered.

"You're pretty feisty, aren't you?" Daniel continued. "I like that. Usually my staff listens to everything I say."

"I'm not one of your little bimbos," Sarah retorted. "If you don't check on room 143, I'll report you to the head of the department."

As Daniel put down the script, he smiled. "That was pretty good, Sarah Cho. I got to say—I'm quite impressed."

"Really? You think so?" Sarah's eyes lit up. "I'm honored you think that, Mr. Producer."

"I think you'll do wonderfully," Daniel said, nodding. "You know, there are some actresses out here who've been taking classes for years and don't have a fraction of the charisma I just saw in you."

Sarah was thrilled—and flattered. Aside from being her boyfriend, Daniel was a big-time soap opera producer and his opinion held actual weight. He was an expert in the field, and if there was anyone's opinion she should trust, it would be his. Besides that, Sarah was excited about this rare glimmer of caring from him. This was the first time since she'd moved to L.A. that he'd shown any genuine interest in her career.

"It means a lot to hear you say that." Sarah touched his arm. "Really."

"I wouldn't say it if it wasn't the truth," Daniel said earnestly. "You have a good chance of getting this role."

"I hope so." Sarah took a deep breath. "I learned a lot from the Lifetime gig. It was such a great feeling when I was doing my scenes on the set—like I actually belonged there. I didn't want the feeling to end!"

"It won't," Daniel said. "This is just the beginning."

"Yes . . ." Sarah gazed out dreamily toward the ocean. "The beginning . . . of everything."

15

The weekend went by in a blur for Sarah.

By the time she dropped her bags on the floor of her apartment, she was convinced that she and Daniel had grown closer on Catalina Island. It was exactly what she'd needed to move to that next level with him, and it had far exceeded her expectations.

Of course, she didn't have much time to dwell on it because she had to get ready for her big audition with *Asylum* even if it wasn't until Thursday. This time, she made sure she was dressed to the nines before heading over to the *Asylum* studios. Wearing her Diane von Fürstenberg top and her most slimming black pants, Sarah walked into the *Asylum* studios in style.

The atmosphere at *Asylum* was different from that at any other audition Sarah had been on. For starters, half of the women in California seemed to be trying out for the role. Sarah tried to be nonplussed as she surveyed her surroundings. The casting director's office was a spacious room with a leather couch next to a mahogany desk bearing two Emmys. As she eased her way into the room, Sarah noticed a tall, slinky blonde who could have been a dead ringer for Scarlett Johansson walking into Clyde's office. Sighing, Sarah took a seat on the couch . . . and that was when she looked down at her feet and realized that she was wearing a black, strappy heel on one foot—and a silver stiletto on the other.

Clapping a hand over her mouth, Sarah stifled a scream. She couldn't believe it—how could this have happened? She'd been in such a rush to get ready that morning—as she'd recited her lines for the twenty-first time—that she must not have paid any attention to what shoes she was slipping on. But of all days for this to happen!

"Sarah Cho!"

Looking up, Sarah saw that Regina, Clyde's assistant, was calling her over. As she walked over to Regina's desk and prayed no one would notice her shoes, Sarah suddenly saw Daniel heading toward them. A moment later, he opened the door and all of the women in the room turned around. Some of them flashed him flirtatious smiles while fluttering their eyelashes at him. None of this was lost on Sarah, and she didn't like it one bit.

"Dan!" Sarah waved at him. "Hectic day?"

"Hi." Daniel barely looked at her. "Extremely."

Sarah was taken completely by surprise. What was with the attitude?

One of the women got up and sashayed over to him.

"Daniel Wong, right?" The tall, impossibly skinny Filipina bombshell simpered at him. "I'm Tiffany—we met last year at the suds awards."

Sarah thought she was hallucinating for a second. Who was this girl flirting so brazenly with her boyfriend?

"Yes, I do remember you." Daniel smiled. "Good to see you."

Sarah couldn't believe it. He was friendlier to this floozy than he was to his own girlfriend! Fuming, she marched up to him.

"So, where's your office?" she demanded. "I'd like to check it out after my read."

"I'm not sure if that's going to work." Daniel shifted back into aloof mode. "I've got a booked calendar today."

Fortunately, Sarah was saved a response by Clyde's appearance from his office with the tall blonde.

"Sarah?" he asked.

"Hi, good to see you again." Sarah quickly turned and walked into Clyde's office without saying good-bye to Daniel.

"We met at the twenty-fifth anniversary party, right?" Clyde said. "Pleasure to see you again."

"Yes." Sarah flashed him her brightest smile as she surreptitiously slid her left foot out of sight. "The pleasure is all mine."

"You came with Daniel, right?" Clyde said.

Sarah nodded. "That's right."

"I just saw him outside. It must have been tough for you," Clyde remarked.

Sarah frowned. She wasn't sure what he meant by that statement . . . but she was desperately curious to find out.

"What do you mean?" she asked.

"Well, I know you guys broke up, so it must be awkward for you to see one another," Clyde said.

It was all Sarah could do not to collapse on the sofa in shock. Clyde thought that she and Daniel were broken up? What was he talking about? Was Daniel going around the office telling people that they weren't dating anymore? Sarah suddenly felt besieged with emotions—confusion, anger . . . Was this why Daniel had just acted the way he had? *Calm down, Sarah,* she ordered herself. She needed to elicit more information from Clyde—like exactly what Daniel had been telling people.

"We're fine." Sarah tried to look nonchalant. "I'm just curious to know when you heard that we weren't together anymore."

"Last week," Clyde said blithely. "That's why I said this must be terribly awkward for you."

Sarah clenched her fists. Here she was, thinking that she and Daniel were progressing to the next level of their relationship— and instead he was telling people that they had broken up!

"You have to do what you have to do, right?" she said. "Anyhow, I'm ready when you are."

* * *

The first thing Sarah did when she left the *Asylum* studios was call Chad.

"What is wrong with him?" she demanded. "He told everyone in his office that we were over! I felt like a complete fool when I was at the audition. The casting director kept asking me if I was okay or not, and I had no clue what he was talking about!"

"Wait, the casting director asked if you were okay?" Chad paused. "And when you saw Daniel, he was nonresponsive and flirting with another girl?"

"Yeah, some girl who was batting her fake eyelashes at him. The worst thing was that he was paying more attention to her than he was to me. When I asked him how he was, he just kept telling me how busy he was." Sarah shook her head. "Sometimes, I wonder if he's thirty-four or fourteen."

"That is really weird." Chad sounded as bewildered as Sarah felt. "When are you going to confront him? But before you tell me—how did the audition go?"

"The audition was great." Sarah took a deep breath. "Clyde was so sweet. He's probably one of the nicest casting directors that I've ever met— Hold on a second, I have another call. It's that agent I told you about," she said, looking up from her caller ID.

Sarah clicked over to the other line. "Hello?"

"Sarah, this is Lucas. I know I haven't been in touch, but I've got a great audition for you. I just got off the phone with the casting director of *One Life to Live*, and he says she's looking for an Asian female for a recurring role for their college story line," Lucas said.

One Life to Live? All of a sudden, all her troubles evaporated.

"Hang on a second," Sarah said quickly. "Let me get off this other call." She switched back to Chad.

"Chad, I have to go," she said hurriedly. "I'll call you right back—I have potentially tremendous news."

"I love tremendous news," Chad approved. "Ciao for now!"

Sarah quickly clicked back to Lucas. "Okay, so what exactly is going on?" she asked.

"Well, I had a talk with Ross Lane, the casting director of *One Life*, and he wants you to audition for the show. Apparently, he remembers you from some workshop you did a while back. You would have to fly back to New York next week for the audition, though," Lucas said.

Sarah blinked. "Omigosh—wow, I'm not sure what to say right now. I think I'm a bit overwhelmed," she said as she clutched her phone like a lifeline.

"Don't be—you're hot right now," Lucas advised. "And we definitely have to strike while the iron's still hot."

New York? *One Life to Live?* Sarah couldn't even comprehend it—what a dream come true that would be! It was all so unexpected, too. After all, she'd been in L.A. for only about six months and was finally feeling that she had acclimated to the Hollywood lifestyle. And then there was Daniel. Thinking about him, Sarah felt a stab of doubt about what would happen with them. All of a sudden, she felt confronted by a multitude of decisions.

"Sarah, I'm telling you," Lucas urged. "It's rare a casting director calls me about an unknown to read for something. It's a really good sign. Do I need to spell this out any further for you?"

Sarah swallowed. She knew this was a rare opportunity, and normally, she would have said yes in a heartbeat. But she felt a strange hesitancy. Was it really because of Daniel? Because if that was the case, it shouldn't be—especially since she was still furious at him. Still, a part of her knew this was all merely a misunderstanding that they could sort out. . . .

Come on, Sarah, you owe it to yourself to go to this audition. If there's anything that really matters, it's your career.

So she did the only thing possible.

"I'll book a flight and be out there next week," Sarah decided. "Tell *One Life* to FedEx me the script."

"Atta girl!" Lucas cheered. "Done and done. I have a really good feeling about this."

* * *

It was an unusually busy Thursday afternoon at the Stinking Rose, but Sarah was so preoccupied that she didn't even notice. Between the *Asylum* audition, Daniel's behavior, the casting director's conversation with her, and her amazing call from Lucas, she could barely keep her thoughts focused. She mechanically went through the motions of greeting customers as her mind zigzagged among all these competing events.

"Crazy day today?" E.J. asked during a rare lull in the evening.

"Can you tell?" Sarah ran a weary hand through her hair.

"It's only written all over your face," E.J. replied. "Is everything okay?"

"I'm fine." Sarah nodded. "I just have a lot on my mind."

"Talk to me," E.J. urged. "Not only am I your manager, but you know I'm also your own personal on-call therapist."

Sarah laughed. "I just don't know where to begin," she admitted. "Let's see . . . Well, in a nutshell, I auditioned for *Asylum* today, found out that my boyfriend who works there has been telling everyone that we broke up, and I got a call from my agent afterward saying that *One Life to Live* wants to audition me, but back in New York." She paused. "I actually have to ask for a few days off because of that."

E.J. brushed aside her concern. "First of all—congratulations! *One Life to Live* is amazing! I'm not a soap opera kind of guy, but I know my sister watches it all the time."

"Thank you." Sarah smiled.

"As for your boyfriend, why would you want someone who would tell his friends that you guys broke up when you didn't? How old is he? Fifteen?" E.J. said. "If you were my girlfriend, I would show you off to the world and bring you a sunflower every day for making my life so bright."

Sarah laughed, touched. Even though that was typical over-the-top E.J.-speak, it was still one of the sweetest things someone had ever said to her. Far sweeter than anything Daniel had ever said. After all, five hours had passed since her audition, and she still hadn't heard from him.

"You sure know how to make a girl feel better," Sarah said, smiling. "Why aren't you an actual shrink again?"

"Hey, I'm just speaking the truth," E.J. declared as he waved at some departing customers. "You're young, beautiful, and I know you came out to L.A. to make it big in Hollywood. The great thing is that you're on your way now. It's probably just disorienting because you finally got used to living here. Plus you got this boyfriend of yours, although I don't think he sounds like much of a prize. You just need to remember why you came out here in the first place."

Sarah nodded. "I know you're right. And I know I have to clear things up with Daniel."

"It shouldn't be that hard to date you, Sarah," E.J. advised. "Remember, know your worth."

"I know, but I really do have feelings for him." Sarah sighed. "He's not just some run-of-the-mill jerk. I think he has a good heart—he just won't show it to me sometimes."

"Maybe, but do you want someone who isn't actually there for you when you need him?" E.J. asked. "That's what a real partner does. They're supposed to be there for you—and that means all the time, not just on a weekend or a Friday."

Sarah blinked. E.J. was completely right. Why couldn't she see that? She saw Daniel only twice a week, and every time she suggested they spend more time together, he would say he was busy. Sure, they'd just had a magical weekend together, but that hadn't seemed to translate to real life. On some level, Sarah had always known this, but she'd put him on a pedestal for so long now. . . .

"I can't argue with anything you've said," Sarah admitted. "I still haven't talked to him yet. Do you think I should call him?"

"No." E.J. shook his head. "Because he'll call you shortly—I know it."

"Thank you." Sarah gave him a grateful smile. "I appreciate the free counseling."

E.J. grinned at her. "You bet. I have to take off but I'll see you next week. Good luck on the audition!"

It was evening when Sarah finally got home.

As she got out of the car, she was startled to see Daniel leaning against her doorstep.

"Hi," he said.

"Hi." Sarah pulled her sweater more tightly around herself. "How long have you been here?"

"An hour or so," Daniel replied. "I tried calling you, but you didn't answer your phone."

"Gee." Sarah raised an eyebrow. "What does that feel like?"

"I know you're mad at me," he said. "I talked to Clyde today."

"Did you?" she said as she opened her door.

"Let me explain." Daniel followed her into her apartment.

A part of Sarah had no desire to speak to him, but at the same time, a part of her was chomping at the bit to tell him the good news about *One Life to Live*. It was strange how she'd dreamed of this moment—and now that it was here, there was none of the sweet triumph she'd imagined there would be.

"I actually do want to hear your explanation." Sarah slammed her apartment door shut. "Let's start by you telling me why you ignored me at the audition today."

"I wasn't ignoring you." Daniel ran a hand through his hair. "I was juggling a million things today. And you were preoccupied, too. You didn't come and see me afterwards."

"Are you kidding me?" Sarah's voice rose. "You're the one who started talking to some skank and telling me that *you* were so busy. And after the lovely conversation I had with your casting director, why would I want to see you?" She ran her hands through her hair. "Why did you tell Clyde that we broke up?"

"Because I didn't want to ruin your chances of getting the job," Daniel said.

That stopped her. "What?"

"If I had told him that you and I were dating, that might have prejudiced him against you." Daniel gazed at her as if that were self-explanatory.

Sarah shook her head. "Why do you think you would have anything to do with me getting a role on *Asylum*? I thought you were the one who said I was so talented."

Daniel sighed. "You're getting it all wrong. My point is that if I told everyone that you and I were still dating, some people might think that I was the reason why you got the audition."

"But you weren't!" Sarah exclaimed. "Stop being so self-absorbed! I'm not sure how you decided that you hold my acting future in your hands, but I do know that you telling everyone we broke up makes it seem like you're embarrassed by me."

"That's not true," Daniel protested.

"Isn't it?" Sarah demanded. "Tell me something—why is it that I haven't met any of your friends in the entire six months that we've been dating, except for that dinner full of posers? And why is it so hard for you to call me your girlfriend?"

"I told you I like you—," Daniel began.

"Stop saying that," Sarah cut him off, shaking her head. "That sounded nice the first week we were dating—but not six months down the road!" She took a deep breath. "I need you to tell me right now, Dan, are you in or are you out? I can't deal with this half-assed thing we have going on, where one minute you're taking me to Catalina Island and the next minute you're telling the world we're not together anymore."

Daniel turned to gaze silently out the window.

"I thought Catalina Island was great," he said finally. "And I think we were both happy that weekend. The problem is, I don't think I'm making you happy any other time—and you deserve to be."

Sarah blinked. Damn right she deserved to be happy all the time, she thought furiously. But her anger was dissolving quickly into sadness, because she knew that Daniel's acknowledgment signaled the beginning of the end. Because she knew then that he wasn't going to fight for what they had.

"I do," Sarah muttered.

"I'm sorry," Daniel said quietly. "I've been thinking all day about this. It's not that I don't want to be in this relationship—it's just that I don't know if I can. All I do know is that I'm not giving you what you want."

It was ironic. The more Daniel agreed with her, the more Sarah could feel her eyes welling up.

"I still don't understand." She sniffled. "If there's a problem, we can fix it. Is there someone else?"

"No." Daniel shook his head vehemently. "That's not what this is about. I really care for you, Sarah, but I don't know if I can ever commit to you the way you want me to. I'm sorry—I just can't do it. I know I'm probably a selfish bastard . . ." His voice trailed off. "I'm so sorry."

Sarah tried to hold on to her anger. At least when she was angry, she felt strong, invincible. But now . . . now all she felt was a strange hollowness in the pit of her stomach. That was when the tears came.

"That's it?" Sarah wiped her eyes. "Is that all you can say?"

Daniel stood there, silent. Even now, at the very end, he had nothing to say to her. And that was when Sarah became angry again.

"I can't talk to you anymore," she gasped. "I want you to leave right now."

"Sarah—," Daniel started toward her.

"Did you hear what I said?" Sarah screamed. "Leave!"

Daniel stopped. Then he nodded and headed to the door. Wrapping her arms around herself, Sarah watched him go. If this were a soap opera, she would trash her apartment, smash a vase, and throw some sentimental keepsake from him at the door. But because it wasn't, all she did was throw herself on the couch and cry herself to sleep.

16

Wearing sweatpants, a Gap regulation T-shirt, and no makeup whatsoever, Sarah boarded her plane to JFK on Tuesday.

It was funny how different this was from how she'd imagined her homecoming to be. She'd always dreamed of waltzing home, looking impossibly glamorous and exuding success as she returned to her apologetic and properly appreciative family. Instead, here she was coming home alone and still jobless. She hadn't had a chance to tell her parents even that she was coming home, let alone about her *One Life to Live* audition. She'd been too miserable all weekend to do anything but cry her eyes out on her balcony and wonder how everything had gone so wrong so fast.

As she sat in the plane before take off, she flipped open her phone to see if there were any messages from Daniel. Nothing. Sarah threw down the phone in disgust. *He didn't call you when you were dating,* she told herself, *why would he call you now?*

Picking up her phone again, she decided to call Chad to tell him what time she would be arriving so he could pick her up.

"I'll be landing by six," Sarah mumbled.

"Sarah, listen to me," Chad urged. "I know you feel like shit right now, but when you come home, you'll feel all better. I'm going to come get you and cheer you up big-time!"

Sarah sniffled. "I can't wait to see you. It'll be good to be home."

She snapped her phone shut. After she'd tucked her flimsy airplane pillow under her head, she closed her eyes, determined to sleep until she got to New York. She didn't want to think about what was ahead—at least not for now.

"Oh, it feels so good to be home." Sarah leaned back in her seat. "I never thought I would miss shoving my way onto a subway car, but I was in such a good mood that I even bought M&M's from the homeless guy on the D train."

"Wow, that's something." Chad raised an eyebrow. "Well, we missed you, too. And I did meet up with that friend of yours, by the way. Giselle. She's a darling."

Sarah smiled wanly. "I knew you'd like her. So far, she's the best thing that's come out of L.A.—well, for a while Daniel was, but we all know how that turned out."

"I always did think his smile was a little too Pepsodent from your pictures," Chad said. "I'm glad you guys broke up."

Sarah took a swig of her wine. "I really don't want to talk about him. I just get so mad every time I think of him . . . and I still don't know how things went so one eighty on me. Two weekends ago I was on cloud nine, we were in Catalina together . . . and now it's all over."

"Focus here, Sarah," Chad ordered. "Remember why you're in New York in the first place, and think about how far you've come. The last time you were in New York, you had no acting prospects whatsoever, and now you're auditioning for a recurring role on a major soap opera. Where are those lines? Give them to me—let's read them together."

Chad's words immediately brought to Sarah's mind the last time she'd read lines with someone—Daniel in Catalina.

"He and I read lines a couple of weeks ago," she said, sniffling. "Everything seemed so perfect, so full of promise back then."

"Come on now," Chad admonished. "No more tears over that worthless man. If you're staying with me, I can't have these negative vibes polluting the ambience."

Sarah took a deep breath. "I'm sorry. I really do appreciate you letting me crash here because I'm definitely not ready to see my family yet. I mean, I can't even hold it together with you— how am I supposed to face the Spanish Inquisition?"

"That does sound terrible," Chad said with a shudder. "Well, why don't we call Owen and we can have a couple bottles of Pinot tonight—"

"No!" Sarah jumped up—then stopped.

Chad stared at her. Sarah swallowed.

"I didn't mean it that way. It's just . . ." She paused. "The last time I saw Owen, there was this awful fight with Daniel. It's not that I'm ashamed to tell him about what happened with Daniel. It's just . . ."

"Just that you're not ready," Chad finished.

Sarah nodded, not able to meet her friend's eyes.

"It's okay," Chad said. "I only have enough wine for the two of us anyway."

Sarah smiled at him. "Right now, that's all I can handle."

Even though she didn't feel like it, Sarah did her primping best for her big *One Life to Live* audition. As she brushed on her thickest mascara, she promised herself that she wasn't going to let Daniel ruin this moment for her. Taking a deep breath, she smeared on more concealer and tried her best to hide the unsightly circles under her eyes.

"Nice to meet you again." Ross Lane, the casting director of *One Life to Live*, shook her hand.

"Likewise." Sarah smiled at him. "I didn't think you would remember me. Thank you so much for calling me."

"I thought you were great in that workshop you did, which is why I've been keeping my eye out for something for you," Ross revealed. "Ready to read?"

Sarah nodded with as much confidence as she could muster. "Sure am."

Ross turned his attention to the script. "How has college been treating you?"

"Okay," Sarah responded. "My parents are going through this really bitter divorce right now, so I'm glad to be away."

"Understandable." Ross nodded. "When did you find out?"

"Just a few weeks ago," Sarah said. "I still don't get it. Just last week, we were one big happy family on vacation in Italy and everything was fine. I couldn't believe it when they sprang this on me . . . all I've been thinking about lately is how I want to run away from all of this."

"Running away from your problems is not the way to live your life," Ross said.

"Yeah." Sarah sighed. "I know."

And she did. Who knew better than her that running away only ended in more pain and problems? The only way she was ever going to get through this was to face her demons. Sarah knew all this . . . but somehow, work was the only thing she could face at the moment.

Unfortunately, work could provide a distraction for only so long, because two days later, Sarah was back in L.A. again.

Sitting on her balcony, she sipped a glass of Chardonnay and watched the sun set over the Pacific. It was a breathtaking sight, and once upon a time, it was all she'd needed to be ecstatically happy. Funny how things changed. All she could think about now was being home back east—even with the noise and the people and the four-hundred-square-foot apartments. If she were in New York now, she could be having dinner with Chad, smoothies with Giselle, dim sum with her family, a Chianti with Owen . . .

Sarah closed her eyes. Even though she'd kept telling herself she would call her family and Owen before she left New York, something always came up. She'd ended up spending all her time with Chad, who was kind enough not to question her avoidance. At least with Chad, she didn't have to come face-to-face with her twin failures: her acting dreams and Daniel.

Her phone beeped. Without looking at who was calling, Sarah answered it. "Hello?"

"It's official—you're the next Susan Lucci," Lucas said. "Guess what? *Asylum* made you an offer."

Sarah gasped and jumped up. In her excitement, her glass got swept off the railing and smashed onto the balcony floor. She barely noticed.

"You're kidding me!" she yelped. "How could this be true?"

"Because you're awesome," Lucas responded. "How does it feel to finally make it, baby?"

Sarah gazed out at the water, her heart beating double time. Once upon a time, this would have been the answer to all her prayers. She'd spent her entire adult life braving her family's disapproval and enduring Balloon Burger humiliation, all in the hopes of reaching this moment. But now that the moment was here, why could she think only about New York? After all, she'd always dreamed about living in L.A., and there were so many things here that she adored—the weather, the beach, her spacious apartment. When would she ever have a balcony in New York? But L.A. also had its drawbacks—most notably, Daniel. She'd spent so much time with Daniel that everything evoked memories of him—the local bistros, the Promenade, even the Starbucks on the corner. New York would be a continent away from the ghost of Daniel, but would it feel as if she were regressing somehow? As if she were going back in time instead of forward? And then there was her family and Owen . . .

That was when E.J.'s words came back to her: *Know your worth.* And that was exactly what she needed to do.

"Lucas," Sarah said, "start spreading the news, because I know where I belong."

* * *

Walking into the *Asylum* studio on Monday, Sarah thought back to her childhood. Ever since she could remember, she'd been obsessed with *Asylum*—more so than any of the other soap operas. Who could forget the straitjacket serial killer story line? Or the time Sebastian and Desiree made love in the padded room? Growing up, Sarah had wanted nothing more than to don one of the chic little white coats that all the *Asylum* doctors sported.

She found Daniel's office easily enough. It was just the way she'd imagined it would be—sleek, stylish, filled with expensive designer furniture . . . and completely impersonal.

He was on the phone when she walked in, but the minute he saw her, his eyes widened and he mumbled something into the receiver and hung up.

"Sarah!" He jumped up.

"Hello, Daniel," Sarah said.

Daniel quickly scooted over toward her. "I meant to call you—"

"I guess you heard I got the job," Sarah said. "Bet that must have been a surprise, huh?"

Daniel shook his head. "Not at all. Sarah, regardless of what happened between us, I always knew you would make it one day. Really."

Looking at him, Sarah realized she believed him. Deep down, he probably did have faith in her; after all, there had to be something that drew him to her in the first place, right? Even though she'd griped about his lack of overt support, that was never really the problem with them.

"I know," she said finally. "I know you believed in me."

He smiled, the relief evident in his eyes. "I'm glad. I didn't want to be the reason for you not to take the job. And I want you to know that our past relationship will never be an issue here at work for you—"

"I appreciate that, Daniel," Sarah interrupted. "I really do. But you don't need to worry about how things will be at work. I'm not taking the role."

Daniel's jaw dropped. Sarah didn't think she'd ever seen him look so stunned, not even when she'd confronted him about their relationship.

"What?" He gaped at her. "But why? This is what you've always wanted—it's what you've been working so hard for."

"That's true," Sarah acknowledged. "There was a time when I would have given anything for the chance to be on *Asylum*."

"Is it because of me?" he demanded. "Because if it is, you shouldn't let me stand in the way of your career."

Sarah sighed. "As hard as it may be for you to believe, Daniel, not everything is about you. I just realized that L.A. is not the right place for me, so I'm moving back to New York." She pulled out a set of keys and placed it on Daniel's desk. "That's why I'm here. I was packing and came across the keys to your sister's apartment. I guess I never returned them to you."

Daniel glanced down at the keys. "Uh . . . thanks. I don't think my sister even noticed they were gone. She's such a scatterbrain."

"I would have liked to meet her," Sarah said.

Daniel looked up. As Sarah met his gaze calmly, he turned away.

"Sarah—," he began.

Sarah held up her hand. "It's okay, Daniel—really. I just wish . . ." She paused.

That caught his attention. He looked at her curiously. "What? What do you wish?"

What did she wish? Where would she begin? To become a star, to make her family gaze at her with pride, to find her true love . . . to understand how it had all gone wrong.

She licked her lips. "You know, since I moved out here, we never did end up having dim sum again. Six months and not a single dim sum outing . . . why is that?"

Daniel's gaze was confused. "You're asking me why we didn't get dim sum?"

"Just tell me," Sarah said.

He stared at her for a long moment, then finally shrugged. "I don't know. I guess there were just too many other things going on."

"Yes," Sarah said slowly. "I think you're right." She took a deep breath. "Well, anyway, I just came over to drop off the keys. Please tell Clyde thank you and that I really appreciated him giving me a chance."

She turned and was almost at the door when Daniel called out after her, "Sarah—be well."

Sarah glanced back at him, and for a minute, she could have sworn there was something like sadness on his face. Maybe— just maybe—in his own way, he really had cared about her.

She smiled. "I will be—I'm going home."

After she exited his office and was on her way out of the studio, Sarah waited for the regret to settle in.

Strangely, it wasn't as bad as she'd imagined. Yes, as she wound her way through the corridors, she couldn't help feeling a certain sadness at how this was likely to be the last time that she would grace these hallways. She could still remember how excited she'd been her first time here, the little squeal of excitement she'd had to suppress as she made her way through wardrobe, makeup, the soundstage . . . But an even stronger feeling was the overwhelming sense of relief she felt. No longer did she have to worry about running into Daniel. No longer did she have to endure that little stab in her heart every time she heard his name mentioned. No longer did she have to live with that ever-present feeling of disappointment and frustration that seemed to accompany every encounter she had with Daniel.

As she got to her car, Sarah paused and turned back to gaze at the studio one last time, thinking about all the things that could have been. . . .

Her phone chirped in her purse. Sarah glanced at it and picked it up.

"Hey, Lucas," she said. "What's up?"

* * *

"Ay-yah!" was the first thing that Sarah's mother said to her.

After spending the past few weeks packing, subletting her apartment, giving notice to E.J., and making sure to take the time to make a proper transition back east (unlike her hasty, seat-of-the-pants move to L.A.), Sarah was back in New York.

"Sarah!" Kim exclaimed. "You so skinny—and pale! I know you don't eat good food in California. This what happen when no soup and vegetables!"

She started picking at Sarah's hair while muttering to herself. Sarah smiled as she let her mother usher her into the kitchen of their family's home. Already, she could smell the fragrant aroma of crispy chicken with scallions, steamed sea bass, sautéed vermicelli with salted pork . . .

"Sarah!" Lin rushed in from the living room and enveloped her in an all-encompassing embrace.

"I am so proud of you!" Lin cried. "My sister—the big-time TV star! And I can't believe you're going to be on *One Life to Live*. You know that's the only soap I've ever liked."

Sarah laughed. "Yes, I know. Guess what—now I'll be able to give you actual spoilers about what's going on."

"Oh, please." Lin waved Sarah's words away. "Who cares about spoilers? I'm just so happy to see you—and what a success you are."

Looking up at her sister, Sarah suddenly remembered the last time they'd seen each other. They'd been standing on the street, enmeshed in the spiderweb of lies that Sarah had told, and she'd begged her sister not to tell their family the truth.

"Thank you," she whispered. "Thank you for not telling them."

Lin paused. "It wasn't my place to tell them. This is a story you're going to tell them yourself."

Sarah took a step back. "I don't know about that—"

"I do," Lin said. "Maybe not tonight or tomorrow or next week. But one day, you'll tell them everything. Okay?"

Sarah looked at her sister, then slowly nodded. As Lin smiled and squeezed her hand, Sarah saw Stephen and Amy hovering in the background. Stephen came forward first.

"I'm so excited for you, Sarah," he said. "We're all so proud of you. And we're even more happy that you're home now. Who needs *Asylum* when you can be on *One Life to Live?*"

"Yes," Amy said. "Congratulations. It's strange, though, that you never told us you were auditioning for *One Life.*"

Sarah looked at her sister and smiled, so happy to be home that she didn't even care about the grudgingly skeptical tone in her sister's voice.

"Thanks, guys," she said. "And Amy, I guess I just wanted to surprise all of you."

Kim pushed them all aside as she bustled over to Sarah and grabbed her arm.

"You sit down and eat *mantous* and soy milk," she ordered. "Or you want dinner now?"

Sarah nodded. "Let's have dinner. I can't wait to have some real, honest-to-goodness Chinese food."

It was strange. All her life, whenever she'd imagined that first day on the set of her first soap opera, Sarah had envisioned something akin to stepping into Oz—a magical moment when time would be suspended and everything would spring into magnificent, vibrant Technicolor. But as she walked into the *One Life to Live* Brooklyn studio that first day, Sarah felt as if she were slipping into a comfortable pair of shoes—albeit a gorgeous pair of ruby slippers that had been tailor-made for her.

Still, there was a tiny measure of intimidation in taking those first, tentative steps, which was why she had come prepared with her own support network. As she walked onto the set, she was immediately enveloped by Chad, a ridiculously handsome man with finely chiseled features who had to be Davis, Giselle—and Owen. Even though guests were usually not allowed on set, Ross had agreed to make an exception for Sarah's first day.

"Hey, girl!" Chad swept her up. "How's the hottest new star in soapdom doing?"

Sarah blushed. "She's doing good—and she really likes the sound of that."

"I hope you don't mind." Chad gestured toward the man beside him. "I had to bring another fan to meet you. Sarah, this is Davis."

Davis beamed and stepped forward with an outstretched hand. "I'm a huge fan of *One Life*, and of you. Chad talks about you all the time. I'm so excited to finally meet you."

"Likewise." Sarah ignored his hand and hugged him. "Welcome to the family."

Giselle came forward, smile radiant. "I'm so happy for you!" she cried. "But I always knew it would happen. Why else do you think I bothered to talk to you in class that day?"

Sarah laughed. "Giselle, I still can't believe this is happening. Weren't we just playing geisha hostess and French maid to those drunken businessmen?"

"Ah, good times." Giselle chuckled. "Too bad you'll be too busy with your new job for us to reprise our roles!"

"Yeah." Sarah shook her head. "The shooting schedule is pretty intense. We shoot forty to fifty-five scenes a day! Can you believe that? On that Lifetime movie, we only shot a few scenes day. I'm totally going to have to get some pointers from you—no time for screwups with just one take!"

"You're going to be great." Giselle hugged her. "And you know I'm never wrong."

Sarah smiled and hugged her back. "Thanks, Giselle."

As she pulled away from Giselle, she saw Owen hanging back awkwardly. Squaring her shoulders, she walked over to him.

"Hey," she said.

"Hey." He lifted his head.

For a moment, they just stood there in their little sliver of silence on the crowded, bustling stage set. Looking at Owen, Sarah had a sudden flashback to that time in L.A. when he'd left her apartment in the middle of the night because he'd been so disgusted with Daniel. Thinking back to that moment now, Sarah couldn't believe she'd let him go.

"Congratulations, superstar." Owen fiddled with the belt loops of his jeans. "I knew this day would come. I would have called earlier with congrats, but I figured you were sipping Cristal with George and Brad and the rest of the *Ocean's Eleven* crew."

"Shut up, wise-ass." Sarah broke into a smile. "Thanks, though—I appreciate it. And I want to say that I'm really, *really* sorry. I acted really shitty to you when you came to visit me."

"You did act really shitty," Owen acknowledged. "I have to say, I never figured you to be the type to flip on a friend for a good lay."

Sarah hung her head. "I never thought I would do that, either, and more than anything, I really regret doing that."

"You know what was worse, though?" he said. "You not sharing your life with me anymore. Like why didn't you tell me about *One Life?* No one would have been more excited than me about your audition."

"I know." Sarah sighed. "It's just . . . I felt like a loser. I felt so bad about taking Daniel's side when you came to visit that I couldn't face you. Can you forgive me?"

For what seemed like an interminable moment, they just stood there. Then:

"Oh, stop it—you know I'll always love ya, babe," Owen said. "And you know I would never blame you for anything that douchebag did. I could never really blame you for anything—period. Whatever happens, you know I got your back."

Sarah looked up. Owen's familiar blue eyes were kind, and suddenly it felt just like old times.

"So I heard from Chad that you got a producer job at Fox," she said softly.

He nodded. "Yeah. I guess I figured if I was ever going to be a producer, it was time to get going on it. You're not the only one who can chase their dreams, you know."

Sarah smiled. "I know."

"All right," Chad announced as he and Giselle appeared at Sarah's elbow, "this is no time to be exclusionary. We all want a piece of our Sarah!"

Sarah laughed as her friends enveloped her in the comforting warmth of their arms. Pulling back, she looked at them all—Chad, her cheerleader; Giselle, her guide; and Owen . . . her true self.

At that moment, a P.A. called over to her, "Sarah, you're wanted on the set!"

Sarah nodded, then turned back to her friends.

Owen nodded at her. "Go get 'em, superstar."

They all cheered. Smiling her thanks, Sarah ran off. She took her place in the scene and turned to get her cue, then closed her eyes briefly as the director called, "Lights, cameras, action!"

Finally, she was home.